DIGGING FOR DEATH

A Mac and Maggie Mason Mystery - **Book 1**

CHARLES P. FRANK

iUniverse LLC
Bloomington

DIGGING FOR DEATH
A MAC AND MAGGIE MASON MYSTERY - BOOK 1

Digging for Death is a work of fiction. References to real people, events, products, establishments, organizations, or locales are intended only to provide a sense of authenticity, and are used to add fictional interest. All other characters, incidents, and dialogue, are drawn from the authors' imaginations and are not to be construed as real.

iUniverse books may be ordered through booksellers or by contacting:

iUniverse
1663 Liberty Drive
Bloomington, IN 47403
www.iuniverse.com
1-800-Authors (1-800-288-4677)

ISBN: 978-1-4917-1847-6 (sc)
ISBN: 978-1-4917-1848-3 (e)

Printed in the United States of America.

iUniverse rev. date: 12/20/2013

3 1969 02250 1372

About the Authors

CHARLES P. FRANK IS A pseudonym for a husband and wife team in Florida and their good friend in North Carolina. Separately, the authors have published a number of other books in the genre of memoir, history, and theology. *Digging for Death* is their first journey into the realm of the novel. *Digging for Death* is a story of relationship and romance wrapped around mystery.

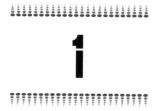

1

2004

THE NEW MOON PROVIDED NO light. Dark clouds hovered overhead. The total darkness at 2 AM made the small rubber raft on the black waters of Pine Island Sound almost invisible. The only whisper heard by the two men was the soft murmur of the paddles as they passed through the water. No one would hear the sound during the early morning hour. It was off season and there were only a few year-round residents on Joseffa Island.

The paddles dug deeply into the calm water as the raft slid noiselessly toward the shore. The two figures in the small vessel were dressed totally in black from their water shoes to the black ski caps that covered their faces, leaving only their eyes visible. Even the area around their eyes had been darkened.

Both men paddled in rhythm, but were constantly on the outlook for the unexpected. The south end of the island was their destination. Their targeted landing spot was near a large stand of mangroves. The man in the front of the raft was large, his muscular arms straining at the thin material of his wet suit. "Keep it quiet," he murmured. "We don't need to be heard by anyone that might be a light sleeper."

"Who do you think would be at this end of the island and awake at this hour?" the smaller companion asked. "Are you absolutely sure he is on the island?"

The larger man replied, "You know the answer as well as I do. I don't know more than you know. The boss said the man was here."

The men continued, each knowing he was skilled in his own right. They had been a team for several years after having been selected and trained for missions such as the one they were now on.

Approaching the shoreline, the smaller man asked, "What does he do here?"

"The man says that he's a groundskeeper and staying in a small apartment near the reception building."

The men eased from the raft into the shallow water a few feet from shore and lifted their craft to hide it in the midst of the mangroves, covering it with fallen branches. They looked around, listening for any sounds. The silence was deafening. The pitch blackness of the night was total. No light shined anywhere on this deserted end of the island. Then they heard the first rumblings of thunder.

"Looks like we are in for a storm," one of the men said as the initial flicker of lightning lit the sky.

A soft rain began to fall and the thunder boomed louder.

The men moved northward in the shadows, avoiding the main sandy path until they could see the outline of the main dock and the reception building nearby. Skirting the small buildings that housed a laundry facility and the administration offices, and watching several small cottages for any signs of movement or light, the two moved toward a walkway that loomed above the reception building. As they cautiously and silently climbed a narrow stairway, they listened for any intrusion on the night's quiet. There was none. They moved along the second level decking that faced the main dock below. Apartment 1, Apartment 2, Apartment 3, they read as they approached Apartment 4. They stopped. The larger of the two, clearly the leader, stopped, signaled again for silence and reached for the door knob. It felt cool in his calloused hand. He turned the knob slightly, testing. It was unlocked.

2

The Present

MAC TURNED OVER IN THE large king-sized bed. He reached over and felt the emptiness of Maggie's side of the bed. Gradually clearing his sleep-fogged brain he remembered. Mags was away but would return today. Looking at the ceiling of the bedroom, Mac saw the projected time. 5:45 AM. He grimaced, barely remembering the days long ago when his body and nature would allow him to sleep later.

Swinging his legs over the side of the bed, he sat for a moment clearing his head. He then stretched and stood. Mac still had an imposing body for his sixty-plus years. At slightly over six foot and a firm 190 pounds, he looked younger than more than six decades.

He thought, "A jog this morning, or a workout in the small gym?" He remembered the time he and Mags had disagreed about how to use that extra bedroom down the hall. Smiling, Mac recalled that he compromised with Mags: a gym for him and a cruise for her.

He opted for the jog and donned a pair of shorts, a tee shirt and his running shoes. Grabbing his wallet and house keys, he dutifully did the recommended stretches as he made his way out the front door. He looked around the cul-de-sac on which they lived. The neighborhood was a nice but unassuming single family development in the small town of Venice, Florida. It was a quiet neighborhood with the residents split equally between retirees and those who were still employed. Having completed his pre-run exercise, Mac began a slow jog making several turns until he reached an avenue that provided a wide bicycle path where he could run for miles safely.

The weather was perfect for this November day, a slight breeze and a temperature in the mid-60's. Lost in his thoughts, Mac ran east until he came to a small church. He circled the church's parking lot and began his run back home. He knew that his total distance would be around five miles. His rapid breathing convinced him that it had been a long time—a year, two years?—since he had routinely measured the distance of this run and begun his daily regimen. By the time he got home, he was puffing. "Getting old is hell," Mac thought. "I shouldn't be huffing after only five miles."

Returning to the house, Mac unlocked the front door to the insistence of a ringing phone. Rushing to his office, he grabbed for the phone. "Mason here," he answered.

"Mac," the voice said, "Don't retired people usually just say 'hello?'"

Mac smiled, recognizing the voice. "Old habits die hard, Jim. How are you?"

"Doing okay, Mac, just too many hours and not enough sleep. I'm not sure whether to thank you or curse you for recommending me for this job."

No one other than Mac's family called him by his given name, MacKenzie. To his friends and Maggie, he was just Mac, a nickname he had picked up forty years earlier during his years in the Navy. Mac had been discharged after having served in D. C., attached to the Naval Investigative Service during the Viet Nam conflict. Conflict, hell, it was a war, plain and simple. Not a popular war, but a war none the less. After his discharge, Mac joined the Miami Police Department and rose through the ranks quickly becoming detective in four years and eventually the head of the Major Crimes Division. Having just retired, he was still acclimating himself to his new life.

Returning his thoughts to Jim and wondering why his friend had called, Mac asked, "What's up Jim. It's only 6:30 and I just left you yesterday. Did the bad guy get away?" Mac reached for a towel to wipe off some Sunshine State sweat.

"Nope, he's still in lockup and still won't say a word. He's lawyered up so we are just letting him stew for now. But, thanks for your help in finding him. I guess you'll be consulting with us often now, at least until I get my feet a little wetter."

"Jim, your feet are more than wet already. You were my second for the past eight years. You can do my old job blindfolded. I know that, and the Chief knows that. So, what's up today? Why the call?"

"Honestly, Mac, Mary asked me to call. She is concerned about Mags. Is she okay? Mary hasn't heard from her in a while and you know, with all that you've been through, she worries."

Mac switched the phone to his other ear. "I know, Jim. I appreciate the concern. Mary and Mags are like sisters. But, tell her Mags is fine. She's in New York this week and comes home today. And, man, am I glad! I'm running out of Hungry Man dinners. Let's try to meet somewhere soon and catch up. OK?"

After the good-byes, Mac hung up the phone and headed for the shower. "Yes," he thought: "Mags would be home today and I couldn't be happier." He thought he had lost her a short two years ago. One chance in four of living and she was still with him. Cancer was a bitch, but Mags had beaten the odds. He was grateful to a miraculous God and a fantastic medical team.

3

MAC BEGAN HIS MORNING RITUAL, shower, shave, and dress. He chose a pair of khaki shorts, a pink polo shirt and brown sandals. Pink was Mags' favorite color and although it had never been Mac's, he wore the color for his wife often. It was early November and Weather.com promised temperatures in the high 60's to low 70's, so shorts were the order of the day. Mags would be dressed warmer since she was flying from New York and even if not, she could not tolerate cooler temperatures after two dozen chemo treatments.

In his office, Mac moved to his desk. Desk? It was really two old writing tables put end to end. When he brought them home, he told Mags: "They are the best ones in any Goodwill Store in town!" She had good-naturedly groaned, but helped him polish them up. It hardly mattered if they sparkled. Mac kept them covered with papers, discs, magazines, post-it notes and whatever else did not accidentally slip into the wastebasket.

Settling into his chair—"the best one in any Goodwill Store in town"—he decided to check his email for any important messages. After rummaging through the usual assortment of jokes and invitations to get money left him by some foreign prince, he found a note from Jim Travis with whom he had just been talking, thanking Mac for the consultation on a capture recently made in Miami and inquiring about Mags, a repeat of their earlier conversation. There was also a two word text message from Will Marks.

Will was the head of the anthropology department at one of Florida's top universities. The text message was short and concise, typical of Will. It simply read, "Call me." Mac thought, "I can do that on my drive to the Tampa airport." He looked at his watch, 8:15. He had plenty of time to get to Tampa before Mags' plane arrived. He moved to the kitchen and poured a bowl of cereal and put a slice of bread into the toaster. Not normally a breakfast person Mac remembered the urgings of his mother and also Mags, "Breakfast is the most important meal of the day!" How many children had heard that throughout their lives! Mac ate while looking over the front page of the *Sarasota Herald-Tribune* he had picked up from his driveway on the return from his jog. He found nothing of major interest and turned to the Venice section to review news in his small community. Again, nothing. He'd look at the *Miami Herald* and the *Wall Street Journal* later this afternoon or evening. Those papers were like old friends, hard to leave behind even after all the years.

Cleaning up the dishes he had used, he grabbed his sun glasses and car keys and headed for the door, 9:00 and still plenty of time to drive to Tampa for Mags' noon arrival.

Mac entered the garage and thought about which car to take to the airport. He could choose the pale blue Chrysler Sebring convertible or the white Toyota Camry Hybrid with the plush beige leather interior. He decided on the Camry. After raising the garage door, Mac looked at the gas gauge and saw three-quarters of a tank, far more than enough to drive to Tampa and back. He again smiled at his decision to buy the Hybrid. Being an avid record keeper, Mac was pleased with the 38-40 miles per gallon the car had averaged and the comfort it provided on road trips.

Knowing the best route to the Tampa International Airport well, Mac still keyed in the address into the car's GPS system. "Hmmmm, which route to take? I could take Highway 41, Tamiami Trail, most of the way, or I could take Interstate 75 straight to the exit for the airport," he thought. "Traffic would be slow through Sarasota so maybe the Interstate would be best." Mac headed out north on

Jacaranda Boulevard. As he approached a round-about, he grimaced and proceeded carefully. If other drivers would just obey the yield signs and get into the correct lane, the round-about would be a benefit to traffic flow. That was not always the case. Mac followed the outside lane and successfully executed the half circle. He continued about a mile until he reached the onramp for I-75 North.

Mac accelerated on the interstate until he reached the seventy mile per hour limit and set the Camry's cruise control. Then he remembered Will's message, "Call me." He pushed the voice activation button on his steering wheel and a female voice from a speaker said, "Enter your voice command."

Mac said, "Call Will Marks." The sometimes-less-than-friendly female voice responded, "Cell or office?" Mac, looking at the car's digital display, responded, "Office."

After two rings, a familiar voice answered, "Dr. Marks, how may I help you?"

Mac replied, "Dr. Marks, how is my favorite archaeologist?"

"Fine, Mac. How is my favorite retired cop of whom I am very jealous?"

"Great, Will, just heading to Tampa to pick up Mags from the airport."

Will replied, "Where has she been? I hope not to Houston again, not to that cancer place, that hospital, again."

"No, Will, I make those trips with her. This one is business and she's doing so well she thought she could do this on her own."

Margaret Mason (Mags) was a fifty-five year old, semi-retired, top flight model. Still able to pull off a number of modeling assignments, she limited herself chiefly to her line of cosmetics. She retained a business manager in New York as well as a close relationship with the labs that turned out her cosmetic products.

Mags had been in New York planning the introduction of her new perfume that she had decided to call Mmmm, a clever play on the fragrance and her initials of her full name, Margaret Marie Miller Mason. Bill Banks, her business manager, handled most of the day-to-day decisions, but Mags still insisted on monthly meetings either in New York or Florida.

Mac teased, "Will, you sent me one of your long and very complicated messages late last night, 'Call me.' What's up?"

Will responded, "I know your schedule might not permit it, but you and Mags seemed to enjoy the dig we did on Joseffa Island last April so I thought you might like to be involved again. As you know, we weren't able to complete the South Ridge project and are going to continue it in late November. Think you could make it?"

"Will, I can't give you a final answer until I talk to Mags. Do you know the exact dates yet?"

"Right now, I'm thinking the last week of November, sometime after Thanksgiving and during the first week of December. The weather should be good then. It's the dry season and the temperature should be pleasant."

"Let me get back to you after I talk to Mags. We have a scheduled trip to Houston, but that's in mid-November. And, we are confident that the results of that trip will be good." Quite unconsciously, Mac made a small frown, knowing somewhere deep within his heart that the news might not be what they wanted to hear.

"OK, just let me know. Give Mags our love."

Mac responded, "And you give Kate our love. I hope we can see you guys again on the dig." The call ended.

Mac thought as he drove. "What two perfectly matched professionals!" Dr. Will Marks had earned the reputation as one of the best, if not the best, archaeologists in the country and certainly in Florida. His wife, Dr. Kate Marks, also an archaeologist, had a reputation that rivaled Will's. Both worked and taught at the university as well as immersing themselves in their frequent archaeological digs.

Mac had met Will and Kate professionally when the couple had been speakers at a forensics conference in Miami several years past. Mags had accompanied Mac and over a dinner following the conference, the two couples became close friends. Mags was in the middle of the health crisis of her life, and Kate was a great comfort, having fought her own cancer battle some years earlier. Kate had defeated breast cancer, still wore her pink bracelet and said she had never taken it off in almost ten years. Mags' cancer was colorectal and during the time she and Mac met the Marks, she was undergoing bi-weekly chemotherapy sessions. He remembered that Mags had said: "It is kind of strange. Having chemo is not the best time to be a friend, but it surely is the best time to have a friend!"

Mac looked at the digital clock in the car and noted that he was ahead of schedule. There was time for a quick break and a cup of coffee. Mac took an exit north of Sarasota and pulled into an easy to access convenience store.

4

HAVING PURCHASED HIS OVERLY SWEET cup of the strongest coffee offered, Mac returned to his car. That was a constant conversation, if not bone of contention, between Mags and Mac. Mac would mix a spoon full of sugar and two more of an artificial sweetener in every cup of coffee. He then added a small amount of cream. Mac said that was for the color more than the taste. Mags was constantly grimacing and encouraging cutting back on the sugar. Mac replied that it was a habit from the days when he worked an important case and went without sleep for days. The coffee got him through, but the sugar gave him the boost he needed. Mags relented, but Mac did notice that when Mags prepared a cup of coffee for him, it was never as sweet. Mac would think, "Keep trying, Mags, maybe someday." But he doubted it.

Mac let his mind wander. What did a guy like him do to deserve a wife as beautiful and totally wonderful as Mags? As he drove north on the interstate he allowed his thoughts to ramble back a dozen years to that day in 2001 on Fifth Avenue in New York City. He had been attending a law enforcement conference at the Plaza and returning from a quick lunch at the Three Guys Restaurant. He could never pass up the opportunity to enjoy their renowned Corfu Salad, a pleasing blend of romaine lettuce, oranges, onion and black olives, with just a touch of cayenne pepper.

As he walked he looked ahead and in a split second, he saw a tall, slender man run from an alleyway, grab a woman's purse, knock her against a building wall where she collapsed. The man, dressed in jeans and a sweatshirt ran toward Mac. On well-trained police instinct, Mac reached out, tripped the purse-snatcher and placed a heavy foot on the man's chest. Within seconds, a police officer pulled a squad car to the curb, jumped out and handcuffed the offender.

Mac looked and saw the woman still lying on the sidewalk, her head bleeding from the impact with the building. Assorted onlookers leaned over her and asked if she was alright. With the offender locked in the backseat of the squad car, the officer and Mac ran to the injured woman. Mac remembered saying, "You okay, ma'am?" but getting no answer.

The woman began to stir, looked up with dazed eyes and said, "I'm not sure …a little dizzy."

"No wonder," said Mac, "You took a pretty hard fall. Your head is bleeding."

The New York police officer quickly inserted, "I can have an ambulance here in a minute."

Mac responded, "That's a good idea. I'm sure she has a concussion and I'm not sure she won't need stitches."

The ambulance arrived. After giving the policeman a quick report and contact information, Mac decided that he would ride to the hospital with the woman and the attendants. As Mac sat beside the woman lying on a stretcher, he thought, "Wow, what an attractive woman, even as disheveled as she is now."

After arriving at the hospital, Mac waited until a doctor in blue scrubs came to him. "Are you a relative?" the doctor asked. Mac replied, "No, I was on the scene and wanted to make sure she's okay."

"She'll be fine, just a mild concussion and some superficial bruising, but we'd like to keep her overnight for observation."

"May I see her?" Mac asked.

"I think that would be okay," the doctor responded. A nurse directed Mac to a room, and he entered tentatively. Mac approached the groggy but beautiful woman. He explained what had happened and after hearing the story, the woman asked, "How can I ever thank you?"

"First, by telling me your name," Mac replied.

"Margaret Miller," the woman replied, "and yours?"

"Mackenzie Mason, but please call me Mac. Only my Mom called me Mackenzie and only when she was angry. Is there anything I can do for you?"

"Could you call a couple of people for me? I understand I'll have to stay here until tomorrow and I'd like my business manager to know. I have a meeting at eight tomorrow morning, and it will have to be rescheduled."

"I'll be glad to call. May I ask where your meeting is?"

"It's with an advertising agency that handles a product I promote. The offices are in the World Trade Center."

Mac would never forget the date. It was September 10, 2001. This Margaret Miller would not be at her meeting in Building One of the center at eight the next morning. Miracle or fate? Mac thanked God that Mags' injuries were no more serious, but also thanked God for the cancellation of a meeting that could have been her last.

Prior to Mac's leaving the hospital, Mags made him promise to come back and allow her to take him to dinner to show her appreciation for his help.

Mac smiled as he drove on toward Tampa in awe of how chance, or God, or whatever brought Mags into his life. They had had their first date that next evening—9/11/2001- in one of the Plaza Hotel dining rooms. He still felt a little guilt for having such a joy come into his life when tragedy and fright and randomness tore into the lives of others.

They saw each other every evening that week. Mac even extended his stay in New York through the weekend, watching the developing news on the bombing and attending the nearby John Street United Methodist Church together, praying with others for the victims and families of the tragedy. That initial time together began a series of plane flights from Miami to New York City and from New York

City to Miami. Eight months later, Mac and Mags were married, bought the house on the cul-de-sac in Venice and began the best dozen years of Mac's life. His first try at matrimony had succumbed to the pressures of work and finally, his wife, Ruth, had said, "If you had rather be married to your job, so be it!" She left. Again he thought of Mags and their life together, "Wow, how could one man be so blessed!"

5

2004

No door chains. No shriek of an alarm. Nothing but stillness. No light showed through the small window. As the thunder rumbled and the lightning lit up the otherwise dark balcony, the two men entered the apartment, their 9mm Glocks drawn.

Shots rang out, muffled by the booming thunder.

Now the dead had to be disposed of and the apartment cleaned. There was blood on the tiled floor. A quick scrubbing with bleach would hide any evidence. An old floral patterned rug was rolled in the corner of the apartment, waiting to be discarded. Perfect! There was a maintenance golf cart and trailer parked below. The rug was rolled around a body and carried to the waiting trailer. A tarp was in the trailer and conveniently used to cover its grisly contents. The deserted south end of the island would be perfect. There was even a shovel in the trailer.

All seemed quiet with no one stirring in the early morning dark. The sandy road gave no clue as to this gruesome trek. Once the cart reached a spot near some mangroves, the digging began. The sand was soft and the three foot deep hole easy to excavate by shovel. The burial complete, the sand was spread and raked smooth so that no disturbance was obvious.

It was time now to leave the island.

6

The Present

MAC TOOK THE 228 EXIT onto I-275N; he looked into the tray next to his seat, knowing he'd need change for the toll as he approached Spruce Street. It was still thirty minutes before Mags' flight would arrive, so he drove to the cell phone lot to await her arrival. She would call him, and he'd meet her at the curb of the arrival area. Mac felt like a teenager on his first date. Mags still had that effect on him.

Mac parked in the cell phone waiting area. Mags' flight should arrive soon. Mac tuned his SiriusXM to the classic radio station. An old 1950 *The Saint* mystery starring Vincent Price was airing. Mac had no sooner gotten into the plot of the story when his cell phone rang. "Hello, Darling, are you near?" Mags' voice asked.

"Be there in five, Hon," Mac answered. He backed out of his parking space and followed the signs that read 'Arrivals.'

Mags was standing with her two suitcases nearby. "Why does a woman need two suitcases for a three day trip?" Mac wondered but wasn't about to ask again. When he had asked once before, she just gave him an eye roll for which she was famous. "No, I won't ask again," Mac thought. He parked at the curb, threw his arms around Mags and gave her a welcoming kiss. As he lifted her two suitcases into the trunk, he shook his head again. Mags had already gotten into the car. Mac slid behind the wheel, signaled his exit from the curb and followed the signs that read "Exit" and "I-75."

"How was the trip, Hon?" Mac asked.

"Great, but I am really beat." As if to prove her point, Mags rubbed her shoulders and yawned. She made no effort to cover her mouth.

"How's Mmmm coming along?" Mac asked.

Mags smiled and said, "Testing is complete. We'll start production within the next couple of weeks. I hope we can roll it out by February in time for Valentine's Day. It'll make a great gift for wives and girlfriends. The fragrance is so subtle that I think it will also do well in the teen market. I brought samples of Mmmm and thought I'd give one to a few people over the next weeks. It's a little different, you know, so I'd like their response to the new fragrance. How's your week been?"

"I drove down to Miami to help Jim with a problem, but only stayed one night at Jim and Mary's. Mary asked about you and wants to get together as soon as we can. You know, Miami has its good points, but it was great to get back to Venice. I spent the remainder of the time watching ESPN. Duke has begun its preseason games and you know the rule." Mags smiled. Mac had gotten his Masters Degree in forensic pathology at Duke, and the rule was simple. Mags was #1 with Mac unless Duke was playing basketball then it was Duke that was #1 in his life. Mags had actually become a major supporter of the team as well. In fact, she was more vocal during games than Mac. She had favorite players and even went as far as yelling at them when they didn't play well and getting up from her recliner to pat them on the head when they made a good play. Mac loved her enthusiasm.

"Coach is adjusting again for a whole new team. I think we are going to have some problems with our inside game, but our perimeter players are fantastic." Mac knew every player and the statistics. Within the first few weeks of play, Mags would too.

As an eighteen-wheeler sped past them, with the windows down on the Camry, diesel fumes wafted into the car.

"Oh, drat!" exclaimed Mags. "I was hoping you would notice I was wearing a sample of Mmmm, but now you will think it smells like truck fuel!"

"Oops," Mac pondered to himself. "I should have said something about how lovely she smelled, but too late now! My bad."

Mac decided that his best strategy was a change of subject. "Oh, I got a call from Will. He wants to know if we can join him and Kate on a continuation of the South Ridge dig in late November. I told him we had a scheduled trip to Houston in mid-November but thought the end of the month was free. What do you think?"

"I'd love it. How long will we stay this time?" Mags replied.

"Probably two weeks, if you can arrange that."

"I'll block it out. It will be good to see Kate and Will again. Oh, how's Sam?"

Sam was the third member of the Mason family. The beautiful orange and white cat was loved by them both. Sam just showed up at the house some five years earlier. Mags took him in. Mac and Mags lived on a small lake and it was not unheard of for an alligator to call the lake home. So, the feisty feline was not allowed to roam outside. Mags first kept Sam on the enclosed lanai but he soon gained entrance to the house. Mac had to acknowledge that Sam was the smartest cat he had ever seen. Sam answered when called, followed commands and was constantly "talking." Mac and Mags laughed when he even seemed to be answering a question with a meow that sounded very close to "Yes" or "No."

"Sam's doing well. He had to have his drink of water from the bathroom faucet throughout the day. Turn the faucet on, turn it off, turn it on, and turn it off again. And, he really lets you know when his food dish is empty. Sometime I wonder whose house it is. I think he just lets us live there," Mac laughed.

"Did you remember to clean his litter box?" Mags asked with one eyebrow raised. Mac remembered the two words his father taught him to say when questioned. "Yes, dear," Mac said with a grin.

They sat quietly for a few miles. Mags gently reached over and let her hand rest on Mac's leg. He smiled and said, "I love you, you know." She smiled and gave his leg a playful pinch.

The exit signs signaled that the turn toward home was not far away. The passing scene seemed more and more familiar. They had passed the exit for Myakka State Park, a special place where Mac and Mags had taken numerous out-of-town visitors. It was a special treat to stop near a bridge in the park and look down at the water below and never fail to see several seven to eight foot alligators. A few miles later they pulled off at Exit 193, Jacaranda Blvd.

Finally, Mac asked, "You know we leave for Houston on Sunday, the 18th. Do you want to fly or drive?"

Mags responded, "You know I prefer to drive. It's two days but fun to travel by car with you," Mac said. "It's almost like an extended date!"

"Driving sounds good to me. We need to get some books on CD. I enjoy that so much."

"I'll make the hotel reservations when we get home. We'll stay in Daphne, Alabama, going and returning if that's okay with you."

"Or maybe we could stop and visit with Adam and Kelly in Biloxi on the way. I'm sure they'd put us up for the night," Mags suggested.

Kelly was an old friend of Mags from her early modeling days. Adam was Mac's 32 year old son. Adam had graduated from West Point, served four years in the U. S. Army Special Forces, and been recruited by the DEA. After a number of very successful years as a special agent, he transferred to the Federal Bureau of Investigation and was stationed in Biloxi. Now he was the Section Head of the Southern Louisiana and Mississippi division. Mac and Maggie had introduced Adam to Kelly three years previously, and within a year they were married.

"And maybe we could visit Beauvoir while in Biloxi" added Mac. Mac loved history and seeing the retirement home of Jefferson Davis was on his bucket list.

Mags replied, "We'd have to leave a day or two early so that we could spend time in Biloxi."

"That's doable" replied Mac.

The car pulled into the driveway of their home a little after 2 PM.

"It's good to be home," Mags said with relief. She laughed, "You know what they say: 'New York is a great place to visit but I wouldn't want to live there!'"

Mac thought to himself, "You don't know how good it is to have you home."

The lid of the trunk popped open, and Mags reached in to grab one of the bags.

"That can wait for a moment," Mac said. "Some things take priority." With that, he placed his arm around Mags' shoulder and pulled her close to him. His kiss was tender and lingering. Then, he added, "Welcome home, my love."

They lugged the suitcases into the house and Mags began the tiresome work of emptying them so she could pack for Friday's trip to Houston. Not knowing what the cancer check-up might reveal meant she did not know exactly how to pack: How long would they be there? What outfits would be right? What if...she would not let herself complete the question.

Finally, the bags were packed—two for Mags, one for Mac—and Mags and Mac collapsed, exhausted, into bed. He put an arm around her and nuzzled her neck.

"How tired are you?" he whispered.

"I'm not *that* tired," she giggled.

So, Mac snuggled a little closer to show her how happy he was to have her home.

7

It was Friday and time for Mac and Mags to leave for Houston. One of Mac's quirks was his inability to sleep the night before a trip. He climbed out of bed at four in the morning and finished packing the car. Mags got up, took sausage and egg biscuits from the refrigerator, and warmed them in the microwave. Mac made coffee and poured it into their two Duke travel mugs.

Mags reached for a mug of coffee, smiling and asking, "Is this mine? I don't want that syrup you call coffee."

Having previously arranged for neighbors to take care of Sam, their feline son, while they were away, Mags and Mac checked on food and water for the still slumbering cat and, carrying their coffee and biscuits, climbed into the Sebring. This would be a good time to enjoy the convertible. They hoped Texas weather would agree! At 5:15, they pulled out of their driveway.

The route to Houston from Venice, Florida was simple. Mac, with amusement, often stated that it only required four turns before entering their destination city, three turns in Venice before reaching I-75 North then turn left on I-10 West and drive straight to Houston.

Mac, in his analytical mode, announced with confidence while looking at the GPS, "Exactly 1046.9 miles to Houston!" Of course, on this trip they would take the exit to Biloxi, Mississippi, and the visit with Adam and Kelly, so Mags in mock horror exclaimed, "No! No! Don't forget Biloxi!"

Mac smiled and answered, "Gotcha, didn't I? You are so easy."

Mac and Mags had a routine for these long trips; it involved a trip to Cracker Barrel where they could rent audio books—good companions for the passing miles. This time, they rented two novels on CD. They chose the latest Patricia Cornwell novel for Mac and a novel by Nora Roberts for Mags. They also purchased an easy crossword puzzle book. Mac was a visual person, and Mags could read the clue to Mac and tell him the number of letters and he could visualize the answer. They enjoyed the driving trips together, one reason they preferred driving on an extended trip over flying.

"Is there any place you'd like to stop along the route today?" Mac asked.

"Do you mean other than every rest area between here and Biloxi?" Mags asked, with a grin on her face. Mac was known to need frequent restroom breaks "You have to stop more often than any woman I know," Mags joked.

"Ha Ha," replied Mac. "Seriously, any place you'd like to see?"

"You know, we pass the exit for the Suwannee River while in the panhandle of Florida. I love Stephen Foster's music and have heard there is a nice museum there dedicated to him."

Mac replied, "Yeah, I've been there. The song Foster composed, 'Old Folks at Home,' mentions the Suwannee River but did you know that he never saw the river? He chose the name Pee Dee River in North and South Carolina, but later changed it to Suwannee. I'm not sure why. He actually misspelled Suwannee, putting Swanee instead of the correct spelling."

"Wow, you are just a wealth of knowledge, aren't you?" Mags said with yet another smile.

"That's me, Encyclopedia MacKenzie. I'd love to stop there but there is one surprise awaiting you when we visit, but I'll let you wait and see what that is."

Both were quiet and reflective for a few miles. Finally, knowing of the controversy surrounding some of the songs, Mags said, "You know, some of these old songs are really from another time, aren't they? I hope we have all learned a thing or two about how to live with each other."

She pulled out the sausage biscuits and handed one to Mac, and she inserted the Patricia Cornwell CD into the player. The couple settled back to enjoy the drive and listen to the book on CD.

Several hours later, having completed the fourth CD of the Patricia Cornwell novel, Mac stopped Mags from putting in CD five. "Let's hold off on that one, Mags. We should be getting near the Suwannee River exit." Sure enough, about ten minutes later, a green sign appeared on the side of the highway. It read "Historic Suwannee River" and below were the actual notes of the first line of "Old Folks at Home."

Mags began to hum and then with a smile she sang, "'Way down upon the Pee Dee River'. It just loses something that way, doesn't it? I'm so glad Foster decided to change the words."

Mac took the exit towards White Springs, Florida, and followed the signs to the museum. Mac paid the $5.00 per vehicle park entrance fee and drove on to an imposing two story yellow building with six white columns highlighting a wide front porch. Mac parked the car and they walked to the building. As they walked, they heard music playing and recognized it as another of Foster's compositions. Upon entering the building, they asked about the music. A volunteer at the welcome counter explained that what they heard was a 96 bell carillon that plays throughout the day.

Mac and Mags began the tour of the museum, viewing demonstrations of quilting, blacksmithing, stained glass making, and other crafts. There was a small gift shop and Mags said, "I want to buy a magnet from here to add to our collection of travel magnets and then maybe a tee shirt."

After their purchases, they walked outside and down a hiking path to the river. "Now, what was the surprise you said I'd find here?" Mags asked.

"I'm surprised you haven't noticed it. Is your smeller off?"

"Oh, I do notice a foul odor. Yuck! What is it?" Mags asked.

"The springs near here have a very high sulfur content. It's the sulfur you smell. There used to be a health spa at the springs where people could wade in and sit in the water. The sulfur is thought to have curative powers. I guess you thought you were cured if you smelled bad enough!"

"Fascinating," Mags replied. "And let me add that my nose is indeed surprised!"

After strolling the hiking path a short distance, Mags and Mac returned to the car.

Mags said, "Let's put the top down for a while. The weather is so pleasant. A little breeze would feel great."

Donning her silver sequined ball cap, Mags got into the car. Mac pushed the button to lower the top and put on his blue ball cap with DUKE emblazoned across the front.

Mags asked, "How much farther to Biloxi?"

"Oh, we have quite a distance to go. We'll probably not get to Adam and Kelly's until 6 PM. Don't forget the time change. They are in the Central Time zone. Maybe you should call them and tell them we'll call again when we are about thirty minutes out. It will probably be before 6 since we pick up an hour."

Mags reached for her cell phone and punched in the speed dial for Adam and Kelly. The familiar voice answered, "Hi! The charcoal is ready for a match! We can't wait for you to get here. We've got some news for you. What time will you get here?"

Mags laughed. "I forgot that you had caller ID. No wonder you gave me all the details before I said a word! And what is your news? It sounds like a big secret!"

"Now, it would hardly be much of a secret if I told you now, would it?" Kelly joked.

"Oh, I suppose not," Mags said, "but you surely have me curious!"

"Curious about what?" Mac whispered, unable to hear the cell phone chat.

Mags spoke to Kelly: "We get there about 5:30 or so, your time. Is that okay?"

"Sounds just right. Adam has the salmon and steaks marinating and we'll pop them onto the grill when we see you drive up."

"Sounds like a plan," Mags replied. "See you soon!" She clicked off the phone.

Mac repeated his question: "Curious about what?"

"She wouldn't tell me. Maybe one of them has a new job. Maybe they are moving. Maybe she's pregnant. I guess we'll have to wait to find out!"

Mac sat quietly for a while, but before they could start the fifth CD in the Cornwell novel, he said, "Oh, good! The sign says the next rest area is just five miles away!"

"Why doesn't that surprise me?" Mags said with the eye roll she so often used.

Mags and Mac opened their doors and got out of the convertible. "I think I'll walk around while you're inside," Mags said as she headed towards a small gazebo. She watched as several people exercised their dogs in the pet area. Mac headed for the Welcome to Mississippi Visitor's Center and the restroom.

Upon getting back into the car, Mac said, "Off we go again. We have less than thirty minutes to Adam and Kelly's. After a quick "we're almost there" call, they started the CD again even though they had to turn the volume up due to the wind noise that was unavoidable in the convertible.

At the I-110 exit, Mac turned south towards Biloxi. Following the GPS directions, Mac crossed a bridge spanning an inlet from the Gulf. Approaching the US Highway 90 or Beach Road, he turned on his left signal and made his turn.

"Wow, how beautiful," Mags said as she looked to her right at the beach and the Gulf. It was a calm day and waves washed gently onto the white sand. "Look at those beautiful wood carvings in the median."

"Those were carved from the stumps of trees that were broken by Hurricane Katrina," Mac responded. "The Mississippi Department of

Transportation cut the trees down to the level you see and a chainsaw artist by the name of Dayton Scroggins fashioned the sculptures."

"My, you are a wealth of knowledge!" Mags said in awe.

"No, just information Adam gave me after Katrina."

Making several turns, Mac came to McDonald Street where Adam and Kelly lived. Finding the ranch style home on the right side of the street, they noted that many of the trees were still showing the results of the hurricane that had caused so much damage just eight years earlier.

"You remember that Adam and Kelly's house was built on the foundation of a home destroyed by Katrina."

They had bought the house shortly after they got married. The house was so beautiful that friends said, "Your place looks like a real estate ad." The couple had spent countless hours landscaping the yard and repainting the shutters, even installing a swing on the front porch facing two rockers they had purchased from Cracker Barrel. One rocker had the crest of West Point Military Academy on it and the other showed the crest of Duke University in honor of the family's favorite basketball team. Since the men's coach at Duke was himself a West Point graduate, the academy chair had double meaning.

As Mac and Mags pulled into the double-wide driveway, Kelly came running from the front porch where she had been sitting in the swing. "You're here", she said excitedly.

2004

THE BREAK OF DAWN CREPT over the eastern horizon. There was no time to delay. Those eager for early morning fishing and quick wake-up jogs on the beach would soon be around. This departure must have no witnesses!

As quietly as the raft had arrived during the night, so now it offered no sound as soft strokes moved it slowly away from its hiding place among the mangroves. As the shore slowly became more distant, a quick glance back revealed nothing. No one watching. No one wondering. No one.

The newly dug grave held its secret. Small island birds began to munch at the insects that stirred in the carefully replaced grass. The soft light of the morning sun showed the clearing skies, but revealed nothing more at Apartment 4 than a closed door. It would be a long time before anyone noticed that the apartment was no longer home to Jimmy Barber.

Sometimes the sea will swallow its intruders. This time the raft made its way to a fishing boat that was ready to welcome it.

9

The Present

Kᴇʟʟʏ ᴇᴍʙʀᴀᴄᴇᴅ Mᴀɢs, ʜᴜɢɢᴇᴅ Mᴀᴄ, and then tried to wrap her arms around them both at once. They all laughed and arm in arm in arm moved toward the side door.

"Don't we get the honor of coming in the front door?" Mac said with a big grin.

"The front door is for guests. You guys are family in more ways than one."

Adam stood in the open doorway. He clasped Mac tightly around the shoulders and then turned to Mags. "Hi, Mom," he said, as he kissed her on the cheek.

Mags loved it when Adam called her "Mom." Once she had described that special joy to Mac this way: "When Adam calls me 'Mom,' I rejoice that love can mean as much as biology!"

The four made their way into the kitchen where they were greeted by Edgar, the labradoodle that Adam had named for the one-time director of the FBI, J. Edgar Hoover.

"I think he is asking how Sam is doing," Kelly said.

Mags reached down and patted the dog. "Sam sends his best meow to you, Edgar!"

Adam turned toward a pan of salmon that was on the counter. "I know the expression is, 'It's not good to eat and run.' Is it okay if we run and eat? I need to get these salmon steaks onto the grill. The steaks are already cooking."

"Your secret marinade?" Mac inquired, already knowing the answer.

"Oh, yes," Adam answered, as he always did. "I got the recipe from a nun who was once the head chef at a convent. I promised never to tell the secret ingredient."

"Oh, a secret ingredient?" Mags asked.

Kelly mouthed the word: "H o g w a s h" so that Mac and Mags could see.

"Mouthwash?" joked Mac. "Did you say the secret ingredient is mouthwash? I wonder which brands you use."

Adam threw his arms up in amused dismissal at this line of thought. "I'll get this on the grill while you two get washed up."

"Sometimes I feel washed up," Mags whispered to Kelly. As Mac stepped into the bathroom, Mags spoke quietly to Kelly. "These trips to Houston always make me worry about the least little thing."

"Have you not felt well?" Kelly asked.

Mags hesitated before she replied. "Yes, but I'm sure you know how it is. One pain or one cough and I worry that the cancer has spread. Mac takes it all in stride and doesn't seem to be concerned at all."

"Oh, Mags, you just have to keep those positive thoughts and know that God still has a lot for you to do. Keep up the prayers and He and those wonderful doctors in Houston will work miracles."

This was heavy talk and there was a moment of heartache before anyone spoke again. Kelly knew she needed to move to some new topic.

"How is the new fragrance, Mmmm, coming along?" Kelly asked.

"As you know, I just returned from New York and the testing phase is complete. It will be on the market within three months. We're also producing a number of other products under the name, Mmmm. I think the distinct fragrance is going to be very popular. I have samples of the perfume and I brought you one."

Kelly took the small bottle from Mags and removed the top and sniffed. "Mmmm, I think the name you've chosen is great: your initials and just what folks will say when they get a whiff. I love it. Thank you."

Mac joined Adam as he brushed the salmon and checked the four steaks on the grill. "How is work going, Son?"

"I've been really busy lately. Ever since 9/11, we've been monitoring all activity up and down the coast. It seems that some questionable characters have been coming into the states by way of the Gulf."

"Are you looking for illegal aliens, drug traffickers or terrorists?" Mac asked.

"Well, all of those, but my office's emphasis is on threats of terrorism and human trafficking; but, as you know, the FBI portfolio covers much more than that!" Adam answered.

"Son, just how much time are you having to put in?"

"Some days I only get home to sleep a few hours and then back to work."

"Adam, how is Kelly handling your work schedule?"

"She's a trooper. She really understands what my job requires."

Mac, with a look of concern, replied, "Just remember what happened to your mom and me. I don't want you to lose Kelly due to your work. No job is worth it. NO JOB!"

"I know, Dad; that's why I've taken a couple days off while you're here."

Adam had set the timer on his watch and said to himself, "Eight minutes on a side" and returned his attention to the salmon and steaks.

"How about a beer while the food cooks?" Adam asked Mac.

"Sure, sounds good," Mac replied, adding, "Surf and turf? It looks to me like you're cooking for an army."

"No, just for my favorite people," Adam said, smiling at his father. The two men settled into patio chairs and watched Edgar lazing under a huge shade tree in the back yard.

Adam, looking down at the beer he was holding, asked, "Have you heard anything from my sister?"

Adam had a younger sister, who had been born three years after Adam. Because of the difficult separation and divorce when Mac's daughter, Eve, was only twelve, her relationship with Mac had been strained. She had lived with her mother, Ruth Thomas, until going away to college. Mac rarely saw her.

Mac responded to Adam's question, also looking down in obvious distress, "No, I get an occasional phone call, usually at Christmas, my birthday or Father's Day but that's about it. And, at times, I cannot help but feel guilty for deserting her at one of the most formidable times of her life."

"Dad, you've always been there. You helped with child support and also paid a large portion of her college expenses. You shouldn't feel guilty."

Mac smiled, patted Adam's shoulder, and said, "Thank you, Son."

Back in the kitchen, Mags asked Kelly, "What can I do to help?"

"Well, if you insist, you could make the salad. Everything is on the island there," Kelly replied.

Kelly put the fresh green beans into a steamer and checked the brown rice she had on the stove.

"We really miss you guys. It's great to be here." Mags said.

Kelly, with a smile, asked, "Do you have time to stop by here on your way back home?"

"We just might. We have to get to Joseffa Island later this month but we should have plenty of time to pack for that when we get home."

"Adam's told me about Joseffa. Is there something special going on there?"

"Will and Kate Marks have invited us to participate again in an archaeological dig they're doing on Joseffa. You remember that we went on their dig there this past April," Mags replied.

"Oh, yeah, I remember. That should be a lot of fun."

"Fun, yes, but hard work too."

"Salmon and steaks are ready," Kelly heard Adam call from the patio.

"Everything is ready in here too. Let's eat."

The two couples sat down at the large dining room table beautifully set by Kelly earlier in the afternoon.

"Doesn't this look lovely," Mags exclaimed. "We could have been just as comfortable at the dinette table in the nook off the kitchen."

"Well, we never use our dining room and this gives us an excuse," Kelly replied with a smile.

Adam turned to Mac and asked, "Dad, would you offer our blessing?" With heads bowed and holding hands around the table, Mac prayed.

After everyone's plates were served, Mags couldn't hold her curiosity any longer. "OK, you two, what's the big secret you have? I've been guessing ever since you told me you had news."

Kelly looked at Adam and said, "You want me to tell them or do you want to?"

"You go ahead, Kelly."

With a huge smile on her face, Kelly burst out, "Adam's being transferred. We'll be moving to Tampa, effective December 1st."

Mags and Mac almost jumped out of their chairs. "That's wonderful news! That's only a little over an hour from us," Mags exclaimed.

"Is this a promotion for you, Son," Mac asked.

"Yes, Dad, it really is. I'll be the Section Head of the Florida region. I'll be doing the same job but with a much larger coastline to cover and a larger staff to manage. As you well know, I could get called in on stuff in other places."

Kelly added with a smile, "A larger salary too."

"That is just fantastic news. We couldn't be happier." Mac said with a huge smile.

The dinner resumed with warm peach cobbler topped with French vanilla ice cream. After the bountiful feast was finished, the men carried the dishes to the kitchen and Kelly loaded the dishwasher after Mags rinsed the dishes. The two couples settled into the family room and caught up on all the news, returning often to the subject of the transfer.

Finally yawning, Mags said, "I must be getting old. I'm ready for bed."

Mac replied, "Hon, I have five years on you and I'm more than ready for bed. Do you still have that king sized bed in the guest room?"

"Sure do," Adam answered. "Good," Mac said as he smiled and winked at Mags.

Mac was an early riser but found it hard to leave Mags' warm body as she cuddled next to him. He slipped out of bed and headed towards the kitchen, hoping he could find the coffee and a lot of sweetener when he smelled the rich aroma wafting from the kitchen. Adam was there with a cup of strong coffee straight from the Keurig coffee maker sitting on the island. "When I heard you get up, I put your mug on. And, I have both sweetener and sugar and cream there too."

"You are a wonderful son. Not just coffee…I really mean it. I am more grateful than you could know."

Mags came into the kitchen followed soon by Kelly. "What do you guys want to do today? Kelly asked.

"Well, Mac wants to take in Beauvoir. Have you ever been there?"

"No, we haven't, and we've wanted to see that place. I hear it is really interesting. May we join you?"

"Of course," Mags replied.

Adam already had eggs and bacon on the stove and biscuits in the oven. "Wow, Son, you are becoming quite the cook. I remember when I couldn't even get you to make a PB and J."

Adam laughed, "I wasn't married to the liberated Kelly then."

"Atta girl," Mags said, giving Kelly a high five.

With breakfast over and the dishes in the dishwasher, the two couples walked out to the convertible.

"When did you get this, Dad?" Adam asked.

"Just a few months ago. Call it our late life crisis."

Mags pretended anger and said, "Late life? Speak for yourself, Old Man."

Laughing, they got into the car as Mac lowered the top.

Beauvoir sat on a slight rise facing the Gulf of Mexico. The grounds were beautiful, and on the way to the entrance, the group saw a large statue of Jefferson Davis.

Mac became the guide saying, "I understand that Jeff Davis settled here after he was released from prison after the end of the War Between the States. Leastways, that's what I found on the Internet!"

"Wow, he had a fantastic view from his front porch. Just look at that beach and the rolling surf," Kelly exclaimed. "It just booms and crashes: beautiful."

A docent met the group at the front door and invited them inside. They moved from room to room, marveling at the sights until they completed their tour.

Upon returning to their car, Mags said, "The things that were most interesting to me is that small bath tub, the man and woman's recliners, and the fact that they each had a bedroom."

"Don't get any ideas, Mags," Mac said in jest.

"No wonder the south lost the war," said Adam with a laugh.

After a nice lunch on the beach front, the couples returned to Adam and Kelly's home.

"I think Duke is playing a game today. Think it will be on TV?" Mac asked.

"Yep, I checked the listings. They're playing Louisville in some kind of a pre-season tournament game." Adam said.

All four settled in the family room and watched the game together on the large sixty inch flat screen TV. All four cheered, but no one louder than Mags. The game was close but Duke pulled out the victory on a final three point shot with only seconds left.

"Whew, great win." Mac exclaimed.

"And you expected less?" Mags chided.

The evening progressed with a great dinner and more visiting. Mac spoke up: "Mags told me that Kelly asked if we could drop by on our way back. If that is still okay, we could come by and spend the night, but we'll need to leave early Thursday morning."

"Of course it's okay," Adam responded. The couples retired to their bedrooms.

As usual, Mac arose at 5:00 but was surprised to find Mags already awake and dressed.

"Are you feeling okay, Darling?"

"I just didn't sleep too well. I've had some small pains."

Mac with concern said, "Why didn't you tell me?"

"Oh, I don't think it is a thing to worry about. I think the sleeplessness is because of the wonderful time we've had here. I've been reliving our visit."

Mac did not say anything, but any hint of a sneak attack from cancer kicked him into his worry mode.

The couple slipped out of the house carrying their luggage, having told Adam and Kelly that they would leave early and get breakfast on the road. It was Sunday morning.

10

THE CRISP FALL AIR FELT good, blowing over the windshield of the Sebring. Mags leaned back, rested for a few blocks and then suddenly sat up straight, banged Mac on the arm and said, "Don't you think we ought to give this car a name?"

"Good grief! Where did that come from?"

"I was just thinking," Mags said, "that we ought to have a contest—just you and me—to see who could come up with the best name for the car."

Mac's mind was still wandering around the thoughts of what Mags called 'small pains.' Thinking about car names was the last thing he wanted to consider.

Mags continued. "For example, since this was the second car we got, we could call it 'Junior.'"

Mac looked at her quizzically.

"Or, since we drive it without a top, we could name it 'Bubbles LaVoo.'"

"Bubbles LaVoo?"

"Yeah, you know," Mags went on enthusiastically, "Bubbles LaVoo sounds like a topless dancer."

"I guess I'm just not into giving names to cars," Mac explained. "Why don't you work on it and tell me what you decide."

Mags pondered for a few moments and then said, "The King? It rhymes with Sebring. Or, Sea Breeze—like the wind blowing on us."

Mac smiled, but said nothing. He thought, "She must be worried about those pains. Why else would she go on about naming this silly car?"

Neither of them made an effort to load the remaining CD from the Cornwall novel. Mac was absorbed in wondering about the days ahead. Mags was silent in her own reflections.

Finally, Mac asked, "Hungry?"

"OK," she answered. "Next exit?"

About two hours after leaving Biloxi, the two left the Interstate and headed toward the Golden Arch. "Drive through?" Mags inquired.

Mac grinned. "No, me thinks I best go in to the facilities."

After Mac returned from his rest break, he joined Mags at the counter. A young man, whose face looked like the "before" picture for an anti-acne cream advertisement, posed the standard question: "How can I help you?"

"Go for it," kidded Mac to Mags. "It's a long way to lunch!"

"How can I help you?" the youth repeated.

Mac looked at the menu board and said, "I'll take the big breakfast with hotcakes and orange juice and coffee and two extra sugars and a cinnamon bun and..." Before he could complete the sentence, Mags interrupted. "And that will be all you're having!"

Mac laughed. "You do care about me, don't you, Mrs. Mason!"

"How can I help you?" insisted the clerk.

Mags said, "Fruit and maple oatmeal, and a small orange juice."

As Mac paid for the order and waited for the tray of food, Mags scouted out plastic ware, napkins, and a table. "I picked this spot at the window," she remarked when Mac joined her. "Since we left our worldly possessions in the back seat of an open convertible, I thought we might keep a watch on things!"

Locals began to filter in. Rather than chatting with each other, Mac and Mags enjoyed people-watching. With a casual nod of the head, Mac pointed out the woman whose hat appeared to be a large serving of fruit. He scratched out a note on a napkin: "When you can, look up Carmen Miranda on the web." Mags smiled.

At the next table, a man and a boy were talking, the man trying to keep his voice down and the boy speaking loudly. "I want another muffin," he said. "I'm still hungry."

The man answered softly, "Billy, that's all the money I have. I can't buy you another muffin."

The boy said, "But, Daddy, I'm hungry. You said I'm a growing boy. I'm almost five years old. Please buy me something else to eat."

"Son, I wish I could. I'm not even sure we have enough gas to get all the way home. I spent our last bit on your breakfast muffin."

The boy stopped begging, but his tear-touched face told the story that this was not the first time his daddy had told him there was no more money. "I wish we weren't poor," he said, not speaking quietly.

Mags reached into her purse. "I'm going to buy that boy another muffin," she said.

Mac laid his hand lightly on Mags' arm. "Don't, Hon," he said. "It might embarrass the father, and it might just be a scam."

"What has the world come to when you can't help somebody?" she asked.

Before Mac and Mags walked back to their car, she approached the manager, handed him five dollars and nodded toward the table. The manager smiled his understanding.

11

As the Sebring pulled out of the parking lot, instead of turning left to go back to the Interstate, Mac turned to the right.

"The Interstate is the other way, isn't it?" Mags insisted.

"Yeah, but I want to check out something." Mac drove slowly a few hundred yards and pulled in front of a small church. He said, "I feel the need for us to do this. OK?"

Mags, knowing that she felt some stirrings of her own anxiety, nodded. "Sure. That would be nice."

"I saw this church from McDonalds and thought we really might stop."

There was only one other car at the church. "Early maybe?" Mac wondered out loud.

Mags read the sign board in front of the small frame building. "Welcome to Harmony Baptist Church. Sunday at 10:00. Wednesday at 7:30."

"Early," she said.

"Maybe down the road," Mac said. "I still want to go to church today."

A few blocks farther, Mac turned. The church driveway was gravel. There were a few well-worn parking spaces in the grass that formed the side yard. A large oak tree offered the only possibility for shade, but there were several picnic tables that sat waiting for the next covered dish lunch.

"Sort of homey, isn't it? Not exactly like the five hundred people per Sunday place we go. This is kind of nice, but I guess not today. We're still too early" Mags shook her head "Yes" as Mac pointed back toward the Interstate.

Although they resumed playing the Cornwall audio book, both Mac and Mags alternated between listening to the closing portions of the recorded story and thinking about the yet-to-be-revealed story of their own lives. This journey to Houston might well have a happy ending…or not.

Around 10:30 that morning, Mac said, "Why don't you play with the GPS some and see if you can find a church that is not too far off the highway?"

"How do you do that?"

"Key in 'church,' when it asks you to enter the destination, I think it will direct us to several nearby churches."

That is exactly what happened and at 10:55, Mac and Mags pulled into the parking lot of Babble Creek Community Church. They closed the top of the convertible. Mac said, "This one is at 11:00, so I think we are on time!"

"Babble Creek is surely an interesting name," Mac said, as they stepped to the single door that led to the sanctuary of the brick church. "Wonder how it got its name."

An elderly man was playing a medley of hymns on an electronic keyboard as Mac and Mags accepted a bulletin from an usher and took a seat two rows from the back of the sparsely attended worship service. Two or three people turned to look at them, but no one spoke.

Mags whispered to Mac, "Do you think we are dressed okay for these people? They all look like they are in their finery, not in their driving clothes!"

The service unfolded in ways familiar to Mac and Mags. The hymns were what they called "oldie but goldies" and they sang with gusto. In fact, Mags leaned over to Mac and said in an undertone, "Am I singing too loudly? That woman over there keeps looking at me." Mac shrugged his shoulders.

Mags looked at the small stained glass windows that went down both sides of the sanctuary. One was a picture of Jesus holding a lamb. At the bottom were the words "In Memory of Graham Babble, 1910-1965." She studied another window, a design of Noah and the ark. The words read "In memory of Jason Babble, 1908-1990." From her pew, she could see one other window, an open Bible. The small rectangle at the bottom said, "In memory of Alice Babble, 1897-1950."

Mags could not resist murmuring to Mac: "I think I know how it got its name!" She cut her eyes toward the windows and Mac read the dedications and shook his head in agreement.

The pew smelled of furniture polish. The cushions were in a red that matched the carpet. The hymnals appeared worn with love. The little pockets held offering envelopes and tiny pencils. In the pew rack was a bulletin left from an earlier service. The soft light from the chandeliers gave off a peaceful glow. As the pastor offered prayer, Mac reached over and held Mags' hand, and they both seemed to be just where they wanted to be.

At precisely twelve noon, the blessing "Go in the name of the Father and the Son and the Holy Spirit" dismissed the congregation. When Mac and Mags turned to step from their pew, a plump woman began moving toward them with haste. "That's the woman who kept looking at me," Mags said.

The woman approached. She was wearing a polyester flowered suit. In her left hand was the bulletin, but she extended her right hand and said, "Hello. I am Gertie Babble. Are you somebody?"

Mac waited a split second and then answered, "Well, yes, I suppose all of us are somebody."

Gertie responded with some agitation, "I wasn't talking to you. I was talking to this young lady. Are you somebody?"

Mags hesitated and said, "I'm not sure what you mean."

"Well, I was just telling Helen that you look like somebody I've seen before. Are you famous?"

"Famous? I don't think of myself that way."

"But I've seen you somewhere. Are you sure you are not on television? Do you do one of those…"

Mags broke in. "No, I am rarely on television. I am Maggie Miller Mason. I do some modeling occasionally."

Gertie stood stock still. "Lord, have sweet mercy!" she bellowed. "That's where I know you! You were on the cover of my *Vogue* magazine. You were the woman in that skin moisturizer ad. You… oh, my! I want your autograph! Here, would you sign my bulletin?"

Mags seemed puzzled but took the bulletin. She reached for a pencil from the holder in the back of the pew. Still a bit mystified by this attention, she wrote "Maggie Mason." "I used to be Maggie Miller, but this is my married name. Happily married. This is Mac, my husband."

"Pleased to meet you," Gertie said rather dismissively. "Oh, Helen is going to be so jealous! Thank you, thank you!" She gave Mags a hug and ran off to tell her friends about her discovery of a real live celebrity.

By the time Mac and Mags got back to their car, Gertie was pointing toward them and talking rapidly to a number of other women. Mags heard one of them ask, "Do you think it would be all right if I took her picture?" Mags instinctively brushed her hair out of her face and tried to straighten the outfit she was wearing.

Six or seven women gathered around the car, each one holding out a bulletin for an autograph or stepping for the best angle for a photograph with a cell phone camera. "Miss Gertie said you were a friend of hers and that it would be okay to take your picture," one said.

"I'm not a Babble, but I've been going to this church for thirty years," another offered.

Gertie walked over, a bit proud of her connection with Mags. "Now you two stop here again anytime you want to!"

Mags smiled and said, "That would be lovely. But, before we go, can I ask for your help?"

The women all nodded and Mags continued: "I'm bringing out a new perfume called Mmmm. It's not on the market yet, but I have some samples. May I give each of you one? All I ask is that you use the card that is attached to the sample and let the folks back at the office know how you like it. You will be part of our test market!"

Mags asked Mac to open the trunk of the car and she took samples from a box and gave one to each of the ladies. "Other products with the same fragrance will be introduced next year: bath oil, soap, shampoo and a number of other items. We think the Mmmm product line will be very popular."

The ladies gushed their appreciation and all smelled their sample and exclaimed on how much they liked it. Gertie said, "I'll make sure every one of these ladies sends a card back in." Mags smiled her appreciation. It was time to go.

Mac helped Mags into the car. He giggled to himself when he heard one voice say, "Oh, isn't she so graceful when she gets into a car!"

The top came down again. As soon as they left the church parking lot, Mac let out a big sigh of relief. "Well," he began, "that surely was different!"

"I'm embarrassed," Mags responded. "You deserve something special. We must stop at Family Thrift when we get to Houston."

Mac leaned over and gave Mags a kiss on the cheek. "I love that place! You know I do!" He headed toward the highway, happy to be going toward his favorite consignment store. He could not help but laugh at the memory of the three hours he spent there on one trip to Houston.

"Family Thrift for me and Pappasito's for you!" Mac enthused. "I can shop and you can eat!"

The miles passed quickly. The warm Texas sun welcomed them. And after Mac had spent thirty minutes shopping for a pair of trousers he did not need, Mags and Mac enjoyed the cheese enchiladas, the refried beans, and margaritas that highlighted every visit to their favorite restaurant.

In spite of the long drive, they were not particularly tired as they parked their car at the Rotary House International, the hotel owned by MD Anderson Medical Center. They stopped for a moment and each took a deep breath. They were there at MD Anderson and they both knew why they had come. They just did not know what came next.

12

2004

THE WAVES FROM THE STORM had died down, but it was still difficult to pull the raft near the fishing vessel. Several hands reached down, and slowly the rubber craft tumbled onto the deck.

Tentative greetings were exchanged. Everyone on the fishing boat did not know the code, so it seemed like friendly chatter when one asked "Did you catch any fish?"

A calm voice answered. "Sometimes you catch the fish. Sometimes the fish catch you."

"Is everything handled?"

"I'd have to dig deep for an answer to that," came the enigmatic reply.

The fishing boat continued its trip away from the island. Some on board knew what was left behind. Others simply piloted the vessel toward its home port.

13

The Present

AFTER CHECKING INTO THE ROTARY House, Mac moved the car to the parking garage, knowing he and Mags probably wouldn't need it until departure in two days. The hospital had a number of cafeterias and the hotel had a fine restaurant. And, if Mags was exhausted after her tests, there was always room service. He raised the roof of the convertible and made sure anything valuable was stored safely in the trunk.

Mac then took an elevator to the eleventh floor and room 1113. Mags had arranged for the bellman to take their luggage to the room and she was unpacking one of her suitcases, putting clothing into the closet and dresser drawers.

"I'm glad I packed in such a way that I don't have to bring both of my suitcases to the room," Mags stated.

Mac began to unpack his suitcase. He hated living out of a suitcase even for two days.

"How are you feeling, Darling?" Mac asked. "Have you experienced any more pain?"

"I'm tired. The pain hasn't been out of control, but yes, I do feel discomfort."

"Hon, I'm glad we are here in case there are any issues. You'll be fine. I'm sure of that. Maybe your body is responding to two cheese enchiladas, the refried beans and that zesty picante sauce, not to mention the margarita."

Mags' face revealed nothing, but she didn't understand Mac's seeming disregard for the possible implications of what she was feeling. She was sure that the pain wasn't caused by dinner. Was she being overly emotional or was Mac taking this visit far too casually?

After unpacking, Mags showered, donned an oversized pink Duke tee shirt and slipped between the sheets. Mac followed her lead and prepared for bed. Tomorrow would be a long day and a good night's sleep was called for. They turned on the TV briefly but Mags soon turned it off as Mac fell asleep. Mags felt the dread that she always had before her visits to Houston. She laid there in the large king sized bed, staring at the ceiling, and finally fell asleep an hour later.

Mac, of course, woke up before 6:00 AM, quietly dressed and went down to the lobby where he knew he'd find coffee. Mags' first appointment was not until 10:00, so there was no reason for her to get up. Mac prepared his coffee and took the complimentary *USA Today* and settled into a plush chair in a room adjacent to the lobby, turning immediately to the sports pages. There was an article on the Duke-Louisville game and predictions that Duke could possibly be the team to beat this year. Mac smiled, knowing that his favorite time of the year was here, five months of Duke basketball. Now, if they just got good news from Mags' tests at the meeting with Dr. Holt tomorrow everything would be great.

Around 8 AM, Mags walked into the sitting room where Mac was checking email messages on his cell phone. "Anything important?" Mags asked.

"We have an email from Adam and Kelly, letting us know we are in their prayers, and we also heard from Will and Kate. They wanted you to know they are thinking of you today also."

Mags made a cup of black decaf coffee. She was allowed this on the day of tests but could not have breakfast until after the blood work was completed. "Do you want some breakfast?" she asked Mac.

"No, Darling, I'll wait and eat with you. Mags, everything will be okay today. No matter what the tests show, you can handle it. You're the strongest woman I've ever met."

Still not feeling a great deal of support from Mac, Mags simply said, "Thank you."

At 9:30, the couple took the elevator up one floor and began the walk across the sky bridge to the hospital. Although this was their fourth trip to Houston, Mac and Mags were still in awe of the size of the medical center. It had multiple buildings and each was at least eight floors. The elevators began at Elevator A and were lettered through Z and then began again at AA. They had no idea how many elevators the hospital had. They both agreed that this medical center was like nothing they had experienced before. The service personnel were amazing. If you looked lost, someone would always step up and ask to help. Even passing doctors had offered them assistance. Mags often recounted to others that she felt more like a guest than a patient. Mac agreed.

Taking the escalator near Elevator A to the second floor, the couple walked to the Diagnostic Center where Mags checked in. They waited for Mags' name to be called. Within five minutes she was called, blood was drawn and within ten minutes, she was out and ready for breakfast. She had two hours until her next appointment.

Mac and Mags returned to the first floor and the cafeteria. It was huge and each chose from the vast assortment of breakfast goodies.

After breakfast and having looked through several shops on the first floor of the hospital, Mac asked, "We still have over an hour until your next appointment. Do you want to go back to the room?"

"No," Mags replied, "Let's just go to the appointment. Maybe they can get me in earlier and, if not, we can read."

Both Mac and Mags had brought their Kindles and enjoyed reading. Mac was in the middle of a complete history of the Revolutionary War and Mags was enjoying a Lorena McCourtney mystery. Taking Elevator C to the third floor, they arrived at Diagnostic Imaging where Mags would go through two hours of preparation for the CT Scan that would target her chest, abdomen, and pelvis.

Before this procedure, Mags was required to drink two large bottles of imaging contrast. She chose banana flavor this time and commented that it wasn't that bad. As both Mac and Mags waited the required time, they each read in silence. Sometimes they would enter into conversation with other patients and their families. The number of cancer patients at the medical center was astounding, and they were from all over the world. It was as if all the patients were part of a club, but the club was far from exclusive. Every age, walk of life and nationality seemed to be represented. Cancer was an undiscriminating invader.

Mac looked into the hallway and saw a man dressed in robes from head to toe. Following him were three women dressed in all black with their faces covered. Mac nudged Mags and indicated the direction with a nod. "Do you think that is an Arab sheik with his harem?"

"I don't know," Mags replied, "but I don't think he is from Babble Creek!"

"Margaret Mason?" a nurse called out from a doorway. The time for the CT Scan had come and Mags rose to follow the lead of the woman in blue scrubs. Mac smiled and blew her a kiss.

Mags was allergic to the iodine in the dye usually used before the CT Scan, so she had to be given Benadryl. The Benadryl always made Mags tired and somewhat loopy. After the scan, she came back out; Mac stood and took her by the arm. They began their walk back to the hotel. Mac was always amused at the way Mags reacted to the Benadryl. She stared wide-eyed out the windows and at the ceiling with a silly grin on her face.

"You're sure cute when you're loopy," Mac smiled as they crossed the sky bridge.

Upon entering their room, Mags immediately fell into bed, pulling the covers over her head. She was asleep within minutes. Mac just looked at her thinking, "I'm sure the luckiest man alive."

After Mags woke up and reported that she was feeling fine, the couple went to the hotel's restaurant. They both chose the buffet and enjoyed a wonderful meal.

"What time is your appointment with Dr. Holt tomorrow?" Mac asked.

"10:00 AM," Mags replied.

Mac responded, "We should be out by 11 and on the road. We won't get to Adam and Kelly's until around 7. I'll pack the car early tomorrow morning and we can call them about our estimated arrival time."

After dinner, the couple returned to their room, packed for the return trip home and settled down on the bed to watch a movie on TV. It was *War Horse*, a movie based on a book Mags and Mac had listened to on a previous trip to Houston. After the movie, Mac turned off the TV and fell immediately to sleep. Mags again stared at the ceiling concerned over what tomorrow's report would be.

The waiting area on the seventh floor of the hospital was full. Within a few minutes, Paula, Dr. Holt's RN, came to Mags smiling. "Hi, Mrs. Mason; let's go back and Dr. Holt will be with you soon." The trio entered a small examination room. Paula took some information from Mags and just looked down as Mags told her about the pains she had been experiencing. She left the room promising that Dr. Holt would be in soon.

There was a gentle knock on the exam room door and Dr. Holt entered. As Dr. Rachna Holt had become a friend as well as her doctor, Mags stood to hug her. The physician was petite, with black hair and dark brown eyes. Standing only 5'2" with a dark complexion, short skirt and four inch heels, Mac would describe her as exotic. She was East Indian by birth and had married her husband during medical school in the states. She had recently given birth to a baby girl and her PA had even emailed Mags the news at Rachna's request. Mac and Mags had sent flowers and a card of congratulations.

After some pleasantries were exchanged, Rachna sat down at her computer and began bringing up files and images. "Maggie, the news isn't good. It looks like there are two new growths. They're located here" pointing to two shadows on the computer screen.

"I was afraid of that," Mags said gripping Mac's hand tightly. Both of them trembled slightly.

"What do we do?"

"I'm not sure yet, Maggie. Your platelets are so low that I'm hesitant to have you take any more chemo. I want to think about it for a day or so and then talk to you about a plan of action."

A tear ran down Mags' cheek. Mac said, "Is surgery possible?"

"No," replied Dr. Holt, "the growths are so close to the aorta that I wouldn't want to take the risk."

Mags asked, "You'll call us as soon as you have come up with a plan?"

"Of course I will, Maggie. Of course I will."

Mac turned as he was leaving the exam room, "Oh, one last question, Dr. Holt? We are scheduled to participate in an archeological dig the end of this month. Should we cancel that?"

"I don't think so, Mac. Maggie, you do whatever you feel up to doing. You won't be taking chemo so you'll probably feel better. Just don't overdo. If you get tired, listen to your body and rest."

The three hugged again and Mags and Mac began the walk to the hotel and their car.

Mac drove from the hospital parking garage, following the GPS directions until they reached I-10 East. Neither Mac nor Mags spoke for the first fifteen minutes of the drive.

"I thought this was over," Mags said through tears. "No chemo, no surgery; I feel so completely lost right now."

"I know," said Mac, "but you'll get through this." Mags again wondered if Mac was taking this too lightly. He wasn't using the word "we."

After a short time, Mags put another disc into the CD player. Mags and Mac tried to lose themselves in the story, but it was hard to turn off the voice of Dr. Holt: "The news isn't good."

14

Mid-afternoon, after a short stop at a Waffle House for lunch, Mac said, "You might want to call Kelly and tell her that we'll arrive around 7 PM."

Mags pulled out her cell phone and made the call. When asked about the appointment, Mags just said, "We'll tell you when we see you" and disconnected the call.

The GPS was exactly on target with the arrival time, so at 6:55 PM, they turned onto McDonald Street and pulled into the driveway.

Kelly ran out the door and gave Mags a huge hug. Mac took their suitcases out of the trunk and following Kelly and Mags, carried the luggage into the house.

"What's the news?" asked Kelly.

"Where's Adam?" Mags asked.

"He had to work late tonight but promised to be home by the time you got here. I expect him any minute. Now, what's the news?"

Mac replied, "We'd rather wait for Adam and tell it once. OK?"

"I'm worried now," shared Kelly.

The three heard the front door opening and Adam calling out, "I'm homeee Lucyyyy!"

Laughing, Kelly said, "Your Desi imitation needs work, Hon. We're in the family room."

"Hi, folks. Have you offered Dad and Mom a drink?" Adam asked.

"They just got here. I've got a bottle of Zin cooling. How about a glass of that?"

Mags broke in with, "I could sure use that."

Adam went into the kitchen and returned with two full glasses of wine for Kelly and Mags and two bottles of Amstel Light for him and Mac.

"OK, now can we have the news?" insisted Kelly.

Mac, seeing Mags' hesitancy, spoke, "Well, it's not good. Mags has two more growths, small, the size of a nickel and a dime but in a difficult place. It's next to the aorta so surgery isn't possible. Her platelets are very low and Dr. Holt doesn't want her to take any more chemo. You know, she has had twenty-four already."

"Well, what treatment is possible?" Kelly implored with tears in her eyes.

"We don't know. Dr. Holt is going to contact us when she has some suggestions."

Mags began to cry and said, "You'll have to excuse me," and rushed from the room. She opened the door to the back patio and went out. Kelly followed her, signaling Mac and saying, "I've got this."

Kelly walked up behind Mags and put her arms around her waist. "I know how hard this is for you. You fought so hard and thought you had the battle won. What can I do, Mom?"

Mags turned around and put her arms around Kelly and hugged her close. "Oh, Kelly, there's nothing anyone can do now except keep praying. And, I wish Mac ..."

She stopped in mid-sentence. "Mom, what do you wish about Mac? Tell me."

"OK, Kelly, I don't think Mac takes this seriously. I don't really feel any sympathy from him at all. Oh, he says the right things, but he just doesn't seem to see the possibilities of what might happen."

"You've been married to Mac for twelve years. I've only been married to Adam for two, but I've learned something. Here's what I think. They are Mason men. They have spent their adult lives in law enforcement, often in life and death situations. They do not ever show weakness. Mac has to remain strong. He has to feel like he has this whole thing under control. I know from what Adam has shared with me that Mac has been worried sick about you since your first diagnosis. He is your advocate, your strongest supporter, but he won't show you his concern. I believe he thinks you will worry more if he shows his concern.

"Oh, Kelly, you are so right. With everything I have on my mind, I didn't even consider that. I should have put that together myself. I'm an emotional wreck right now. I'll give him an extra big kiss and hug tonight and maybe a little more when we go to bed."

They both laughed and returned to the family room. Mags went straight to sit on the sofa next to Mac and placed her hand on his knee giving it a gentle squeeze. "Love you, Darling," she said.

"I love you, too," Mac said, leaning over and kissing her cheek.

At that moment, Mags' cell phone rang. Running to the table near the entrance of the house where she left her purse, she found the cell phone and answered.

"Maggie Mason," she answered.

"Maggie, it's Rachna Holt. Do you have a minute?"

"Definitely," Mags said, walking towards the family room and mouthing the name, "Dr. Holt" and putting the phone on speaker.

"Well, after you left I started thinking more about your case. I looked at the images again and remembered an radiation oncologist friend of mine who is tops in his field. I forwarded your records to him for him to study. He has already gotten back to me."

"What did he say?" Mags got up her nerve to ask.

"He says he can target those two growths and feels he can kill them with radiation."

Mags broke into tears and handed the phone to Mac. "Dr. Holt, this is Mac. I'm afraid that Mags can't talk right now. Your news is a miracle. What are we supposed to do next?"

"Well, I want Maggie to take a break from the chemo, rest her body and prepare to come back here in six weeks. You'll need to be prepared to stay here for two months for the radiation treatments. Any more questions?"

"No, Dr. Holt, I can't think of any for now. You have made our day. Thank you!"

Goodbyes were said and Mac took the crying Mags into his arms. Adam and Kelly stood and wrapped their arms around the couple. Happy tears were shed by all four.

The following morning Mac and Mags got up at 6 AM, visited with Kelly and Adam over a light breakfast and loaded up for their remaining eight hour drive home. The glimpse of the morning sun said exactly what they were thinking: it is a new day; maybe there is hope.

15

Mac and Mags continued their drive back to Florida. Having completed their discs of Patricia Cornwell's novel, they began listening to a shorter novel by Nora Roberts, one of Mags' favorite romance authors.

"Oh, good!" Mac exclaimed. "Rest area in two miles!"

Mags stretched her arms. "You woke me up! I dozed off."

"Were you dreaming about me?" Mac teased.

"Now would that be a dream or a nightmare?" Mags laughed.

As they pulled into the rest area parking lot, Mac noticed something unusual: there were four cars in a row, all with Vermont license plates.

"What are the odds of that?" Mac commented.

When they returned to their car, Mags noticed that one of the Vermont cars now had a couple standing next to it. "A long way to Vermont," Mags said with a smile.

"Indeed," came the non-committal answer.

Mac approached the couple, "Vermont: beautiful state. Hope you enjoyed your sojourn down our way. We're from Florida, leastways now."

"It was hard to enjoy this trip. We have been to Texas for a funeral. My grandmother. She lived to be 99 and died just two days before her 100th birthday."

"I'm sorry," Mags said softly.

"Are you traveling together?" Mac asked, pointing to the Vermont tags.

"Yes, I guess we wouldn't get lost on our own, but we just need to be close to each other. It sort of helps our grief."

There were persons now at each of the long-way-from-home cars.

Mac said, "If it is okay with you, I want to do something I have never done before. I mean, I've never done it in a parking lot with complete strangers."

"What is that you want to do?"

"If all of you can gather close by, if you don't think I am some kind of religious weirdo, I'd like to have a prayer with you."

A tear slipped down the face of the man with whom Mac had been speaking. "Would you?" he asked.

The group held hands and Mac offered a simple prayer: "Lord, these people are hurting. Travel with them and give them the peace that passes understanding. Thank You for the long life these travelers remember. And even now walk with them in the shadows of death. Amen."

Some got back into their cars without saying anything. Some came over and gave Mac a hug. Some stood quietly, adding their own silent prayers.

The Masons gave a wave of good-bye and got back into their car. Mags said, "As usual, Mr. Mason, I am so proud of you. That was a beautiful thing to do."

The miles seemed to dissolve quickly.

It was late afternoon when they reached Exit 193 and turned onto Jacaranda Boulevard.

"It always feels so good to make this exit and know we are near home," Mags commented.

"Five minutes and we'll be there," Mac responded.

Mac and Mags pulled into their driveway and began unloading their car. Mac insisted on carrying all the heavy luggage. Mags smiled, knowing that Mac was concerned about her health. She knew that he did care and loved him all the more because of his concern.

Mac and Mags unpacked their suitcases leaving dirty clothes in the laundry room for Mags to wash. Mags wouldn't allow Mac to wash any clothes. When Mac asked why, Mags replied, "You would just throw all the clothes into the washing machine. You don't sort." "They get clean, don't they?" Mac replied. "Yes, if you don't mind pink underwear. I swear. Men!" Mac just laughed.

The next morning, knowing they'd need to leave in a few days, Mac and Mags began making plans for their trip to Joseffa Island.

Mac remembered and said, "I haven't confirmed to Will that we are coming for the dig. I need to call him."

"It will be good to see Will and Kate again. It's been seven months," Mags replied. "And you should probably call Bob also. I don't know if he and Susan will be on the island, but it sure would be good to see them again". Bob and Susan were the owners of Joseffa Island and good friends of Mac and Mags.

"Are we taking the Joseffa Island shuttle over to the island or are we taking *The Mistress*?" Mags asked. *The Mistress* was Mac and Mag's 39 foot Bayliner Motor Launch. It slept four comfortably with two staterooms, a full galley and two baths.

"*The Mistress*, if that's okay with you. We can stay on her and save having to find a cottage available to rent," Mac replied. "That reminds me. I'll need to call Pat Jefferson also to arrange for docking of *The Mistress* and also to reserve a golf cart for island transportation." Patrick Jefferson (Pat) was the CEO of Joseffa Island and was much more than just a business acquaintance of the Masons. Mags and Mac had become members of the Joseffa Island Club some years earlier so now they had access to the private island.

"That will be fine. I'll just need to shop for groceries to stock the boat," Mags offered. "I'm headed to Walmart to stock up on all the groceries we'll need for two weeks."

"Don't forget the toilet paper," Mac said with a smile. "We don't want to have to buy it on the island."

On a previous trip, the couple had run out of TP and were stunned to find out that one roll of single ply toilet paper had cost $2.59.

"Oh, I definitely have that on my list," laughed Mags.

16

2004

THE WAVES SEEMED TO SETTLE down as the activity on the boat settled down. The crew relaxed as the vessel moved deeper into the Gulf waters. There were eight or ten men on the craft and slowly, one at a time, they slipped below deck to see what the cook had fixed for lunch. Time out on the water seemed to make everyone hungry.

The captain kept a hand on the wheel but the boat almost seemed to choose its own course. Wherever it was going, it was going to be away from the island, far away.

One man, his skin rugged from exposure to the daily sun, slipped next to the captain. Both of the men seemed lost in thought, but neither of them spoke. Another man joined them and it was as if they each knew what the other was thinking. Slowly, they joined hands in kind of a congratulatory circle.

The radio antenna whipped in the breeze as it sent a signal to some far off receiver. An answer came back: "Message received."

17

The Present

MAC MADE THE NECESSARY CALLS to Bob Gardner, the owner of Joseffa Island. "Hi, Bob. Mac here."

"How are you, Mac? When are Susan and I going to see you two again?"

"We hope we'll see you soon. Are you going to be on Joseffa for the archaeological dig next week?"

"We do plan on being there at least part of the time. Are you and Mags going to help this time?"

"Yes, we'll be there for the entire two weeks if Mags is up to it," Mac replied.

"How's she doing, Mac? We've been concerned."

"We have some news, but if you don't mind, we'll share it when we see you."

"OK, I'll tell Susan and we hope you can join us for dinner at the Inn or the cottage while you're here. Are you staying on *The Mistress?*"

"Yes, we're coming over Saturday and should be there early afternoon. We'd love to have dinner with you and Susan. I need to get off now and call Pat about docking and a golf cart. You have a great day."

"You have a good day too and tell Pat to let you use our extra cart. We only need one when we come. It silly for you to rent one," Bob offered.

"Great, and thanks, Bob. Goodbye for now."

"Bye, Mac."

Mac then called Pat Jefferson, the CEO of Joseffa, and made arrangements for docking *The Mistress* and for using Bob's golf cart. He also called the Venice Yacht Club where he docked *The Mistress* and arranged for fueling and readiness for their departure Saturday. When the receptionist at the Yacht Club began to hang up, she said, "And have a happy Thanksgiving!"

Mac said, "I love Thanksgiving in Florida. There's no snow, when over the river and through the woods, to Grandmother's house we go!"

They set up a table on the lanai; using candles shaped like turkeys and added gold napkins. It was a tradition from Mags' family to place a few kernels of corn on the table, a reminder of how the early settlers gave thanks even when life was simple, almost barren. Because they were leaving Saturday for Joseffa Island, they planned a simple holiday lunch, just the two of them.

"Does a turkey sandwich qualify as a Thanksgiving banquet?"

Mags answered, "Only if you have a side dish of canned cranberry sauce."

A few potato chips completed the meal, although there was peppermint flavored ice cream in the freezer if they decided to go full tilt.

"I am thankful for you," Mac said.

"And I am thankful for you."

They reached across the table to hold hands while Mac said a blessing, but before he could speak, there was an insistent ring of the doorbell.

"Who could that be on Thanksgiving Day?" Mac put down his napkin and headed for the door.

When he opened the door, a woman stood there, maybe thirty years old.

"Eve!" shouted Mac. Then he called out to the lanai, "Mags, its Eve!"

The woman did not step in but said in a straight-forward voice. "I prefer that you call me Evelyn."

By now, Mags had made her way to the front of the house. With a friendly sweep of her arm, she said, "Eve, come on in!"

"My…name…is…Evelyn, Evelyn Thomas." She walked into the entry way and said, "You know that you named me 'Eve' because you thought it was so clever to have a son and a daughter named Adam and Eve."

When Mac and Ruth had divorced, Ruth chose to revert to her maiden name. Eve, in anger, chose to adopt her mother's maiden name as well. This decision on Eve's part hurt Mac deeply, but he tried to respect his daughter's decision.

"Whew." Mac let out a long sigh. "I didn't know you were coming. I didn't know you were in Florida."

Evelyn crossed her arms and muttered, "Where I am and where I go is my business, not yours, Daddy-dear." She spoke with a tone bordering on venom.

"We were having a bite to eat—not much, really—but we'd love for you to come and share Thanksgiving lunch with us," Mags invited.

Mac rushed to the kitchen and made another sandwich while Mags set another place at the table. They all gathered on the lanai.

"How is my perfect brother?"

"Adam is okay."

"And his perfect wife?"

"Kelly is okay."

"And their perfect dog?"

"Edgar is okay."

There was silence as each munched on the turkey sandwich, unsure what to say next.

"You may wonder why I am here," Evelyn said.

"What you tell us is up to you," Mac replied.

"My counselor said I needed to get on better terms with my father. So, instead of spending Thanksgiving with Mom, I decided to visit you. Plus, I also have a friend in the area. So, here I am."

Mac and Mags exchanged glances.

"What's that look supposed to mean?"

"It means that you are welcomed here for as long as you can stay."

"Thank you. I can only be here today." Evelyn twisted her napkin in her hands and then added, "I really do want to get on better terms with you, Dad. I know that your splitting up with Mom does not have to mean that you and I split up." And then she gave a broad grin. "And for starters you can call me Eve! But remember Daddy Dear, it is still Eve Thomas. "

They all relaxed a bit, but they all knew that this journey of reconciliation was far from over.

The following day, Evelyn, AKA Eve, insisted on calling a taxi. She only smiled when they asked if she were going to the airport or train station or bus depot. "My counselor also said not to move too fast," she added to her smile. The cab came and with waves of good-bye, this surprising Thanksgiving visit was ended.

The following morning, Mac loaded the Camry's trunk with the suitcases he and Mags had packed, as well as the many bags of groceries and necessities they required for their two week stay on the island. Having arranged for Sam's care, including a special catnip treat, they left home for the drive to the Venice Yacht Club.

Arriving at the Yacht Club, they were met by a member of the staff. They loaded up a two-wheeled cart. It was large enough to transport all their luggage and grocery bags to *The Mistress*. Having put all the supplies and suitcases onto the deck of the boat, Mac began carrying everything below for Mags to organize. Mags began by putting the cold items into the two Nova Kool refrigerators and the freezer. Other items were placed in a surprisingly large pantry.

Mac checked to make sure that the three hundred gallon fuel tank was topped off and that the two hundred gallon fresh water tank was full. A dock worker loosened *The Mistress'* mooring lines as soon as Mac started the twin 330 hp Cummins diesel engines. Mac, piloting from the flying bridge, eased *The Mistress* from the dock and proceeded slowly away from the marina, adhering to the "No Wake" signs posted in the harbor.

From Venice, it was about a 45 minute cruise to Joseffa Island. The day was pleasant with the temperatures in the upper 70's. Mags was wearing a pair of capris and a warm sweater. Since the chemo treatments, any temperature below 70 seemed very cold to her. She knew the wind would make it seem colder than it was. Mac was in shorts and a tee shirt. His silver gray hair was blowing in the wind as he accelerated, having cleared the harbor. Mags stood on the top deck feeling Mac's arm around her waist as they picked up speed. Her blonde hair was tied back in a pony tail. Few people realized it was a wig. Her loss of hair was caused by the twenty-four chemo treatments she had received. Only Mac had seen her shaved head, and he still thought her the most beautiful woman he had ever seen.

The couple loved their time together on *The Mistress*. Mac slowed as they saw a pod of bottle nosed dolphins on the starboard side of the boat. He eased the boat towards the dolphins; the pod began following the boat, jumping and swimming in the wake as Mac accelerated again. Mags marveled at the beauty of the magnificent creatures.

Mac pointed up as they passed Boca Grande. Mags looked and saw an osprey nesting platform with a huge nest atop it.

"Look," said Mags, "how big that nest is."

"Do you remember the time we saw the baby ospreys?"

"Yeah, but this is not the season."

Mac giggled. "I remember you said they were 'cute-sy wute-sy.'"

"I don't talk like that!"

In a baby-talk voice, Mac said, "Awww. Look at the cute-sy wute-sy baby birds. They are just precious, just precious!"

"I don't talk like that!"

"Oh, yes you do, Mags-sy Wag-sy!"

Mags shook her head, rolled her eyes and then gave Mac a playful slap on the cheek. Then, she leaned over and said, "Aw, poor baby! Let Mama kiss it and make it all better!" She gave him a light buss.

They both laughed.

The cruise ended all too soon as Mac and Mags saw Joseffa Island appear in the distance.

Mac radioed the Joseffa Harbor Master and received instructions as to where to moor *The Mistress*. Mac slowly entered the indicated slip, dropped over dock bumpers, and threw the bow and then aft lines to harbor attendants who quickly tied *The Mistress* in place.

The Harbor Master, Phil, approached Mac and spoke. "Welcome back, Mr. Mason. It's been a while since we've seen you."

"Thanks, Phil. We'll be here for two weeks. We'll be staying on the boat."

"That's what Mr. Jefferson told me. If you need anything for your boat while here, just let me know."

Mac and Mags walked up the long, main dock to the Welcome Center and Administration Building. "Just wanted to check in with you," Mac said to the young man at the front desk. "Is Pat in?"

"Yes, he's in his office. Go right back. I know he's looking forward to seeing you."

Mac and Mags walked back to Pat's office and found him on the phone. When that call ended, Mac asked. "How's it going, Pat?"

"Going well here. How about with you two? Maggie, how are you doing?"

"The fight goes on, Pat. We have to go back to Houston after the first of the year for radiation, but we're just blessed that we're confident that we'll beat this thing. It's just more insidious than we could ever have thought."

"You know all our prayers are with you. I hear you'll be here helping the Marks on the dig."

"Yep, hopefully for the entire two weeks," Mags replied.

"Did Bob call you about using one of his golf carts while we are here?" Mac asked.

"He did, and it's out front, all charged up and ready to go," Pat responded.

"Great, I know we'll see you around. Is Bob on the island yet?"

"No, he and Susan are expected any time now. I'll let them know you are here when they arrive."

"Being a woman and unable to see a fine young man like you without a significant other, I have to ask. Is there a woman in your life now?" Mags asked with a smile.

"Well, there is someone. I'll tell you about her."

Just as Pat was ready to divulge the new woman in his life, his phone rang. After listening to Pat's side of the conversation for a moment, it was obvious that he would be on the phone a while. Mags and Mac waved goodbye and mouthed, "See you later!" and left Pat's office.

Mac and Mags returned to *The Mistress* and ate a ham and Swiss cheese sandwich, chips and enjoyed diet sodas. They tried to talk about Eve's unexpected visit but they were as mystified as they had been on Thanksgiving Day. Mags was feeling tired after arising early, loading and unloading and then the trip over to the island, plus the tension of yesterday's unusual family reunion.

"Think I might lie down awhile," she said.

Mac replied, "I might just join you." They moved to their stateroom in the aft of the boat and both were soon asleep.

18

WHEN MAC AWOKE IN THE late afternoon, he began to reflect on the island. Why was it such a special place?

Joseffa had a long and fascinating history of ten thousand years. At the conclusion of the ice age, what is now Joseffa Island was not an island at all but was part of the mainland of what is now Florida, lying sixty miles inland from the coast. As the ice melted, the island was formed. Now it was located six miles off the coast, separated from the mainland by Pine Island Sound.

Ten thousand years? In the mid-1980's a Santa Fe point, most likely used on a spear, was found on the island. Will Marks was shown the point and after some research, was able to date it to a period a thousand decades ago.

The island was first inhabited periodically by the Calusa Indians. The Calusa were an extremely advanced tribe of Native Americans who used Joseffa for a seasonal home. The Calusa had a strong religious faith. Even the Spanish priests visiting the island were unable to convert the Indians to Catholicism. The Calusa lived off the land and sea. They were known for their ability to make tools from shell and the bones of sea life. It was even thought that Joseffa was the site of a tool making industry. Sadly, the Calusa eventually became extinct due to disease brought by the Spanish, wars with neighboring tribes, and hostile actions perpetrated by the Spanish. The few remaining Calusa travelled south to Cuba and were assimilated into that culture.

The island had been the home to a number of fishing ranchos populated by the Spanish and Cubans. Mullet were netted, salted, and exported to Cuba. Joseffa had also been the location of a small fort that housed a contingent of soldiers active in the Seminole Wars in Florida. The fort was also manned for a brief time by northern soldiers during the Civil War.

Joseffa had been owned by a number of well-known entrepreneurs from the eighteenth century until the present. It became a vacation and fishing spot for many famous politicians, industrialists, actors, and authors during the nineteenth century. However, no owner had held claim to Joseffa longer than its present owner, G. Robert Gardner, or Bob, as he was known to Mac and Mags. Bob had bought the island in the mid-1970's, finding it a virtual jungle with cottages and outbuildings in a poor state of repair. In the past thirty-seven years, Bob had turned Joseffa into a paradise, sporting over one hundred and twenty homes, a hotel/restaurant, a bar, a fitness center, and a small museum that had been honored as one of the finest small museums in the state.

The archaeology digs performed by Will and Kate Marks had uncovered artifacts dating back thousands of years as well as a number of human remains identified as Calusa. The remains were proven to be over six thousand years old.

Mac smiled as he thought of the history of the island. "No wonder I love this place," he mused.

Mac took a tall glass of iced tea to the deck of *The Mistress*. He held his electronic reader opened to the book, *The American Revolution, a History*. He heard sounds from below and then a voice. "Mac, are you on deck?" Mags called out.

"Yeah, up here. Come join me, Hon."

"Oh, it's a beautiful evening. It's hard to believe we are only six miles from the hustle and bustle of the mainland," Mags said.

"I love this place. We don't come here often enough."

Mac and Mags had been so intent on looking out at the water that they didn't hear the approaching footsteps on the dock. "Permission to come aboard, Captain," a cheerful voice called. Looking to the right, Mags and Mac saw Will and Kate Marks approaching.

"Permission granted," Mac called out.

"When did you guys get here?" Mags asked as Mac held out his hands to assist Kate and Will aboard.

"We came over yesterday and have been working at the dig site and deciding how we should proceed Monday morning," responded Will. "We are so glad you all could make it. We'll have help each day from Pine Island volunteers but it's good to have you two who already know the ropes."

"Did the island staff do a good job covering the pits from the April dig?" Mags asked.

"There was some erosion in the area of the test pit but nothing major," Will responded.

"OK, enough talk about the dig for now. Tell us how you are doing, Mags. We've been concerned since your Houston trip last week," Kate asked with apprehension.

"There's good news and bad news, Kate. The bad news is that they discovered two new growths, and Dr. Holt is afraid to prescribe any more chemo. The good news is that she has referred me to a radiation oncologist who feels there's a good chance he can kill the two tumors. She wants me to recuperate from the chemo for six weeks and return to Anderson for an extended stay," Mags shared.

"Mags, I know how disappointed you must be. But, as you know, you are getting treatment from the best cancer research hospital in the world. They cured me and I have every confidence that they'll cure you," Kate offered. "But, is it okay for you to be digging now?"

"Dr. Holt says I can do anything that I feel up to doing. She just cautions me to listen to my body and rest when I feel tired or over-heated. I actually feel pretty good now. I do tire easily but have been looking so forward to this time on Joseffa, being with you two and helping with another dig. Oh," Mags added, "that reminds me. I have something for you."

Mags turned and went down the ladder into *The Mistress'* living quarters.

Mac jumped up and quickly sputtered, "I'm a lousy host. Would you like something cold to drink? We have Zinfandel, Coors Light, and sodas in the fridge. What can I get you?"

"I'll take the Zin," said Kate.

"A Coors Light for me," added Will.

"I'll have Zin, too," Mags called out as she climbed the ladder back to the main deck.

"Wasn't going to miss you, Hon. Be right back," Mac said with a smile.

"I've got something for you, Kate," Mags said as she held out a small white box with the monogram, Mmmm, on the cover.

"What is this?" Kate asked.

"Open it and see. Now, it's just a sample but it passed testing earlier this month and won't be on the market until February, but I wanted you to give it a test and tell me what you think."

"Mmmm, that's a clever name. It's another Margaret Marie Miller Mason product!" Smelling the fragrance, Kate added, "and it is definitely Mmmm. Not sure it is appropriate to wear on a dig but if Dr. Marks will ever take me out somewhere, I will definitely wear it."

"Think you're in trouble, Marks," Mac whispered to Will.

"Looks like it," Will frowned.

The two couples visited, sharing memories made over the years. Then Mac spoke up, "What are you two doing for dinner? I have some mighty good looking rib eyes down below. Why don't you join us?"

Kate looked at Will, smiled and they both responded together, "Sounds great!"

Mac and Will stood over the grill, enjoying their beers, while Mags and Kate went below. The women threw four potatoes into the microwave and began to prepare a salad. After enjoying dinner together and talking even more about the upcoming weeks of the dig,

Kate said, "You know, we have more to do at the site tomorrow. We should probably get back to the condo and get a good night's sleep."

"Where are you staying this trip?" Mags asked.

"The same place. Bob and Susan's condo. As you know, it's just north of their cottage on the Promenade," Kate replied. "Do you have any time tomorrow to lend us a hand? We'll just be setting up the resource table, the screens, and organizing tools."

Mags looked at Mac and replied, "We can come by after lunch. We want to attend the worship service on the beach at ten but then we'll grab a sandwich and head on down."

"Good, see you then. And, thanks for the perfume, the wonderful dinner and most of all, the friendship," Kate said as she hugged Mags and then Mac.

Mac and Mags carried the dishes down below and quickly washed them. Mags headed for the shower and Mac called after her. "Don't forget, we only have three hundred gallons of fresh water before we refill. I want a shower too."

Laughing, Mags replied, "Even I don't use three hundred gallons."

It had been a good day.

19

"Wake up, Sleepy Head," Mags said as she nudged Mac.

"Huhhhhh, what?" Mac said as he opened his eyes and looked up at Mags with a cup of coffee in her hand.

"It's almost 9 in the morning," Mags laughed. "I've been up for a couple of hours."

"Come on, you've got to be kidding. I never sleep 'til nine," Mac said, looking at his watch.

"Well, you did this morning. You must have been exhausted or it's the gentle rocking of the boat."

"Wow, I sure did sleep well. What about you?" Mac asked.

"I slept great. You know, I haven't felt any of that discomfort since we returned from Houston," Mags said thoughtfully.

"I like hearing that, Mags, but don't overdo. Promise me?"

"I promise, Dr. Mason," Mags laughed. "I have French toast and bacon ready."

"Let me throw on a robe and I'll be right in."

Mac pulled on his white terry cloth robe and walked down the narrow hallway through the galley and into the small salon area. Mags had set the table with bright yellow plates and their fishy flatware. Mac laughed when Mags bought the set of forks, knives, and spoons. The ends of the handles were shaped like a tarpon's head with a hole where the eye would be.

"I still can't believe you found these, Mags," Mac laughed again. "All this looks great!"

After breakfast, Mac and Mags dressed in shorts, tee shirts and their running shoes. "Glad we don't have to dress up for church today." Mac said.

"Mac, this *is* dress up on Joseffa," Mags smiled.

The couple locked the cabin door, and Mac gave Mags a hand as she climbed onto the dock. It was a beautiful morning with very moderate temperatures and a blue sky with just a scattering of puffy clouds. They walked down the dock to the water front. Mac reached in his pocket, retrieved a key and pointed to a golf cart. "Your chariot, my dear," Mac offered.

Mac put the golf cart in reverse, backed out of its space and headed to the beach on the windward side of Joseffa. A quarter of a mile down the beach, the couple saw a dozen or more people talking and laughing among themselves. Mac parked the cart, and he and Mags walked towards the group.

"Mason, good to see you," a man about Mac's age spoke up. Others in the group began to welcome Mags and Mac.

"It's like coming home, Mac," Mags commented.

"I agree," Mac replied.

Chairs had been set up on the beach, compliments of one of the beach front residents. A small handmade booklet was handed out and an older gentleman stood at the front and said, "Let's turn to page five and sing this old favorite."

Mac and Mags turned to page five and saw the hymn, "Shall We Gather at the River?"

Mac smiled at Mags and said, "Close but no cigar." They both laughed.

After the hymn, a period of sharing followed. When those assembled told of joys and concerns in their lives, Mac simply shared the names, "Adam and Eve." A couple of people looked puzzled at the timing of this biblical reference. A woman, who appeared to be in her early twenties, led in prayer.

Then the older gentleman, whom Mac didn't know, stood and spoke. He had prepared a short homily on God's creation and the beauty of the earth and how we, as stewards of the earth, were blessed with the beauty of Joseffa and our responsibility to protect it. Another well-known hymn, "Just as I Am," was sung in closing. Mac and Mags approached the older gentleman who had led the service and introduced themselves.

"I'm Paul Peterson," the man offered. "I've only just moved to the island but quickly found myself volunteering to lead services one week. It is so good to meet you two."

It's good to meet you also, Paul. We'll probably see you around. We'll be here for a couple of weeks," Mags said.

Paul asked, "Staying at the Inn?"

"No," responded Mac, "We're on our boat, but we are members of the island here. Hope we see you around."

Mac and Mags returned to their golf cart and Mac asked, "It's only 10:45. Do you think Will and Kate are at the dig site yet?"

"Why don't we drive down and see?"

Mac drove down the beach, past the Inn and swimming pool and then turned onto the Promenade just to the left of the museum.

"I'd like to go through the museum again this trip. It's really some kind of place," Mags commented, looking at the white building that had been converted from a cottage into a museum in 1994.

"I'd enjoy that too," Mac said.

Mac continued down the narrow Promenade toward the south end of the island. There were cottages on both sides of the drive. Mac and Mags always were amused at the term "cottage", because the residences were larger than their home in Venice. For that matter, the label "Promenade" seemed a bit much for the path that was no more than four feet wide.

As they rode toward the location of the dig, Mac and Mags commented on the beautiful foliage on both sides of the path as well as the small ponds populated with ducks and other Florida water fowl. One pond contained a fountain in its middle, spraying water in an arc. Trees in front of cottages often were decorated with pots containing orchids and midnight blooming cereus.

"You just can't possibly describe the beauty of this island. It must be seen to be appreciated," commented Mags.

"Pictures can't even do it justice," added Mac.

After the path curved to the left, Mac and Mags saw another golf cart parked under a tree on the right side. Working nearby were Will and Kate.

"Hope you can still use us," Mac called out.

"Good morning. Yes, we still have a few things to do. Let us tell you our plans for this dig. As you know, we started with a test pit and extended it twelve feet last April. We want to continue digging at that location to a depth of about six feet. We should continue finding artifacts dating back approximately three thousand to thirty-five hundred years ago. But, we'd like to dig another test pit ten feet to the south paralleling the first."

Will continued, "The grounds keepers did a good job of covering April's dig with plywood. There was some erosion in the area of the test pit. We'll have to clear that out keeping the sand and debris separate from what we excavate deeper. We don't want the 'finds' contaminated."

"So, what can we do to help?" asked Mags.

"First, we'll measure off the new test pit. We want it to measure thirty inches by thirty inches. I have stakes to mark the corners and then we'll tie this yellow cord between the stakes, measuring to assure a constant depth to agree with all of our Joseffa excavations," Will said, pointing at a ball of yellow string. "Mags, would you help Kate with that while Mac and I move the sifting screens and tools into place?"

Mac and Will began moving two sifting screens to the excavation site that was begun in April. The sifting screens were mounted on waist high supports allowing all sand excavated to be sifted and any artifact larger than one-fourth inch to be bagged and saved for further examination. They also moved one sifting screen to an area next to the location of the new test pit.

Mags and Kate measured and hammered the four stakes into the ground. Kate measured and Mags tied off the yellow string, forming the square that would indicate the extremities of the test pit.

"What's next?" asked Mac.

Will responded looking around, "I think that is about it for today. We're ready."

At that moment, the group heard a golf cart approaching from the north.

"Look, it's Bob," Mags said with excitement.

The golf cart came to a halt on the pathway near the four. "Hey, I thought I'd come down and see if you guys were here yet. Susan and I got in an hour or so ago. Susan wanted me to see if you were here."

"We're ready for tomorrow, Bob. Hopefully, we'll have some residents arriving early to help. The volunteers from Pine Island will arrive on the 10 AM shuttle", Will offered.

"Well, you never know how many of the residents will show up. There's mainland time and there's Joseffa time, but hopefully you will get some help," Bob said with a smile. "Susan wanted me to invite the four of you to our cottage for dinner tonight. I thought I'd throw some chicken on the grill and we could all catch up."

Mags quickly asked, "What can we bring?"

"I think Susan has it all handled, Mags, but thanks. If she needs anything, I'll have her call your cell."

"We look forward to it," Mags offered, looking at the other three. They all nodded their agreement.

Bob Gardner turned his golf cart around and began his drive northward on the Promenade. Mac, Mags, Will, and Kate did one last look around and also began their trip back to the center of the island.

20

2004

THE PORT WAS NOW IN sight, so all hands aboard the fishing boat moved to their duty stations. They bustled with the efficiency of a well-oiled machine and the craft moved steadily toward its home dock.

The captain turned to the right and spoke so that only two or three men could hear: "Are you ready to make a report? You'll need to debrief as soon as we get docked."

The answer came, "Ready, Captain."

"It's a shame" the captain continued, "that…" He stopped, noticing that there were a few eavesdroppers.

There was a bang and a rattle as the vessel bumped against the dock.

There was nothing to indicate that there were some unanswered questions left on Joseffa Island.

21

Present

Mac and Mags spent the rest of the afternoon relaxing on the deck of *The Mistress*. Mags had slipped into her pink, two piece swim suit and applied a generous layer of SPF 30.

Mac, in his jean cut-offs, asked with a sly smile, "Can I help with that?"

"Sure, you can get my back."

Mac took the sunscreen and began to rub.

"I said, 'My back, Mr. Mason!'" Mags said, with her patented eye roll.

"Oh, sorry, Mrs. Mason."

Mac and Mags laid on the towels they had positioned on the flat front deck and turned to their Kindles to read.

"What time are we expected at Bob and Susan's?" Mags asked, looking up from her novel.

"Bob never said, but since we're on Joseffa, time is so unimportant. I'd guess we could go over around 6 PM or so."

"If I go to sleep, wake me around 5:00 so I can get cleaned up and dressed, Mac."

"Will do, Hon."

Mac and Mags, each taking one of the two bathrooms on *The Mistress*, took their showers. Mac pulled on a pair of khaki shorts, a light blue polo shirt and sandals. Mags dressed in a yellow flowered sundress and a pair of white open-toed sandals.

"What's that?" Mags asked, pointing to a paper sack in Mac's hand.

He answered: "Bob's beverage of choice. You know he doesn't drink the strong stuff, but he loves Diet Dr. Pepper. This is that big bottle we still had in the 'fridge from our last time out."

"Nice thought." And then, as they departed *The Mistress*, Mags grabbed a sample bottle of Mmmm knowing she really wanted Susan's input on the new product. They walked hand in hand to their golf cart.

As dusk settled on the island, the warmth of the sun began to slip into the cool of evening. "Should I have brought a sweater?" Mags asked.

"There's more than one way to stay warm." And Mac put his arm around the love of his life. He pulled her closer and moving her gently toward him, he gave her a long hug, peppered with gentle but insistent kisses. "That's the best I can do while carrying Dr. Pepper."

"Have I told you lately that I love you?"

"Hmmm. Sounds like a song."

"Perhaps, but it is also the beat of my heart."

"Mercy, you surely do get romantic when you get on Joseffa Island!"

They both laughed and climbed into the cart.

They moved slowly along the Promenade until they were in front of Bob and Susan's cottage. The sign in front said "Pirate's Cove, Circa 1907." Stepping out of the cart, they walked up the sandy path that was lined with bright flowering kalanchoe.

"It's so nice to see blooming plants here. In New York, all the plants have been moved indoors. Hooray for Joseffa temperatures!"

Mac said, "My dear, you know more about plants than I know about Duke basketball."

"Not likely! Not likely!"

Before they got to the door, it swung open and Bob greeted them with an enthusiastic "Come in, wayfaring strangers! Come in and have some sustenance!"

The living room was ornate, but comfortable. All around were reminders of the globe-trotting vacations that Bob and Susan enjoyed. The tusks of a large elephant stood out from the wall, next to a Chinese gong. A subway map of London was framed and mounted next to a photograph of Bob in front of the Bolshoi Ballet in Moscow.

Mac aimed a finger at the photograph and said, "You never have quite mastered the *pas de deux*, have you?"

"Well, not without a lot of effort!"

Mac handed Bob the sack containing Diet Dr. Pepper. "Ah, good memory, my friend! Good memory! This is the ale of the gods!"

"If you say so, but I might try something from the god Bacchus!"

"Your call. Let's go check on the chicken. Mags, Susan is in the kitchen. She can tell you about a new book store that just opened in Sarasota. And, before I forget, Kate phoned and said that Will received a call from the university. They won't get here for supper but hope to make it in time for dessert."

Mac replied, "Bummer. Having to work on the week-end! I guess the problems do not work on schedule. I'm looking forward to these days with Kate and Will. Now, which way to the birds?"

As the two men stepped out onto the deck and to the grill, Mac said, "This reminds me of my junior high party days. The boys go to one side and do their thing and the girls go to the other side and do their thing."

"I sort of like the way I remember my senior high parties. The boys and girls have only one thing in mind."

"Bingo! You got that right! I'm with them. I'm still in my senior high mode!"

Soon the four settled at a picnic table on the side deck. Plates were generously filled with chicken, cole slaw, potato salad and what Susan called "my buttery-yeasty-pull out all the stops rolls."

"Mac, would you ask the blessing?"

"Sure. For friends, for food, and for Your presence, we give You thanks, O Lord. Amen."

They began to chew more and talk less. Finally, Mags turned toward Susan, sniffed the air, and exclaimed with excitement, "You are wearing Mmmm!"

"The sample you just gave me, my dear!"

"What do you think?"

"The word that comes to mind is 'persuasive.'"

"Whoa! I had not thought of it as being persuasive, but maybe being dangerous."

"Dangerous for us sweet, innocent girls to wear around those ravenous beasts called men!"

The deck filled with good-natured laughter and affirmative nods of the head when asked by Bob, "Would you like seconds?"

"Bob, how are things on the island?" inquired Mac.

"Nothing big going on right now. We did have some teen-ager pranks a few weeks ago. They, shall we say, 'borrowed' golf carts and had a race down on the beach. No harm done except for a few irate residents and one cart that got stuck." He paused. "When are you folks going to move out here?"

"You better believe we think about it every time we renew our membership. Sometimes I think Mags would move out here without me but with our schedules of my consulting and Mags' promoting her products, it is just more convenient to live on the mainland!"

Mags faked a demure look. "If I did move here, I would let you visit on alternate week-ends." Mac playfully kicked her under the table.

"Would you like to move back to the living room for some apple pie? A la mode!"

The doorbell rang. "Perfect timing," Susan said as she went to welcome Kate and Will.

The three couples broke into several simultaneous conversations, as long-time friends do when it is "catch up" time.

Snippets of talk filled the air.

"Dig."

"Diesel fuel."

"The book is a bit lusty."

"Add a little paprika."

"Cat fur everywhere!"

"A soft fragrance."

"He hit a three-pointer."

Finally, Susan said, "The drinks are on the house! What'll you have?"

With glasses and mugs in hand, they all returned to the deck and settled into chairs.

"Let's do the apple pie here on the deck," Bob suggested, as he took a big swallow of Dr. Pepper. The six seemed quite at ease with one another.

"If it's okay, Susan," Mags asked, "why don't each of us fix our own pie in the kitchen?"

So, the six took large slices of the bountiful apple pies, piled on vanilla ice cream, and went back to the deck.

Bob continued his earlier comments. "Yeah, things are going well here. Oh, there is an occasional personnel issue---they come and go---but Joseffa Island is still my idea of home."

22

MAC AWOKE SLOWLY AND GENTLY slipped his arm out from under Mags whose head was resting on his shoulder. He eased out of bed, went into one of the bathrooms and prepared for the day. Moving to the galley, he noticed that Mags was still curled up, sleeping peacefully. Mac took a large pot from the cabinet below the small counter, filled it with water and put it on to boil. He then opened a drawer and took out two one quart zip lock bags. Taking four eggs, he broke two eggs into each bag. He smashed the eggs so that the yokes were mixed thoroughly with the whites. He cut small pieces of ham and placed an equal amount in each bag. He then added a small amount of cheese to the bag he had designated as Mags'. He placed twice as much cheese into his bag. "Never too much cheese," Mac said out loud. He pressed the air from the bags, sealed them and dropped them into the now boiling water, setting the stove timer to thirteen minutes. He then placed two pieces of multigrain bread into the toaster and removed butter and raspberry jam from the 'fridge.

"Baggie omelets?" Mags said as she entered the kitchen already dressed for the day.

"I hope I didn't wake you, Hon. I tried to be quiet."

"No, I woke enough to know you were up and decided it was time for me too. Thank you for making breakfast."

"Well you know, baggie omelets are my specialty right after P B and J," Mac proudly announced. "Ten minutes and we eat."

Mac buttered the toast and spread a generous amount of jam over the melted butter. He then lifted the bags from the hot water and carefully opened each, avoiding the hot steam that gushed forth. He rolled the omelets onto plates with the toast, poured Mags a cup of Cappuccino and himself a second cup of coffee. Holding Mags' chair for her, they sat for their morning meal.

"Isn't this the easiest recipe for an omelet, Mac?"

"It sure is and I'm amused when I think of Frank making these so often for himself since you taught him. I'm not sure he can prepare anything else other than pimento cheese sandwiches."

Frank Vance had been Mac's roommate while they were both undergraduate students at Duke and they had remained good friends for over thirty-five years. Frank taught church history and theology classes at the Theological School at Drew University in New Jersey, but his basketball loyalties remained Duke Blue. Mac and Frank loved to kibitz about the games.

"When do you think we'll see Frank again?" Mags asked.

"I'm not sure. Hopefully he will come for a visit soon or we can make a visit up there, maybe on one of your trips to New York."

"What's the name of that place where he lives? Hoppy something."

"Hopatcong…Hoe…*pat*…kong. It's a Native American term that means 'honey waters of many coves.' —at least I think that is what Frank said."

"That works for me. Do you want more toast?"

Having completed breakfast and washed the dishes, Mags gathered her sun screen and insect repellent and the couple left for the dig site.

After settling into the golf cart, Mac turned to Mags, "Now, Hon, you have to make me one promise. If you get tired, you have to sit down. Don't be proud. Or, if you are really tired, let me take you back to *The Mistress* so you can rest. OK?"

"Mac, I promise, but I do have to say that since I have been over the chemo treatments for the past couple of weeks, I am feeling so much better and so much stronger."

The couple continued driving south on the Promenade until they came to the South Ridge Dig Site. It was 8:30 AM and Will and Kate were already organizing for the day.

"Hey, guys, we're here. What can we do?"

Will answered, "I think we'll let you start taking the top layer of grass and ground cover off the test pit in the new location. We don't need to save the surface debris. You can just dump that. But, don't go deeper than about five centimeters to start. We'll measure when that's done and begin our ten centimeter excavations. If you happen to see anything unusual, just call Kate or me."

Mags and Mac went to the tool area and each got a small garden trowel and a bucket to share. They knelt next to the area marked off for the test pit and began to gently remove the top layer of grass, sand and leaves putting the debris in a bucket for disposal.

Mac swatted at his neck. "Oh, great, the 'no see ums' are back. Do you think your insect repellent will keep them away?"

Will overheard Mac and reached into his backpack and brought a bottle to Mac. "Here, try this. We find it works better than any repellent for the sand fleas. It's Skin So Soft and it seems to really keep the no see ums away."

Mac and Mags sprayed generous amounts on their necks, arms and hands rubbing it on their faces.

Mac and Mags worked together until they had finished excavating the five centimeters or about two inches. They called Will over, "Is this okay?" Mac asked.

"Looks good. Now you can dump your bucket and make sure that it is totally empty. Then, you can begin the next ten centimeters."

"I'm so ignorant about the metric system. Didn't you say last time that ten centimeters was about four inches?" Mags asked.

"Yep," Will answered holding a plastic zip lock bag in his hands. "Here is your first bag. It has the site location marked on it. This one is marked 'shells.' When you find other items like charred wood or pottery fragments, you can make up your own bags over at the work table. Just follow the descriptions I put on the first bag and keep the location codes and depth correct. You remember that from April, don't you?"

"Got it," replied Mac. The couple went back to work gradually scrapping layer after layer of sand being careful to keep the profiles even and straight. The excavated materials were put in a five gallon bucket where it could be carried to the quarter-inch sifting screen.

About 9:45, Will called out, "Mac, can you do me a favor? Would you go down to the dock and meet the 10 AM shuttle? There should be volunteers from Pine Island. Kate will take our golf cart too since there should be five people."

Mac and Kate drove the two carts to the main dock and picked up their passengers. After Mac and Kate returned, the work continued with Mac and Mags working on the new location while the volunteers continued excavating the April dig site. Everyone stopped for lunch around noon and Mac and Mags returned to The *Mistress* for a quick sandwich, chips, and a soda.

The afternoon went smoothly other than finding something interesting at the site of the April dig: a large shell deposit that probably indicated the location of cooking or tool making. The volunteers left on the 4 PM shuttle. Mags and Mac helped close down the site for the day.

On the trip back to *The Mistress*, Mac asked, "Mags, how are you feeling?"

"I'm really feeling fine. It wasn't too hot today and I did rest when I felt tired. So, all's good! Today's score is Mags 1, Cancer 0."

"Let's keep it that way!"

The couple continued the ride to the dock discussing what they might have for dinner. Of course, dinner would come after getting cleaned up from the sand and dirt they had on their bodies and clothing.

❖ ❖ ❖

Mac fired up the grill on the deck of *The Mistress* and after preparing his marinade, he slowly cooked two salmon steaks. Mags made a salad and fried potatoes and onions. A bottle of Zin was opened and the couple enjoyed their dinner on deck.

"It was a good day, wasn't it?" Mags asked.

"It was a very good day. No exciting finds but what is more important is what Will and Kate can learn from what we might find."

"Well, tomorrow is another day. I'm really eager to begin digging deeper in the test pit."

The couple cleaned up the dinner dishes, and returned to the deck so that they could sit and watch the sun set. When Mac saw Mags yawning, he took her hand and led her down below to get a good night's sleep.

"I won't read long tonight," Mac said, also yawning. In minutes, both were fast asleep. Sleep would not have been so sound had they known what the next day would bring.

23

On Tuesday, Mac and Mags arose early, had a breakfast of sausage and egg biscuits, and dressed quickly. They both chose to wear jeans, knowing that they would be on their knees digging most of the day. Mags had brought knee pads but Mac thought them more trouble than they were worth.

As Mac and Mags walked down the dock to their golf cart, Mags asked, "What do you think Will and Kate will have us doing today?"

"Well, yesterday we got down 20 centimeters or eight inches. I assume we'll continue to dig and screen the next 10 centimeters or more. I hope we find something interesting today."

"So do I. It's always fun to find something used by the early Calusa. Remember when you found those pottery shards in April?" Mags asked.

"And people think of the Calusa as being primitive. I don't think so. I'm constantly amazed at their culture, you know--the tools they made, and the pottery. Good stuff. To me, it all seems pretty much up to speed! And remember their strong religious beliefs. The Spanish missionaries were never able to convert them."

Arriving at the dig site, Mac and Mags saw that Will and Kate had already begun. Will, very much in his in-charge mode, said: "Keep on excavating that new pit another ten centimeters."

"Remember to protect the profiles. Don't stand too near the pit or cause the sides to cave in," Kate reminded.

"Yes, Dr. Marks," Mac replied in jest.

Kate did an eye roll that looked awfully familiar to Mac. He threw his hands up and asked, "Did you learn that eye roll from Mags?"

Will quickly chimed in, "Oh, she's had that down pat since I married her. I think it is something mothers teach daughters from childhood."

Mac and Mags knelt next to their pit and began carefully removing another layer of sand, making sure to prevent the sides from caving in. When a bucket was full of sand and shells, Mac carried the bucket to the quarter-inch sifting screen and Mags shook the screen, causing everything under a quarter of an inch to fall through, leaving only larger objects. She was on the lookout for particular shells, charred wood, pottery shards or other finds that might be considered archaic. Strangely, nothing was in the first 30 centimeters but sand.

"I'm finding nothing so far, Will. I thought we would hit something by now," Mags said.

"That is unusual but every site is different. You'll probably find something soon."

Mags returned to the pit and continued working with Mac. They were beginning their fourth ten centimeter level. They were over a foot deep now.

"What is that?" Mags exclaimed as she saw a small white object appear.

"Looks like we've uncovered our first shell," Mac replied. "Get the brush and let's be careful in case it's part of a tool."

As Mags brushed around the object and eased sand away from the edges, she screamed out, "Will...Kate...you better get over here. I'm not positive what I've found but I think maybe we have found the bones of a hand."

"Don't disturb anything. Let me look. Kate," Will called out, "Get the camera."

Will began to slowly brush away sand and sure enough a phalange appeared. He continued brushing and slowly uncovered the bones of a complete hand.

"OK, we have to stop right here. I've got to take over." Will stated.

"What's the procedure, Will? We've never found human remains before," Mags and Mac asked almost in unison.

"First, I will try to determine if these bones are aboriginal or if they are less than seventy-five years old. If they are archaic, I have to call the state archaeologist. If they are more recent, I have to call the Lee County Medical Examiner."

"What can we do to help?" Mags asked.

"There's really nothing right now. This pit is no longer an archaeological dig site. Until we determine the age of this find, we'll have to halt everything. I always hate doing that, but we have no choice." Kate nodded her head in agreement.

Will walked over to the work table and sat in a lawn chair with his phone in hand. He quickly selected a name from the contact list on his phone and pressed the "call" icon.

"Dr. Garcia, please," Will spoke into the cell phone.

"Raul Garcia here," a voice came on the line.

"Raul, this is Will Marks. I'm on Joseffa Island and we've just found human remains. Because of the depth of the find, I'm doubtful that the body is archaic. What do you want me to do?"

"Will, can you determine for sure whether the body is archaic or not? You've found so many ancient burials on that island, there's no point in my getting involved until you're sure."

"We've only uncovered a hand so far. I didn't want to dig anymore until I checked with you. If we find the body to be archaic, I will call the state archaeologist. Is it okay if we uncover more, if any more exists?"

"Yes, why don't you do that and try not to disturb the skeletal remains in case it is a more recent burial," Dr. Garcia responded.

"OK, Raul, I'll call you later and tell you what we have found."

"Good, Will. Think you'll be able to find out today?

"I would think so. I've put the dig on hold for now. I'll call and tell my other volunteers to cancel their trip over until further notice. I've got two experienced people helping now. I think you know Mac

Mason from his time as Head of Major Crimes in Miami. He and his wife, Maggie, are here. Mac is certainly qualified in this area."

"Great, I haven't seen Mac in years. You couldn't have better help."

Will pressed "End of Call" on his cell and turned to Kate, Mac, and Mags.

"Looks like we will be excavating the remains and see what we've got. The test pit might be compromised now so it is no longer an active dig except for these remains. If they prove to be archaic, we can continue to explore this site. If not, we will have to close it down."

"Can we help with this, Will?" Mags asked.

"Yes, we'll all gently continue to uncover any additional remains. Let's just be very careful and try to keep the skeleton in the position it was buried."

"We'll have to expand the pit," Kate remarked.

"Yes, we will. Use your trowels but be very careful," Will cautioned.

Will picked up his cell phone again and called his Pine Island volunteer contact.

"Betty, you'll have to send your volunteers home. I know you are probably near the island shuttle now, but it can't be helped. I'll explain later." Will disconnected.

Kate, Mac, Mags, and Will knelt around the test pit and began to brush sand away from the exposed skeletal hand.

After brushing and removing more sand, Will said, "We do have an arm. Looks like it is the right one. Uh, oh, we don't have an archaic burial here. It looks like this body is clothed and it looks like the upper clothing is made of rubber. I'd better call Raul again."

Will made his call to Raul Garcia and was assured that the doctor was on his way to Joseffa. Before hanging up, Raul suggested that Will continue to excavate the body knowing that no one would know better how to protect it than Will and Kate.

The four continued slowly to remove the sand from the body until Mags exclaimed, "Unless this unfortunate soul has two right hands, we have more than one body. It looks like there's another beneath the first."

"Two bodies? My God!" Kate exclaimed.

24

WILL, KATE, MAC, AND MAGS continued using their trowels and brushes to uncover the topmost body. As Mac had ascertained, the top body was clothed in rubber.

"Looks like a wet suit to me," stated Mac.

"Looks like that to me," replied Will.

As the four got the top body fully uncovered, Will said, "Look at this. I'd say we have an unnatural death here. Look at the skull."

As the group looked at the skull, it was apparent that there was a small hole in the center of the forehead.

"Looks like a bullet hole to me," said Mac.

"You'd be the expert on that, Mac," Kate replied remembering Mac's previous profession.

"Yes, but we still need the medical examiner to state the cause of death. That's the law."

"Dr. Garcia should be here within the hour," Will allowed.

"What do we do about the second body?" Mags asked.

"Let's carefully get as much sand out from around the body as possible. We'll probably have to wait for the forensics team to remove the first body before the second can be totally uncovered," Mac stated.

"Dr. Garcia will call for the Lee County Sheriff and his forensics team when he gets here, but I doubt the bodies will be removed today. There's a lot to do before they can be carried to the morgue for a full autopsy."

"What can we do after we get as much of the sand out of here as we can?" Mags asked.

"Well, I think I need to call Bob and Pat. The Sheriff of Lee County will have to be brought in, and the owner and CEO of the island will need to be apprised of the situation. This is not exactly business as usual!" Will offered.

The Sheriff will probably put up crime scene tape and post security until the site investigation is complete," Mac added.

"How long do you think the bodies have been here?" Mags asked.

Will responded, "It's hard to say. No one knows how long it takes for rubber to decompose, or if it ever completely decomposes. That will be up to the medical examiner to determine."

About an hour later, Dr. Raul Garcia came in a golf cart driven by Pat Jefferson who dropped off Garcia and headed back south on the Promenade. Garcia was a short, stout man with a heavy black mustache. Prematurely gray hair rimmed his bald head. He was dressed in jeans and a tee shirt that read, "Olé, los toros son rey."

Mags whispered to Mac, "What does his tee shirt say?"

"The best I can translate is 'Bravo, Bulls are king," Mac laughed.

But as Dr. Garcia approached the dig site, the scene turned serious, deadly serious.

"Good to see you again, Raul," Mac said as he introduced the doctor to Mags.

"I haven't seen you since that conference at the Ritz-Carlton in Miami."

"That has to have been several years. I've retired since then and Jim Travis is the new Head of Major Crimes. I think you probably met Jim at the conference."

"I'm glad you are here, Mac. You can probably fill Bud Walton in on what we've found here," Raul suggested.

"Bud Walton? I don't think I know that name," replied Mac.

"Bud is the newly elected sheriff of Lee County. I called him on the way here and he will join us shortly. He's calling for a crime scene investigation team assigned to Fort Myers to join him here. Bud is young, but he's sharp. He got his undergraduate degree in Criminal Justice from Florida State and was a deputy until last year when Sheriff Bates retired and he was elected."

Mac, Will, and Raul knelt over the test pit excavation that was much larger and less defined than the original test pit. The two skeletal bodies lay undisturbed in the bottom of the pit. Raul rubbed the stubble on his chin and said, "It's pretty obvious what the cause of death was of the top body. Look at that skull. It looks like a small caliber weapon made that, but I'll know more when I get the remains back to the lab and do some measurements. I will be glad when Sheriff Walton and the CSI team get here. I can't move anything until they give me clearance."

About that time, a golf cart came down the Promenade from the north. It was driven by Bob Gardner. Pat Jefferson accompanied him.

"I got your call, Will. More bodies, huh?" Bob said.

"Yes Bob, but these aren't archaic. These are more recent deaths."

Pat interjected, "How in the world did anyone get buried on this island without our knowing?"

"That's a question I can't answer. All I know is that the bodies have been buried for less than seventy-five years, are dressed in what appears to be wet suits and the top skeleton's skull has what appears to be a bullet hole in the forehead."

"You would find out the information Will just gave you eventually, but I'd like to urge you not tell anyone until Sheriff Walton and the CSI team complete their work. I doubt that we will complete excavating the bodies today. So, this area will be off limits to anyone. The sheriff will probably make this clear when he arrives."

With a worried look Bob ran his hand through his thick hair. "This island is small. Word spreads quickly. The whole island will know something is happening in a matter of hours. We'll do what we can to control the residents, but I'd suggest the sheriff use deputies to cordon off this area."

"I'm sure he will, Bob," Raul responded.

"Finding dead bodies that are not archaic is sure not good for business," Pat mumbled.

"We'd know if an island resident..." Bob looked up and did not complete his sentence.

Bettina McCauley, one of the island's most habitual gossipers, was out walking her Shih Tzu, Puffball. She waved and said, "Morning, folks. Looks like a party! What's going on?"

Pat walked over to her, blocking her view of the excavation. "Hi, Bett. We're just checking out the new pit on the archaeological dig. Nothing to be concerned about. I've been meaning to see you about that meeting of the museum committee that's coming up. Got a minute?" Pat began walking Ms. McCauley north down the Promenade toward her cottage.

Mac commented, "Boy, that was smooth. Good thing that Pat remembered that meeting."

Laughing, Bob responded, "I am not sure there is a meeting. Bett's memory isn't what it once was, but she does love that museum. The question is whether Pat will be able to get away from her in less than an hour."

"Well, it might not make any difference. Here comes the parade."

Two golf carts were approaching. The first carried Sheriff Walton with two of his uniformed deputies. The second carried five men and women dressed in navy blue tee shirts with "CSI" emblazoned on the front and back. The carts stopped. Sheriff Walton approached a young woman in the second cart and took her aside. She was not smiling. Then, the sheriff and young woman approached the group of six: the Marks, the Masons, Bob Gardner and Raul Garcia.

"I still don't understand why there are so many at my possible crime scene," the young woman asked the sheriff.

"Becky, I told you. This was an archaeological dig and these folks are... Oh hell, let Raul introduce everyone to us both."

Speaking to the six gathered, Dr. Garcia began the introductions. "Folks, this is Rebecca Loush. She is the head of the Crime Scene Investigative Service in Lee County. Becky, this is Bob Gardner, the owner of Joseffa Island. I want you to also meet Will and Kate Marks, archaeologists from the university in Cedar Key. And, last but not least, meet Mac and Mags Mason."

Mac stepped forward. "It's good to meet you, Ms. Loush, even under the circumstances."

"That's DOCTOR Loush, Mr. Mason." She then turned to Sheriff Walton and asked, "Who found the body?"

"You need to ask Dr. Garcia that question. I just got here too."

"Dr. Garcia?" Loush questioned.

Walking to the excavation, Raul said, "The bodies were found this morning on the second day of the dig. Dr. Marks immediately called me and I asked him to see if he could determine whether the digs were archaic, which is not unusual on Joseffa. He called me back within fifteen minutes and told me that they were not archaic and that there were at least two bodies."

"Why in hell was the dig allowed to continue? Why are the bodies almost completely uncovered?" Dr. Loush questioned, frowning.

"I told him to continue to carefully remove the sand. We didn't know how many bodies we might have," replied Raul.

"That's my job, Dr. Garcia; you know that!"

At that moment, Will Marks stepped in. "Dr. Loush, we were careful to put everything taken from the pit into buckets and set aside. That's standard procedure when we find human remains of any kind."

"Well, that's something anyway. If evidence of value is in the buckets, I'm not sure proper chain of evidence has been maintained, but that's a question for someone else down the line if this is a homicide."

"Dr. Marks, Dr. Garcia, can you come over here a moment," Dr. Loush requested.

Raul spoke up. "Becky, can we cut out the doctor stuff and go on a first name basis? That could get very confusing."

Loush hesitated for a moment, glanced around the group, and then, for the first time, smiled. She nodded, "Raul, that will work for me. Is that okay with you, Dr. Marks?"

Will smiled, signaled his assent and reached his hand out to shake Becky's.

Becky Loush directed Sheriff Walton, "Would you and your guys secure the area and then our team will get to work."

The sheriff and his two deputies brought stakes and yellow crime scene ribbon from their cart and began to mark off the area surrounding the entire dig site.

"Bill," Loush said to one of her team, "You and Dot begin with the photos. I want pictures from every angle. And, make sure to get photos of those buckets they filled also. We aren't really set up to do this tonight."

Loush turned to Sheriff Walton, "It's getting late. Can you post two of your men here all night to keep the area secure?"

"We are already prepared to do that, Becky."

Bob stepped forward. "Dr. Loush…I mean Becky, will you need us any longer? I'd like to prepare a statement and schedule a meeting with the island residents tonight if possible. If I don't fill them in, we'll have more people down here than you and the sheriff can handle. I won't give them any more information than I have to."

Sheriff Walton spoke up. "And, we'll have to decide how to handle the press. I'm sure their scanners have already picked up on the trip out here."

Bob answered, "We can handle that. No one gets on Joseffa unless it's a resident, member, or someone who is invited, but we might need some help monitoring each of our docks. I can station some of my people around the island."

"Good idea Bob, but we will probably have to schedule a news conference soon or we'll have helicopters and boats all over the place."

"You can handle that, Bud." Bob replied.

Becky came over to the group still assembled. "I think you can all leave now. I'd like you available for questions tomorrow. Is that possible?"

Everyone nodded positively.

Mac and Mags said their goodbyes and walked to their golf cart.

Mac placed his arm around Mags waist and said, "You know? We missed lunch with all the excitement. Why don't we go back to *The Mistress*, have a glass of wine and then dinner at the Inn? I don't think either of us wants to cook tonight."

As the couple got into their golf cart, Mags said, "Great idea Mr. Mason, or can I call you Mac?" They both laughed.

25

SHOWERS COMPLETED, MAC AND MAGS stood before the opened closet door. "I vote informal," Mags said.

"Agreed."

"Does this blue top look okay with the white slacks and the red shoes? I'm afraid I'll look like the Fourth of July."

Mac looked into Mags' azure eyes. "You always set off fireworks in me."

"Shucks, Mr. Mason. One just does what one can!"

The two exchanged a lively hug and then Mac slipped on a polo shirt and khaki trousers. He extended an arm and said, "May I have the pleasure of escorting the Queen of the Ball to the dance?"

Mags chuckled as they walked toward the Inn. "Too pooped to dance tonight!"

The stately Inn loomed ahead at the top of a small hill. As they climbed the wooden steps to the front veranda, Mac and Mags paused to look back toward the water. Mac said, "You know, every time I look out there it becomes my favorite time of the day!"

Mags squeezed his hand as they stepped through the front door of the Inn.

Strolling through the lobby, the Masons were met by a lanky young man. "Good evening, Mr. and Mrs. Mason. Do you want the bar or dining tonight?"

"Dining tonight, Peter. Casual side."

Peter led them to a table for two and handed them menus. "Elyse will be serving you tonight."

Before long, a middle-aged woman approached the table. "Hi, Elyse," Mac and Mags said together.

"Good to see you back," Elyse responded. "Here's water for both of you. May I take your order?"

"The Erastus Foote for me," offered Mac. "I'm in the mood for grouper."

"Chips or fries?"

"Chips. Nothing better than your homemade chips!"

"Chef Salad for me," Mags said. "Hold the onions, but add extra cheese."

"And, if I remember correctly, you want the raspberry vinaigrette dressing."

Mags grinned. "Amazing. You've worked here, what, thirty years? And you have waited on how many tables? And you remember the kind of dressing I like? Amazing!"

Elyse did not say anything, but her glowing face answered for her.

As they waited for their dinner, Mac and Mags rehashed the day's surprising twist. "It won't be long until this whole place will be chattering about the find," Mac suggested.

"Has Bob or Pat made any announcement about a meeting tonight? They had better get ahead of the game."

Mac waited a moment before replying. "I haven't heard any announcement, but it won't be long before folks will notice the security at the dig site."

"Maybe it is my imagination," Mags noted, "but I could swear I heard the people at that table over there ask, 'Were they male or female?'"

Mac laughed. "That question would fit a lot of situations!"

Pat Jefferson passed by the table where Mac and Mags sat. "Hi! I had to go visit the little boys' room. I must have taken one sip too many! If you get a chance, come over and let me introduce you to someone. She's a bit special to me and I'd like you to meet her."

Mags teased. "Little boys' room? Are you old enough to have a special friend?"

"Come on," Pat invited, "while you are waiting for your food."

The three made their way into the formal dining area. It took a while because Pat stopped to speak at almost every table. They came to a table near the window. A single candle radiated from the middle of the white tablecloth.

As they walked up, Pat put his hand on the shoulder of his friend. "Mac and Mags Mason, I'd like you to meet Eve Thomas."

Eve turned.

"Eve!" Mac and Mags shouted.

People at nearby tables glanced to see what was going on.

"Do you know each other?" Pat stood with an incredulous look.

Mac smiled and said, "Pat, let me introduce you to my daughter, Evelyn."

With a shocked expression, Pat said, "Oh my God. Eve, uh, Evelyn, you never told me that you had been married."

"I haven't, Pat. I use my mother's maiden name. Don't ask! It's a long story."

"It's a story I'd like to hear!" Pat then looked at his watch. "Boy, would I like to hear it! But, uh, oh, ten minutes 'til seven. I have to get to the auditorium. I have a meeting with the residents at seven. Eve, you're welcome to come with me, or I can meet you at your condo afterwards."

"I think I'd prefer to go back to the condo and change into something more comfortable."

Pat looked at Mac and Mags. "Since you are a part of this, would you like to join in the meeting?"

"Sure, Pat. Mags and I might be able to answer a few questions since we've talked more at length with Sheriff Walton. However, we'll need to cancel our dinner order with Elyse and eat later."

"I can take care of that," offered Pat, as he turned toward the kitchen area.

Pat walked Eve out to her golf cart and as Mac and Mags watched, he leaned over and gave Eve a very chaste kiss on the cheek and said, smiling, "Your dad is watching."

Eve reached up and pulled Pat's head to her and gave him a deep and passionate kiss.

Walking out of the auditorium toward the Inn and then dining room, Mags said, "I think that went very well. Pat and Bob did a good job of allaying any fears that the residents might have."

"Yeah, he did, and I think giving them as much information as possible will alleviate false rumors," Mac responded. "Did you notice how Bob looked straight at Betinna as he cautioned against gossip?"

Smiling, Mags added, "Yes, I did. It was hard to miss! One good idea that came from the meeting was the suggestion that all off-island members and residents receive a courtesy phone call to insure that all are accounted for. The excuse of reminding them of the upcoming annual members' meeting is a good cover."

The couple continued to the Inn. Elyse came immediately to the table and asked, "Would you like the same items or would you like to see the menu?"

Mac looked at Mags and with her head nod said, "I think we'll have the same but I'd like to add a glass of white wine before the meal. How about you, Mags?"

"Sounds great," replied Mags.

The couple finished their meal, thanked Elyse again for her great service, and apologized for rescheduling their dinner. They walked north on the Promenade. Halfway to the dock, they passed under the largest and most beautiful banyan tree either had ever seen. Mags looked at Mac. "It's amazing how those limbs grow straight down and bury themselves in the ground creating another trunk. I never get enough of this island!"

Arriving back at *The Mistress*, the couple sat on the upper deck, listening to the gentle lapping of the waves against the side of the boat. They watched as the lights of a large yacht passed along the Inner Coastal Waterway. After quietly conversing about the dig, Pat and Eve's relationship, the finding of the bodies, and wondering what the future days would bring, the couple descended into their bedroom, prepared for bed. Both were plagued with more questions than answers, but sleep came quickly. Tuesday had been one exciting day!

26

THE SHRIEK OF THE ALARM clock woke up Mac and Mags at the same time. As Mac bounded from bed he called out, "Lord, how many times has it taken an alarm clock to wake me up! I must have been really zonked!"

"You and me both!" A quick kiss. A quick shower. A quick getting dressed. A quick orange juice. And the two were jogging for the golf cart.

"Do you think it is okay for me to go down to the site?" Mags asked. "After all, I won't exactly be there for professional reasons. You're the pro."

"Better to ask forgiveness than to get permission. Come on and let's see."

They parked the cart at the edge of the yellow "crime scene" tape. They had to pick their way through ten or twelve island residents who were gawking at the activity. "That's as close as you can come," a beefy security man yelled at the Masons.

Sheriff Walton looked up and said "No, it's okay, Larry. We need to talk to these two, both of them." Mac and Mags walked to the dig site. Several people were down on their knees, carefully examining the buckets that contained what might (or might not) be evidence. A woman with a Canon EOS 100 was busy snapping close-up photographs. Every once in a while, she would call up the digital image, would glance at it, and then would resume her work.

"Mac, this will need to be an official on-the-record conversation. Mags, can I ask you to step over to the side a bit? I need to do this one by the book."

After a quick glance at those who were carefully looking through the dig site, Sheriff Walton began: "For the record, please state your name and please acknowledge that you know I am recording our conversation."

Mac nodded his head in affirmation and said, "I am Mackenzie K. Mason. I am talking with Sheriff Walton and I am aware that he is recording our conversation."

"What is your professional background?"

"I am retired from my most recent position, head of the Major Crimes Division of the Miami Police Department."

"I'm impressed. Any other investigative experience?"

"I was an officer in the Naval Investigative Services."

"I have to be honest with you, Mac. I knew all that. I've heard you speak before, and I'm well aware of your reputation. I still had to interview you, so let's continue."

"Where were you on Tuesday, December 1, of this year?"

Before Mac could answer, one of the officers assisting a CSI team member yelled, "Sheriff, you had better come over here! We have something to show you!" The onlooker residents tried to get a better look, but the security team blocked their view.

Garcia and Loush rushed over to the excavation.

"What have you found?" they asked almost in unison.

"I'm not sure. It looks like a medallion on a chain. The chain is broken."

"Well, photograph it as found and bag it. It wasn't on the body?" Dr. Loush asked.

"No, just lying next to it," answered one of Loush's team.

Dr. Loush then turned to Dr. Garcia. "I think we have done all we can do with the bodies and the pit. You can remove them now. Have you arranged for transport back to Fort Myers?"

"Yes, we've scheduled a special island shuttle. All I have to do is call Pat Jefferson when we are ready. How long will you be here?" Dr. Garcia asked.

Loush answered, "I'm not sure. Although I doubt there are any more bodies, we have to make sure."

Mac couldn't help but hear what Becky had said and asked, "You're not going to have to dig up this whole area, are you?"

Loush looked at the area and said, "I hope not, but I do have a problem. Are Will and Kate still on the island?"

Mac replied, "I think so. Do you need them? I can call them."

"Please do," Loush gratefully responded.

As Mac placed the call on his cell phone, Sheriff Walton approached.

"Mr. Mason, did you forget we were having an interview?"

Mac said goodbye to Will and turned to Becky. "Will will be down soon. He and Kate were talking with Bob about the dig and whether it could continue."

"Thanks, Mac."

"OK, Sheriff, where were we?"

"I was asking where you on Tuesday, December 1."

"Well, I spent Monday night on our boat, *The Mistress*, had breakfast and came straight down here to continue digging in the test pit. We had only been working about an hour when we discovered what turned out to be the right hand of the first body. Will called Dr. Garcia. He called you and that's really all I know."

"Do you do any investigative work now, or are you really retired?"

"I often consult with different police departments. I've done some work with government agencies. I also teach investigative techniques at the University of Miami from time to time."

"That's what I was hoping to hear. We have a good department for a county, but we are sometimes spread too thin. Could we contract with you to be available until we sort out this situation?" Walton asked.

"Well, I'm scheduled to be here for the next ten days and I have nothing on my schedule for the rest of the year. I could be available."

"Good, Mac. I appreciate that."

Sheriff Walton then took Mags aside and asked her, "Where were you on December 1, 2013?" He received responses similar to Mac's. He thanked her and turned to watch Garcia and two CSI team members carefully remove the bones from the pit and place them in black, zippered body bags.

At that time, Will and Kate approached in their golf cart.

Dr. Loush walked directly to them. Without so much as a "good morning," she opened with an onslaught of questions. "Do you have your equipment with you? What I mean is: Do you have your equipment that would prevent us from having to dig? Or do you just have shovels? What do you have that would help us see down into this entire area? Deeper? What kind of tools do you have that we could use so we don't have to dig up this entire area?"

Will listened patiently. "Hello, Dr. Loush. The short answer is 'No, we don't have that equipment with us.' The long answer is 'Yes, we can get it here, probably by late afternoon."

Loush, visibly relaxed. "I guess I am a bit nervous. This looks as if it could be something big. That Mason fellow is all in a lather, concerned that we might have to disturb the whole archaeological site. If you've got some way for us to see down into the site without actually tearing it up…"

"If Mr. Mason is so concerned," Will said with a smile, "perhaps he will take us by boat back to the university so I can get the equipment you need. It's called ground penetrating radar."

"How can you get there by boat? I thought you worked at the main campus?"

Will laughed. "No, not for a long time. The Department of Anthropology and Archaeology is at the campus near Cedar Key. You are right in that I used to work at what we call 'that other school.' Now I—should I say, 'we', because Kate is also part of the operation—now we are happily at Florida Coastal University."

Even as Will finished his explanation, Dr. Loush was waving her arms frantically toward Mac. "Over here, Mason, over here!"

Although puzzled by Dr. Loush's insistent manner, Mac stepped over. The leader of the Crime Scene Investigation service (CSI) explained the need for the ground penetrating radar that Will had back at the university.

It did not take long for the Markses and the Masons to move to *The Mistress*, re-fuel, and head out into the Gulf. As they pulled away from Joseffa Island, Mags looked back and said, "Full speed ahead, mate! It looks like everybody on the island is down at the site. FULL speed ahead!"

The Mistress responded to the urgent guidance Mac gave the controls. Soon they were in open water, wind and waves left in their trail.

27

2004

As the dock crew tied the vessel to its storage slip, one man stepped to the aft of the vessel. He fingered his collar, briefly looked surprised, and then reached inside a canvas bag. With a furtive glance, he decided no one was watching, so he simply emptied the contents of the bag into the water. There was a resounding splash and he smiled with satisfaction.

Most of the crew piled off and headed for food and drink, but the one man, empty canvas bag still in hand, was greeted by two others, stubble-faced men with large aviator sunglasses. The smaller one asked the man a simple question: "And?"

"Two less problems but I still need to lay low, very low," the man answered.

The three walked slowly toward the dock restaurant.

28

The Present

"THIS IS QUITE A HOME away from home," Will said as he stood next to Mac on the flying bridge where Mac was navigating.

"What's not to like? We love the water. Living where we do provides us with a great opportunity to sail. God's creation provides the rest! I never forget how greatly we are blessed," Mac replied.

Mags and Kate had put on their swim suits, lathered themselves with SPF 30, and were lying on the front deck sunning.

"When will you return to Houston again, Mags?" Kate asked.

"After the first of the year. Dr. Holt wants me to have time to recover from the chemo treatments I've had over the past six months."

"How are you feeling?" Kate asked, with concern.

"You know, if I didn't know I had those two tumors eating away at me, I'd never know I was sick. I've felt great the past several weeks."

"Now exactly what will they do at the hospital?"

"Well, as I understand it, the radiation oncologist will see me. I'll go through more testing, probably blood work and another CT Scan. Then they will determine the exact treatments I require. Once that is done, I will be tattooed for the exact points they want to target. Then a mold will be prepared to fit my body. I'll lie in that during each treatment."

"Sounds complicated. How many treatments are required?" Kate asked.

"The oncologist will determine that, but I've been told to expect between twenty-four and thirty."

"Wow, how long will you have to be in Houston?"

"We're planning on eight weeks."

Kate looked puzzled and asked, "Where will you stay? Surely not a hotel for that long."

"Mac has been researching places to live. MD Anderson is very helpful in recommending places. Mac has narrowed it down to a number of apartments. In an apartment, we will have shuttle service to and from the hospital, have a washer and dryer, and have a kitchen for cooking our meals. We're leaning toward one that's in the museum area and right across the street from Hermann Park. They have activities going on there year around and a wonderful outdoor theater. That'll help pass some time."

"Will you feel like doing those things?" Kate's voice showed her concern.

"Dr. Holt tells me to listen to my body and do what I feel up to doing. I'm sure I'll have my good days and my bad days during the treatment, but I want to see as much of Houston as possible. We might even make some weekend side trips to places like San Antonio and Galveston. If I'm up to it, I'd like to see some sights in all three cities. I love the River Walk, the Alamo and some missions in San Antonio. I'd like to see NASA and then maybe San Jacinto near Houston. We'll try to take advantage of our time. Mac and I have done that since we've been married but especially since I was diagnosed."

"You were certainly blessed when you met him, but then, so was he."

"Aw, thanks, Kate. It's was the best mugging I've ever endured," Mags said smiling.

Mac and Will had been talking about Mac's consulting, Mags' health, and Will and Kate's move to the Cedar Key campus of Florida Coastal University.

"Why did you choose to move to FCU, Will?"

"I've had a dream for years. This opportunity gave me a chance to fulfill it," Will responded. "Kate and I are both deep water scuba certified. I experienced one archaeological dig in Greece when I was just out of graduate school. I've dreamed of having the opportunity to do marine archaeology again. FCU gave me that opportunity. You know they have one of the best marine laboratories in Florida and a top-notch marine archaeology department, as well. As department head there, I can pretty much choose the digs I want to go on."

Mac motioned to the front deck. "How does Kate feel about it?"

"Oh, she misses our friends back on the main campus and especially her graduate students, but she is always as excited as I am and ready for adventure."

As they were talking, Mac's cell phone sounded the beginning chords of Beethoven's "Fifth Symphony." Mac blushed and said, "What can I say? I love Beethoven." He answered.

The call was from Dr. Garcia. "I've completed the autopsy on our two bodies. Sheriff Walton asked me to call and fill you in. He told me you would be involved in the case."

Mac put the call on speaker and brought *The Mistress* to an idle, cutting the noise down so that Will could hear. "I have Will Marks here. I have you on speaker."

"Not a problem, Mac. The two bodies are male and in their mid-thirties, I'd estimate. The COD, er, cause of death, was a gunshot wound, in both cases. One victim died when the bullet penetrated the squama frontalis, or the forehead. Based on fractures of the rib cage and a hole in the wet suit, I believe the other received a bullet to his chest. I found both slugs and have sent them to ballistics and will add them to the evidence bag. I've also taken DNA samples and sent them to the lab in Miami to see if we can get a hit on CODIS.".

Will spoke loudly into the phone. "CODIS, what's that?"

Dr. Garcia responded, "CODIS is the Combined DNA Index System. For quite a few years now, DNA samples have been taken from many persons arrested. As you know, DNA is a better indicator of a person's identity than fingerprints. No two people, except possibly identical twins, have the same DNA."

Will asked, "When can you expect to get those results? I know the lab gets backlogged and the process takes some time."

"They tell me it may be as long as two weeks. But, Mac, I hope you don't mind, but I used your name. Dr. Wilson knew you and immediately said, 'We'll do everything to speed it up'."

"Wally is a great guy. I've worked with him more times than I can remember. He's tops in his field and I appreciate that he will give this top priority," Mac replied. "Well, we know more than we did."

"Oh, there is one other thing," Garcia added. "Sheriff Walton said that he failed to tell you about one possible piece of evidence that was found. They found a medallion on a broken chain buried next to the bodies. We don't know if it belonged to one of the deceased or whether it could have come from the perpetrator or whoever buried the bodies, if that was someone different. We don't know, of course. I'm sending you an email with a photo of it attached. The medallion has an interesting engraving on it. We wanted you to see it. I'm going to check it for finger prints, but haven't gotten to that yet. You'll have it as soon as I hang up."

"Thanks, Raul. If you discover anything else, let me know. We are going to FCU now to pick up the Ground Penetrating Radar. We should be back to Joseffa tomorrow around noon. We're spending the night at Cedar Key."

"I hope Will doesn't find any more bodies. I heard from Becky and she said Sheriff Walton has the site secured until they can do a full search. Good luck and be safe."

Mac pressed the "End Call" button and turned to Will. "Well, we know more than we did earlier. Let's update the ladies. They've been in this from the beginning and I think it would be okay." Mac kept *The Mistress* idling and called down to Mags and Kate to come to the bridge.

After catching up Mags and Kate, Mac said, "We should be to the FCU marina in about thirty minutes."

Will snapped his fingers saying, "Oh, I almost forgot something. I need to call my office before my assistant leaves for the marina."

Will pressed a selection from his list of contacts on his cell phone. "Marilyn, do you have the equipment ready? We'll be there in thirty minutes."

"Yep, Will, all loaded in the van."

"Great, did you remember to include the RADAN disk?"

Marilyn replied, "I have it right here. See you in thirty!"

Mags looked at Will. "What is RADAN?"

Will replied, "It's the Radar Data Analyzer software. It interprets what the Ground Penetrating Radar has recorded."

The Mistress continued on its northward track until Mac said, "Will, is that the FCU marina off to the starboard side?"

"That's it. The Harbor Master will point you towards a mooring."

Mac idled *The Mistress* and watched as an older man came out on the dock and motioned to an empty slip. Mac slowly maneuvered the 39 foot Bayliner toward the dock.

Will said, "Marilyn isn't here yet. I don't see the department van."

Mags jumped up from the seat she and Kate had been sharing and said, "Why not a soda while we are waiting?"

Mac nodded his head in agreement. "Sounds good, Mags. Maybe Marilyn would like one also. Is that okay, Will?"

Mags poured the four glasses of Diet Coke and kept an extra glass handy. Within ten minutes the FCU Archaeology Department van pulled into the lot adjacent to the docks. A young slender woman with blonde hair pulled back in a pony tail, stepped out.

Mags exclaimed, "Wow, she's young!"

"Young, but would you believe that she earned her PhD at 22 years old? She was graduated from high school at 15, completed her undergraduate degree at 17 and doctorate four years ago. We brought her with us when we were offered our positions at FCU. She is our right hand and our left hand," Kate shared.

Marilyn came down the dock, pushing something that looked like a very narrow three wheeled lawnmower. She smiled as Mac helped her lift the GPR onto the deck of *The Mistress*. "You travel in style, Dr. and Dr. Marks," she grinned.

"It's all in whom you know, Mare. Let me introduce you to Mac and Mags Mason, old friends."

The five sat on the padded chairs on the main deck of *The Mistress* and discussed the Joseffa dig and what had interrupted it.

After an hour of sharing, Will said, "Kate and I know a wonderful seafood restaurant in Cedar Key within walking distance. It's called The Pickled Pelican. Why don't we have dinner there? My treat."

"Sounds good to us, Will," Mags agreed. "How about you, Marilyn?"

"I'd love to, but I have a new fish on the line. He's a little younger than I am, but a sharp doctoral student. We're taking in a movie."

Marilyn left. Mac and Mags locked the recently secured equipment below deck and the four began their walk to The Pickled Pelican.

29

The restaurant had a beautiful view of the Gulf. Since the evening was so pleasant, the group decided to sit on the outer deck. A rather perky young woman came to the table with menus and said, "Dr. Marks," looking at both Will and Kate, "good to see ya'll again."

"Nice to see you again, Peggy. Hope your classes are going well. Marilyn told us that you nailed that last exam. We should have an answer soon to your request for the proctor's position in the department," Kate offered. "We'd like you to meet Mac and Maggie Mason, friends of ours."

"Good to meet you," Peggy smiled at the Masons. "I sure hope my application is approved. I enjoy it here, but I would love to be able to work at the university." She smiled and added, "I'll give you some time with the menu and come back for your order. Can I get you something to drink?"

Will and Mac ordered iced tea. Mags and Kate both asked for water.

"Well, everything here is good and the servings are huge. Even the appetizers would suffice as a meal, but we could share one," Kate suggested.

Peggy returned and Will ordered the Peel and Eat Shrimp and the Cedar Key Clams for the appetizer. Mags chose the Baked Grouper Dinner while Kate selected Grilled Shrimp. Will said, "I'm going whole hog. I'm having the Seafarer's Combo." Mac chose the Fried Shrimp and Oyster Dinner.

"That's great for your cholesterol, Mac," Mags grimaced.

"My cholesterol was 190 at my last physical. I think I can handle a little fried seafood," Mac smiled.

When the food orders had been taken, Will looked at Mac. "Did you get that e-mail from Raul Garcia?"

"I forgot all about that. Let me check," Mac said, taking his cell phone from his shirt pocket. "Yes, I have something here and there is an attachment."

Mac pushed several selections on his phone and brought up an image.

"Hmmm, this is on the medallion that was found next to the bodies. The image on it is so familiar. I know I've seen it before, but I just can't remember where. It will come to me," Mac said as he passed the phone around the table for the others to see.

"It rings no bells for me," Mags said.

Will added, "Means nothing to me."

Kate studied the image for a long time. "It almost looks like some kind of gang symbol, but I have no idea what it is."

Mac took back his phone. "I guess I'll have to keep thinking about it. Wow, look at that food!"

The appetizers eaten, platters overflowing with seafood were brought to the table by Peggy and a helper. "Eat hearty, mates," she said with a chuckle.

As the group was enjoying its meal, Mac looked at Will and Kate and asked, "You are going to spend the night on *The Mistress*, aren't you? I know your home is probably near here, but since you'll be going back to Joseffa with us in the morning, you are certainly welcomed."

Will looked at Kate and with her nod, responded, "That would be great. We brought an overnight bag that we were taking home, but I like your idea better! So, we're set."

"Great," responded Mags, "The guest stateroom is ready for you, as is the second bath."

After some sparring with Mac, Will settled the dinner check and left Peggy a well-deserved gratuity; the four headed back to

The Mistress. "I'm glad we have a little walk. I need it after that scrumptious meal. Will, you were right. The Pickled Pelican is a great restaurant!" Mags beamed.

The following morning Mac, of course, was the first up, showered, and dressed. Will followed him from the guest stateroom and asked, "I sure hope you have coffee made. I'm comatose until I get my first cup."

"There are selections next to the Keurig. Choose your poison. The sweetener is on the counter and milk is in the 'fridge on the right."

Mac began the process of making baggie omelets. "Is Kate up yet?"

"She was stirring when I left the stateroom. She should be out soon."

"Mags was doing the same. I'll get breakfast started."

Mac prepared the four one quart zipper lock bags with two eggs each and set out grated cheese, minced onions, mushrooms, tomatoes, green pepper and ham. "You can choose what you'd like in your omelet. Just put it in one of the baggies and mark it with your name."

"Omelets made in a bag? Interesting," Will said.

"I'm not much of a cook, but I can handle these. They are fast and really quite good."

Kate came into the room followed a minute later by Mags.

"I smell coffee and I'm more than ready for my first cup," Kate stated as she looked around the galley.

Kate was dressed in white shorts and a navy blue long-sleeved sweat shirt with the large white letters FCU across the front. She had on a pair of white sandals.

Mags came into the galley, saw that Mac had started breakfast and giving him a kiss on the cheek, said, "Thank you, Hon, for getting this started."

Mags was dressed in pale yellow capris, a white sleeveless blouse with a green and yellow floral pattern, and sandals.

Mac completed preparing the omelets while Mags put bread into the toaster and began cutting slices of cantaloupe. Mac served the four plates and the quartet sat down around the small table in the salon.

After breakfast, Mags and Kate cleaned up the breakfast dishes while Mac and Will went topside to prepare for the trip back to Joseffa.

After pulling away from the dock, Mac said, "We should get back to Joseffa before noon. When we get back I want to go and see Pat while you and Becky survey the dig area with the equipment we picked up."

"Are you going to check with Pat as to the results of his calls to the members and residents?" Will asked.

"Yes, I'm going to do that and there's something else of a personal nature I'd like to ask him about."

"Have you given any more thought to the image on the medallion that was found next to the bodies?"

With a frown, Mac answered, "Yes, and for the life of me, I can't remember where I've seen that image. I don't think it is a gang symbol. From my time in Miami, I have seen most of those and am pretty sure the image is not a gang symbol. I want to send the image to Jim Travis and see if it rings a bell with him."

"Jim Travis? Do I know him?" Will inquired.

"Jim was promoted to the head of the Major Crimes Division when I retired. He might help me remember where I've seen the image."

"Mac, why did you retire? You don't seem old enough for Social Security," Will smiled.

"Not quite, Will. When Mags was diagnosed, I just wanted to spend as much time with her as possible. My job with the Miami PD didn't leave me with much time. I've never regretted the decision."

"Good for you. I know that I felt pulled in every direction when Kate went through her cancer journey. Fortunately, the university was very understanding and I cut my teaching load back to only two classes."

Mac had headed *The Mistress* south and, after passing the "No Wake" zone, opened up the throttle. Mags and Kate came up to the main deck, chose two deck chairs and watched as gulls swooped down toward the boat hoping for a handout.

Suddenly, Mags called out to Mac on the flying bridge, "Look, Mac, dolphins!"

Mac looked to the starboard side of *The Mistress* and saw several bodies rise out of the water, soar through the air and again, submerge. He slowed the boat and eased his way over in front of the dolphins' path. The sleek aquatic mammals immediately began following *The Mistress*. They proceeded to jump and play in the immediate wake of the boat. Mags and Kate went to the stern and reached out as if they could touch the beautiful creatures. Mags asked, "Kate, why don't we call these things 'porpoise'? Is there a difference between a dolphin and a porpoise?"

Answering, Kate said, "Yes, but most people don't know they are two different species. Dolphins can grow to be thirty feet in length. Porpoises are much smaller. The dorsal fins of each are different. Porpoises have a more rectangular dorsal fin than a dolphin. Dolphins are curved. What we see in these waters are normally dolphin."

"I notice that restaurants no longer have dolphin on the menu."

"No, too many people, especially children, were saying, 'I don't want to eat Flipper,'" Kate said with a smile. "Remember that program? Anyway, restaurants have chosen mahi mahi, the Hawaiian name for the dolphin fish. In Hawaiian, mahi mahi means 'very strong.'"

All four friends continued to watch the dolphins as they cavorted behind *The Mistress* until Mac speeded up and the pod turned, swam away in their continuing search for food.

Mags and Kate returned to their deck chairs, stretched their bare legs out and turned their faces to the sky soaking up the warm sun. Mac and Will looked ahead, both ready for their return to Joseffa. As they approached the island, Mac radioed ahead to notify the Harbor

Master of their arrival. Will called Dr. Loush to let her know they were there.

After tying up *The Mistress*, the four unloaded the equipment they had picked up from Marilyn and walked the dock toward their waiting golf carts.

After loading the Ground Penetrating Radar unit into the back of Will's golf cart, the four began their drive to the dig site. Becky Loush was already there and waiting without much patience. She and Will immediately unloaded the GPR, made some adjustments to the settings and began their sweep of the area.

"If we get a reading indicating a collection of objects, I'd like to mark the area. We have to determine an area for our next test pit since the last one is now contaminated," Will stated.

After covering the entire area surrounding the pit in which the bodies were found, Becky announced, "I am pretty certain there are no other human remains in this area, but let's run the RADAN software just to make sure what we have down there." Will set up his laptop, inserted the software disk, and began to watch the program.

"Nothing seems to indicate anything other than smaller objects, probably shells. But, some of those may be archaic tools. I have a good section in mind for our next test pit."

"I think I am finished here. I got Dr. Garcia's report on his findings. My work here is done. I am releasing the area back to you," Dr. Loush announced, as she took the crime scene tape down.

Mac, Kate, and Mags came over. Each said their goodbyes to Becky as she left the area. Then, Mags coughed. "We best get ready for the locals to come down here to see what they can see! I don't feel much like being a tour guide!"

Mac asked, "That goes double for me. Meanwhile, I assume, Dr. Marks, that we'll start with a new test pit in the area you indicated."

"Yes," said Will, "I'd like Kate and Mags to stake off the area as they did before. I'll call the Pine Island people and let them know they can return to dig tomorrow."

"I bet we will get more volunteers from the residents tomorrow and knowing Betinna, she will be the leader of the group," Mac laughed.

"Nothing like finding human remains to bring out the volunteers," Will agreed.

"I do need to call Pat. I want to meet with him as soon as possible. Can you do without me for a while?" Mac asked.

"Sure, Mac. There's not much to do except get organized for tomorrow."

"I also want to talk to Raul Garcia again. There's a question I failed to ask him," Mac stated.

Mac went to a lawn chair next to the work table and took out his cell phone and pushed a programmed contact number. After speaking to Pat Jefferson, he told Mags, Kate and Will goodbye, got into his golf cart and headed for the Administration Building.

He wanted to hear Pat's response to the phone calls made to the members and residents, but had something equally as important on his mind.

30

ON MAC'S DRIVE BACK TO the Administration Building, he reached again for his cell phone and selected Dr. Garcia's number. He pushed the "Send" button.

"Dr. Raul Garcia," a voice answered.

"Raul, Mac Mason here. Have you got a minute? I forget to ask you an important question."

"Sure, Mac, what do you need?"

"Have you had time to estimate how long the bodies were buried?"

Raul paused a moment. "Mac, I'm getting a second opinion from a co-worker but I have an estimate. Since the bones were completely void of any decay even though they were encased in the wet suits, I'm estimating the burial took place around eight years ago, give or take a year."

"So," Mac asked, "we could say any time from 2003 to 2005. Is that correct?"

"Yes, Mac, I'd be comfortable with that. If my 'second opinion' disagrees, I'll call you."

"Great, Raul. I've nothing more to ask now. Thanks for sending the written report to me, as well as the photo of the medallion."

Garcia interrupted. "Wait, Mac, I have more interesting information for you. There was a partial fingerprint on the medallion. I've run it through IAFIS, the Integrated Automated Fingerprint Identification System, and I got a hit. I'm ninety-eight percent sure the print belongs to Jim Barber, a felon with a rap sheet as long as your arm. I'll send you those results also."

"Great work, Raul. I know Barber's rep. Thanks for everything. We'll talk later."

"Goodbye, Mac, and good luck! Oh, does that medallion image mean anything to you?"

"Still pondering," Mac said, as something began to stir in his memory.

"Keep on pondering. I'd sure like to know who that belonged to, but I'll bet it's Barber's."

"I promise to ponder!"

Mac continued his drive to see Pat.

Mac pulled his golf cart into a vacant space outside the Administration Building and walked to the open door. There was a bowl of water and a bowl of dry cat food sitting next to the door.

"Feeding the residential cats?" Mac asked Nick, the young man at the front desk.

"Oh, that is for Ginger. She is the island cat. No one claims her, so we make sure she has food and water."

"Is Pat in his office?"

"Yes, he just came in. You can go on back."

Mac walked by several desks, down a hallway and into Pat's office. Pat was on the phone but motioned for Mac to sit down. When he hung the phone up, he asked, "What can I do for you, Mac?"

"First, some news. The dig site has been opened up for us to resume the dig. But, I do have a question for you. Have you had a chance to contact the members and residents who are not on the island?"

"Yeah, I put several of the staff on that project to assist me. We've contacted all but four of the people on our list. We used the ploy of reminding them of the annual meeting. We reached all but the four I mentioned. I left messages for those and expect call backs today. If I don't get the call backs, I'll call them again before the end of the day."

"Great, Pat. Let me know the results, please. I doubt the bodies are members or residents since we've dated the burial to 2003 and the latest 2005."

"Then, I'm certain it is not a resident or member. We would have missed them by now," Pat stated emphatically.

"I agree, Pat. Now, I have another request for you. Can you go back and ascertain whether any unusual thing happened during those years?"

"What do you mean by 'unusual,' Mac?"

"Umm, personnel issues, problems, anything out of the ordinary."

"I keep a journal for just that reason. My memory is like a sieve and I keep anything important written down in case I do need to remember an event or a date. I can go through that now and also quiz our staff who was here during those years," Pat offered.

"Great, that is exactly what I want." Mac paused and looking quite uncomfortable, added, "Now I have something of a more personal nature."

"I can imagine what that is, but ask away," replied Pat.

"OK, please understand, it is not that I don't approve. I'm just curious," Mac said uncomfortably. "How did you meet Eve?"

"I was at a cocktail party at a friend's home in Tampa. Eve was there. We started talking and seemed to hit it off, so I asked her out for coffee the following day. Then, I asked her to dinner. She accepted and we've been seeing each other since then."

"Tampa?" Mac questioned. "What was Eve doing in Tampa?"

"Boy, you are out of touch with your daughter! She's lives in Tampa and has for the last several months, I understand."

"Is she working? What does she do?"

"She's an image consultant. I understand that she works as a contractor. She accepts clients who want to do anything from a physical makeover to learning which fork to use to eat a salad. She also works on increasing their confidence where that might be a concern. Lately, she has been working for some major corporation in Tampa that sends representatives to Japan. She teaches them the

Japanese culture and how to interact in their society. I hear she's quite good at what she does."

"Wow," said Mac. "I had no idea. That must be her mother Ruth's influence on her."

"Now, Mac, may I ask you a question? If it is too personal, please just tell me."

"You've shared with me. What can I tell you, Pat?"

"It doesn't take a mind reader to see that the two of you have issues. I care about you and I care about Eve. Can you tell me what the problem is?"

"Oh Pat, it's a long story. The *Reader's Digest* version is this. Ruth and I separated when Eve was twelve years old. Since I was the one to leave, Eve felt deserted. Of course, she thought her mother was blameless and it was all my fault. And, I have to admit, many of the problems between Ruth and me were my fault. I was working so hard on advancing my career at the Miami Police Department that I worked sixteen hour days. I brought my work home with me. It wasn't fun for Ruth. She worried about my safety and I wasn't much of a sharer then. We drifted farther and farther apart until Ruth just couldn't take it anymore. We sat and told Eve we were separating and I can still remember the tears she shed. I left and the divorce followed. During those early years, Eve would come and visit me. But, as she got older, she became more and more distant until she actually became angry. That's where the situation is now. I've tried to tell her that I was wrong, but she can't get over the grief of not having a father during those difficult years. Now, you know as much as anyone. Just do me a favor, please."

"What is that, Mac?"

"Don't ever hurt her. I can't think of a better man for her to be interested in, but don't hurt her. I might have to hunt you down and kill you," Mac said, laughing.

"Mac, things are not serious yet. But, I care about Eve and we both want to take our time and see where things go. I promise you, I won't hurt her."

"That's all I want to hear, Pat."

31

MAC LEFT THE ADMINISTRATION BUILDING and again took out his cell phone. He looked up Jim Travis' direct phone number and pressed "Send."

"Major Crimes, Jim Travis here," a voice said.

"Jim, Mac here. Why aren't you out bringing justice to the world?"

"Mac, how are you? I just have a slow day here. It's rare, but as you know, it does happen. I'm just catching up on reading reports and doing paperwork."

"Well Jim, I've found myself in the middle of a mystery and I'm doing some consulting work for Lee County. I need to call on you for your expertise and probably your memory. Mine seems to be failing."

"What do I need to remember, Mac?"

"Well, a piece of evidence found along with two bodies is a medallion with an image on it. I know I've seen the image before, but I cannot place it. I thought you might recognize it. Can I send the photo of the image to you by e-mail?"

"Two bodies? Two? You don't seem very retired, my friend! Sure, Mac, send the picture and I'll call you whether I recognize it or not. OK?"

"Great, Jim. That's exactly what I need."

Mac continued his drive to the dig site, noting that it was almost lunch time. When he arrived, he found Mags sitting in a lawn chair in the shade with her head between her knees. "Mags, what is wrong? Are you sick?" Mac asked.

"Oh, Hon, I just got very nauseous, and I ache all over. I had to stop for a while."

"No, you're stopping for the day," Mac said, as he walked over to Will and Kate. "I'm taking Mags back to *The Mistress*. I think all this has been too much for her. I want her to rest."

"We couldn't agree more. There's really nothing for you two to do today. And, if she isn't better tomorrow, don't come down here," Kate stated.

Will nodded his agreement saying, "Bettina was down here while you were gone. She says that at least ten residents have indicated that they will be here at nine tomorrow. And, we have four coming from Pine Island. We'll be fine."

"OK, we might need to go to the mainland for a few groceries. Normally, we'd wait until Sunday, but we might do that tomorrow. Could we pick up anything for you?"

Kate replied, "I think we are okay, but if I think of anything, I'll tell you this evening."

Mac took Mags' arm and led her to the golf cart.

As they drove to the dock, Mac took out his cell phone and sent a message to Jim Travis. He attached the photo of the medallion and pressed "Send."

Upon going aboard *The Mistress*, Mac helped Mags down to their stateroom. She quickly removed her work clothes, slipped on a long tee shirt of Mac's and got into bed. Mac asked, "Could I get you anything?"

"Please, Mac, could I just have a glass of water and a couple of Aleve?"

"Sure, Hon; be right back."

Mac had no sooner left Mags than his cell phone rang. He answered as he filled a glass with water over ice and took two Aleve from a bottle in the bathroom.

"Mac Mason here," he spoke into his cell.

Mac continued to the stateroom giving Mags the water and pills.

"Mac, Jim here. Yes, I recognize the image on that medallion. I'm sending you a picture of where you saw it."

"Don't keep me in suspense, Jim. Where did I see it?"

"It was a tattoo on the arm of Jim Barber. Remember, Jim was the guy that you helped us track down on your last trip here."

"Damn, that's right, Jim. I remember now. Can you send a picture of that tattoo and any information you have on Barber? He is still in custody, isn't he?"

"No, we released him on bond. Although we suspect him of other things, we didn't have proof enough to keep him on anything but assault and possessing drugs."

"What about the question of trafficking that we apprehended him on?" Mac asked.

"The witness we had recanted her testimony. I think she was afraid of being sent back to Cambodia. She's applied for a work permit and is working for a diplomat in the embassy here, and he is vouching for her. We couldn't hold Barber on trafficking without a witness or evidence of his guilt."

"So, he is out on bond for the other offenses?"

"Yes, he is. Do we need to bring him in?"

"Send me the photo and we might just bring him in for questioning," Mac suggested. "Call me when you get him. You can hold him overnight, can't you? I could be there tomorrow."

"I can do that. There are a few more questions we'd like to ask him anyway," Jim replied.

Mac disconnected from the call and went to check on Mags. She was fast asleep.

Mac went to the 'fridge and cabinets and began a list of items that were needed to supplement the groceries for the next week. Mac then went up onto the deck of *The Mistress* with his Kindle and began to read.

An hour passed and Mac heard the door to the lower deck opening. Looking up, he saw Mags climbing the steps. "What are you doing up, Darling?" Mac asked.

"I'm feeling a lot better. I think that I just got over-heated, plus the leaning over gets to me after a while. I know it is December, but today seemed unusually warm. My headache and pains are gone and so is my nausea."

"Wonderful, but please take it easy. It scares me to death when you don't feel well," Mac said as he put his arms around Mags.

"I'll be careful. I promise. I forget that my body is still not healed. I felt so good I just forgot to 'listen' to it."

"Now, I do have something to ask you. I don't think it will put a strain on you since you can rest below deck while we cruise to Fort Myers. We need some groceries and I need to go to Miami. Do you think you'd be up to the drive from Fort Myers to Miami?"

"I think so. When will we go?" Mags asked.

"Tomorrow. I'll start out early and you don't even have to get up until we get to Fort Myers. We'll rent a car there and drive on to Miami."

"What do you have to do in Miami?"

Mac updated Mags on his talk with Jim Travis, explaining his need to question Jim Barber.

"Sounds like a good lead you've gotten. Do you think Barber is involved in all this somehow?"

"I have no idea, but I do know that the medallion connects with him. If he's not the one, he just might have ties to whoever is in this mess. Now, Hon, what can the grand chef make for your dinner?"

"I think I'd just like soup and a salad. I think I'd better forgo any rich food tonight."

"I think I can handle that. Do you want to stay up here or go below while I prepare your gourmet meal?" Mac asked with a smile.

"I think I'll stay up here and read." She held up her Kindle.

"I'll call you when it's ready," Mac said.

He went to the galley and organized the ingredients for the salad on the counter. He then took out the fresh mushrooms they had brought with them. He took a can of chicken broth, a small onion, and butter. In a matter of minutes, he had a simmering saucepan of soup and a fresh salad.

"Madam, dinner is served," Mac called up the stairs.

Mags came down to the small table and the couple enjoyed their dinner together, talking about the books they were reading.

Since the next day was full, Mags and Mac prepared for bed. Just as Mac was pulling the sheet over him, his cell phone rang.

"Mac Mason," he answered.

"Mac, it's Jim. Bad news! Barber has skipped. Neighbors haven't seen him come or go in a few weeks. It looks like he skipped bail as soon as he was released."

"Well, it doesn't look like I need to come to Miami."

"No, I'll keep you up to date. We've got an APB out on him."

"Jim, have you sent me a picture of him as well as a copy of his rap sheet?"

"I was going to give that to you tomorrow, but I'll email it right now."

"Great, Jim, and thanks. Talk to you soon."

"Catch you later, Mac. Bye."

Mags had been listening to Mac's side of the conversation. "Guess we just go to the grocery store tomorrow then."

"Yep, that looks like it. We don't need to leave as early. We'll take our time."

32

PAT KNOCKED ON THE DOOR of the condo.

"Come on in. It's unlocked," Eve responded.

Pat, looked at the bags sitting next to the door and said, "I see you're all packed."

"Yes, ready to go."

"I thought if you could spare the time, we'd have dinner on Boca Grande before you drive back to Tampa," Pat offered.

"Sounds good. Where are you thinking about going to eat?"

"There's a very good restaurant, The Pink Elephant, right near the dock where your car is parked."

"Oh, yeah, I remember seeing that when I was there," Eve said.

Pat carried Eve's luggage to a golf cart and they drove to the dock where Pat's twenty foot Key Largo runabout was moored. He helped Eve into the boat and cast off, heading for Boca Grande.

The water was smooth; they made the crossing in less than forty-five minutes.

Pat and Eve exited the boat, each carrying one of Eve's bags. They placed the suitcases in the back of Eve's Toyota Highlander and walked toward the restaurant.

"I had a visit from your dad yesterday," Pat said.

"What did Daddy Dearest want?" Eve asked in a huff.

"Well, we had some business to discuss concerning the bodies found on the dig, but we also talked a little about you."

"Oh, you did?" stated Eve, obviously not happy.

By this time, the couple had arrived at The Pink Elephant and were met by a young man who asked, "How many, please?"

"Two," Pat replied.

The couple was escorted to a table for two at a window looking out towards the waterway where Pat's boat was docked. A waitress came to the table and the two placed their drink orders and began to peruse the menu.

"I think I've lost my appetite," said Eve.

"Why? Because I brought up your father?" Pat asked.

"I lose my appetite every time I think about him. I try to do better, but it just doesn't work."

The waitress came back and both ordered a chef salad and iced tea.

"I don't understand, Eve. I've known your father for years, and I've rarely met a nicer man, and he obviously loves you."

"Pat, stay out of this! You don't know the whole story."

"Eve, I think I do know the story. Your dad told me, but only when I asked him to let me know, as his good friend."

"Then you know, he deserted my mother and me!"

"I'm not sure 'deserted' is the right description, but I do know that he is aware and sorry for what impact Ruth's and his decision had on you," Pat offered.

"Again, I'm not sure you know what you're talking about. Maybe he has changed but that arm candy he married will never be my mother!"

"Is there any indication that Maggie has attempted to be your mother?"

"No, but why did Dad have to leave?"

"Your dad admits that he let his work come between your mom and him. He regrets that happened."

"Oh, Pat, I wish that were true. In all honesty, I have missed Dad. He was my hero as I was growing up and then all of a sudden he and Mom were telling me they were quits. I tried to cover it up, but my heart was broken." She paused. "And I guess it still is."

"I understand, Eve, but try to see past who he was and see who he is. I'd like him for a father-in-law!"

Eve was about to reply when her mouth dropped open. "Father-in-law? Is that what you said? Father-in-law? Did you just propose to me?"

Pat smiled, "Well, not officially. You'll know when I do it officially, but I wanted to plant a seed."

"Plant a seed? You just planted a whole garden. Wow!"

"Something for you to think about, Evelyn!"

Think about it, she did, as they poked at their salads.

In a daze, Eve followed Pat out of the restaurant and to her car. He pulled her into his arms and kissed her with more passion than he ever had. "Have a safe trip, Darling," Pat said.

Eve drove away from Boca Grande with her mind racing, "Wow," was all she could say or think.

33

MAC AND MAGS AWOKE THE next morning at the same time. Mac turned and asked, "How are you feeling this morning?"

"I'm feeling fine. I slept well. How about you?"

"Oh, I always sleep well except for that 3:00 AM trip to the little boy's room. I hate getting old," laughed Mac.

"What do you want for breakfast?"

"You know, a sausage and egg biscuit would be fine for me. Do you want to warm those up while I make the coffee?"

"Sounds good to me. But, I think I'll have cappuccino," answered Mags.

As Mac added his third spoon of sweetener to his coffee, his cell phone rang.

Before he could even answer, he heard Pat's voice. "All residents and members are accounted for, Mac."

"Good, Pat, I can check that off my list. Mags and I are headed to the grocery in Fort Myers. Can we bring you anything?"

"No, I'm good, Mac. Don't forget, you can call the office here if you ever want to save yourself time and fuel. We can shop for you on our daily trip. By the way, I took Eve back to Boca Grande last evening. I'll probably go to Tampa to see her in the next week or so, but she is coming to the New Year's Eve celebration here on the island. Are you and Mags coming?"

"Thanks for reminding me. We've been so busy we haven't discussed it. I'm sure Mags would love to go and, as far as I know, we have no plans yet. I'll talk to her and then call to make reservations. Is the evening still formal?"

"Well, it seems to be getting less formal, but you know the ladies. They like to get all decked out and a lot of the men will be wearing tuxes," offered Pat.

"I'll let you know. How are you coming with that list of occurrences from 2003 through 2005?"

"I've started working on it and should have it for you by the time you return from Fort Myers. Call me and I'll drop it by to you when you get back."

"Will do. We're leaving within the hour."

Mac and Mags sat after their breakfast and reviewed Mac's grocery list. "Looks like you did a good job on this list, Mr. Mason," Mags complimented.

After cleaning up the few dishes from breakfast, Mac prepared *The Mistress* for their trip to the mainland. Within the half hour they were on their way.

"Remind me, Mags, when we get back to Joseffa, to have the fuel and the potable water topped off. I need to dump the holding tanks, too."

"Will do, Captain."

Mac and Mags docked at the marina nearest the large Super Walmart and began their walk there. "This store is so convenient. I'm glad the marina provides these grocery carts; it makes it easier to carry our stuff back," Mags said.

The couple split their list in half and Mags and Mac completed their shopping in record time. After paying, they began their trip back to *The Mistress*.

Within an hour, they were back, docking on Joseffa. "Why don't you relax while I put the groceries away?" Mac offered.

"I think I'll do that. I'm a little tired. I'm not sure why, but I am." Mags said, as she stretched out on the sofa in the small salon and immediately fell asleep.

Mac had completed putting the groceries away when he heard a voice from above. "Permission to come aboard!" It was Pat.

"Welcome! Is that the list you have there?"

"Sure is. There really aren't many items on it. Very little happened out of the ordinary, but I did see a couple of events that might raise some interest," Pat advised.

"I'll look it over after we have a late lunch. Would you join us?" Mac asked.

"No, thank you. I ate over at the Inn and need to meet with a couple of disgruntled residents. It seems that a couple of teenaged boys partied last night and got a little loud. I just need to smooth some ruffled feathers."

After Pat left, Mags woke up and asked, "What would you like for lunch? How about a ham and Swiss cheese sandwich and some chips?"

"Sounds perfect to me!"

Mac settled in a chair in the salon and began to read the list that Pat had prepared.

1. 01/01/03   Teens used residents' golf carts without permission damaging three.
2. 03/10/03   Sous Chef quits after disagreement with Chef. Gave no notice.
3. 09/23/03   Catboat almost sinks during race to Punta Blanca. No one injured. Boat towed in.
4. 11/23/03   Wallace Johnson suffers heart attack and is airlifted to the Fort Myers' hospital.
5. 01/01/04   New Fire Chief begins employment.
6. 03/21/04   John Thomas, grounds worker, vacates apartment and leaves job with no notice, no termination letter, and without pay due him.
7. 03/21/04   Bettina McCauley complained that she just found a very smelly egg from the 2003 Easter egg hunt.

8. 03/22/04 Bettina McCauley complained that no announcement had been made that residents should use only plastic eggs in the Easter egg hunt.
9. 03/23/04 Bettina McCauley sent out notice that she would be in charge of the Easter egg hunt in the future.

Mac continued reading but found nothing that aroused his curiosity. His attention returned to item #2. "No," Mac thought, "a disagreement with the Chef would not cause a murder. Beside, the Chef is still working on the island. But, item #6 is curious."

Mac turned to Mags. "Mags, why would a grounds keeper who had been around long enough to rate an apartment, leave with no notice and without his pay?"

"He wouldn't, would he, Mac? Unless he had an emergency or had to leave in a hurry."

Mac picked up his cell and called Pat. "Pat, what information can you give me about this John Thomas, the grounds keeper who left unexpectedly?"

"I thought that would get your attention, Mac. I've pulled his employment record for you. It's all the information I have on him. You might also want to talk to Rufus Reagan, our Head of Grounds Keeping. He would know Thomas best."

"I'll come right over and get that employment record. Is there a picture of Thomas?"

"Yes, we take pictures of all our employees for their ID badges. That is in the file."

"Be right there, Pat."

Mac walked the short distance to the Administration Building and went straight to Pat's office.

"That didn't take long, Mac. I have a copy of John Thomas' personnel record. He was with us for two years. Strange situation. I've also called Rufus and he will be available tomorrow, if you want to see him."

Mac opened the personnel folder and immediately saw the picture of Thomas. "Well, hello, Jim Barber!" Mac exclaimed.

"You recognize him?" Pat asked.

"Oh, yes; in fact, he was in custody in Miami until last week when he was released on bond. I asked that he be picked up for questioning because I thought he was involved in some way, but he had skipped. We think we found something of his near those bodies; but anyway, he had jumped bond. When Thomas was hired, didn't your background check on him produce anything unusual?"

Pat looked down and, with obvious embarrassment, said, "Mac, we were really negligent about background checks until recently. I suppose that we didn't think grounds keepers were a threat or a problem. We do background checks on all employees now."

"I understand."

Mac took the personnel folder and began his walk back to *The Mistress*.

Mags met Mac on deck and asked, "Have you had a chance to look at the file yet?"

"I haven't read the file, but I have seen John Thomas' photo and we know him as Jim Barber."

"Jim Barber. Is that the man who has the tattoo identical to the image on the medallion that they found?"

"Yep, the very same. I need to call Sheriff Walton and also Jim Travis. I think we need a task force to handle this. It might be bigger than two murders, if that is possible."

Mac sat down on deck of *The Mistress* and took out his cell phone to make those calls.

Before Mac could make his first call, his phone played the familiar chords of Beethoven's "Fifth Symphony," signaling an incoming call. Mac answered.

"Mason here."

Mac immediately recognized the voice of Dr. Raul Garcia.

"Mac, I got the results of the DNA test today and ran the information through CODIS."

Mac was very familiar with the Combined DNA Index System. CODIS contains the DNA profiles of known offenders, as well as other persons of interest to law enforcement.

"Did you get a hit?" Mac asked.

"I got not only one hit, but a hit on both bodies. They are identified as William and Daniel Morrison."

"Those names sound familiar. Who are they?"

Dr. Garcia continued, "They are brothers. The best description for them is that they were mercenaries. A less polite term might be 'hit men'. Their services were available to the highest bidder."

"No possibility of error?" Mac asked.

"None. I got a perfect match!"

Mac thought, rubbing his chin, "Can you send me your findings as soon as possible. That's a major piece of information."

Mac thought to himself: "Glad I heard from Raul before making these calls. I have far more info to support my request now."

Mac picked up his cell phone to select his first person to call: Sheriff Walton. He selected the sheriff's name and pressed "Send."

"Sheriff Walton, this is Mac Mason. I've gotten some updated information on the two murders. I'll email that to you. We know who the deceased are and we've got another man who might be tied to all this. We found something that we are pretty sure belonged to him. It was buried with the bodies, probably by accident. Not proof, exactly, but it surely gives us somewhere to start. But, I think this is going to be bigger than the murders. Would you be willing to call in the FBI for consultation? Plus, would you be willing to be part of a task force to investigate the murders and other felonies that I think might be part of this?"

"Are the other crimes within the purview of the FBI?"

"Yes, definitely. We really need their resources. I'd also like to invite the Miami Police Department's Head of Major Crimes. Again, if my suspicions are correct, this will fall under his jurisdiction. His name is Jim Travis. I'll be glad to make the calls if you would like."

"Yes, Mac. Why don't you make the call to the FBI and also Miami PD? I've cleared you to have official capacity as a consultant to Lee County law enforcement. Just let me know when and where you want to meet."

Mac made a note in the small, yellow pad he still kept in his back pants pocket, a habit that carried over from his pre-retirement days. He selected another name from his contact list: Jim Travis. It surely helped to have personal cell phone numbers when things were in a rush!

"Jim, Mac here. Do you have a minute?"

"Sure, Mac. What can I do for you?"

Mac filled Jim in on what had been discovered concerning the bodies and the one who was somehow tied to the deaths.

Jim let out a heavy breath. "Mac, do you know what this means?"

"Oh, yes, Jim, I think I do. Although we had insufficient evidence to tie Barber to human trafficking in Florida, we might just have more evidence for bringing down the higher ups. We've got to check this out. I'd like to ask you if you would be part of a cross-jurisdictional task force. We can put our information together with Lee County, the FBI, Miami PD, and probably other law enforcement as well."

"Have you contacted the FBI yet?" asked Travis.

"No, but that's my next call. I don't think you know, but Adam has just been transferred to Tampa to head that office. I'm going to call him and see how we should proceed. Sheriff Walton has agreed to bring the FBI into the investigation of the murders since it is in his jurisdiction. But, I want their resources so that we can go deeper."

"I'm on board, Mac. Just tell me when and where to meet."

Mac disconnected from his call with Jim as Mags came on deck.

"You are a busy man up here. I couldn't help but hear you talking to Jim Travis. Are you about to call Adam?"

"I think so, but I had better not share too much of what I've found out until I get all my ducks in a row."

Mags nodded her understanding and disappeared below deck.

Mac again picked up his phone and selected Adam from his contact list. He again pressed "Send."

"Mason here," a voice answered.

"Mason here, too," Mac said laughing. "How are you, Son?"

"Fine, Dad. My first week on the job here in Tampa, but I'm settling in pretty well. I have a great team here."

"Good. Well, this isn't a social call. I need your input, advice, and hopefully assistance."

Without allowing for interruption, Mac shared with Adam the finding of the two bodies, the possible identification of someone who might have been involved with the burial and the identity of the two murdered brothers. When his dad mentioned the medallion, Adam replied, "Maybe I am a bit cautious, but maybe that does not belong to the murderer or to the one who buried the bodies, but might have just happened to be with the murdered men for who-knows-what reason."

"Worth a thought. One murderer? Two murderers? I guess we can't jump to any conclusion based on that medallion until we know how it ended up in the test pit. This isn't simple, is it?"

"OK, Dad, what do you need from me?"

"Since I am under contract to the Lee County Sheriff's Department, I have been authorized to request FBI involvement. I am not sure what your chain of command would say about your being the liaison, but I'd like you."

"Dad, I hold the position of Section Chief and I report to one of the Assistant Directors. I'd have to explain the need to him and gain his approval before I can become involved."

"Can you do that quickly?"

"As quick as a phone call. I'll give him all the particulars and your suspicion that this might be an opening into the problem we are having with human trafficking. For now, that will have to be just a hunch on your part. No evidence. I'll call you back as soon as I have an answer."

"Great, Son! Oh, by the way, do you remember meeting Pat Jefferson, the CEO of Joseffa Island?"

"Yeah, I remember Pat. Kelly and I met him when we went to Joseffa last year."

"Well, he's dating your sister. It looks pretty serious. Eve is also living and working in Tampa now."

"Wow, in Tampa? Who would have thought that we were neighbors? I had no idea. What is she doing now?"

"She's an image consultant and, from what I understand, very good at her job. She's working now with some big corporation, preparing their employees for trips to Japan. She teaches them things they need to know about the Japanese culture so they are better able to do their jobs."

"That sounds right down her alley. Mom certainly prepared her for that with all those etiquette classes Eve took. I bet she is one of the best, Dad!"

"Well, call me as soon as you've talked to the Assistant Director. Make sure he is okay with two people from the same family working together on this case. I'd better get off now. Bye, Son."

"Goodbye, Dad. Later."

Mac looked to the west and saw the sun beginning to set. He called down the stairwell to Mags, "Hon, the sunset looks like it will be beautiful. Why don't you bring some iced tea up here and we'll enjoy it?"

"Coming right up, Mr. Weatherman," Mags called out.

Mags came up to the main deck and settled into a deck chair next to Mac, handing him a tall, plastic glass of iced tea. Mags and Mac looked to the west and saw the beautiful orange across the horizon, topped with purple and then a layer of puffy clouds. As the sun settled slowly over the horizon, Mac pulled Mags closer to him and turned her face toward him. He leaned down and kissed Mags with the passion that his love for her evidenced.

"Mmmm, I need to put that kiss into my new perfume ads. My only reaction to it is 'Mmmm'".

Wiggling his eyebrows, Mac said, "Let's eat a quick dinner up here and then go to bed early. What do you say?"

"Now what could you possibly have on your mind, Mr. Mason?" Mags said with a huge grin.

"I think you know!" Mac replied.

34

UPON WAKING UP THE FOLLOWING morning, Mac looked at Mags and said, "It's Saturday, but Will and Kate are still digging today because of the days we missed earlier this week. We should go down and see them. I may have to bow out of the dig next week. I'll be up to my eyeballs with this investigation. However, you can continue if you want. Don't push yourself. Are you sure you are up to it?"

"I will probably go over there, Mac. I feel we made a commitment and I enjoy the digs anyway. I feel okay."

"OK, but be careful. I feel bad about not being able to help out, but I think Will and Kate will understand. We'll head down there after breakfast."

❖ ❖ ❖

A little later, Mac and Mags headed back to the dig site. When they got to the south end of Joseffa, Will looked up and smiled, saying, "Hello, you two." Then he approached Mags, gave her a hug and asked, "How are you feeling now?"

"I'm great, Will. I just have to be more careful. I have to remember that I'm not really 100%, even when I feel that I am."

Kate walked over to join the three. Always in work mode, she said, "Welcome, ready to work?"

Mags smiled, "Yep, ready, Boss!"

Mac looked at the two and said, "I will probably have to desert you next week. We've made progress in the murder that took place here, and I will probably be up to my neck in the investigation."

Mac updated Will and Kate on the news concerning identification of the possible killer and the bodies. "Maybe I am wrong," Mac continued, "but I surely think that medallion belongs to someone who does not know it was there. The medallion plus dead bodies makes me a touch suspicious!"

"Wow, you were really busy yesterday. Of course, we understand your needing to be away from the dig. We'll keep an eye on Mags, making sure she doesn't work us too hard! Seriously, we'll get her back to *The Mistress* if she needs to rest."

"What can we do today?" Mags asked.

"I doubt we'll have much help today. We had more than we needed yesterday, but I think the excitement of finding the bodies has waned. I'd like both of you to work the new test pit. We've gotten down to about thirty centimeters so you can begin on the next ten," Kate requested.

"Gotcha!" Mags gave an emphatic salute, as she smiled.

Mac and Mags settled into their work. As buckets were filled, Mac carried them to the quarter-inch screen and Mags shook the screen and looked for items that might be of importance.

Around 11:00 AM, Mags called out, "I think I found something. Will, can you come here?" Mags held up a flat object about four inches long and one inch across. It appeared to be worn very smooth. Will came to the screen. He picked up the object and turned it slowly in his hand.

"Good find, Mags. This is a fish net gauge. It appears to be made from a manatee rib bone. This is one of the Calusa's smaller ones."

"Smaller?" Mags asked. "And what's a fish net gauge?"

"Yes, the Calusa made fish net gauges of three sizes. They would wind their material for making nets around this stone and the size of the stone determined the size of the holes in the net. This one was used to net smaller fish. Really good find, Mags."

Mags beamed as she took a special zip lock bag, recorded the location of the find and wrote in large letters, Fish Net Gauge-Manatee Bone.

Mac and Mags stopped for lunch, having brought sandwiches and sodas in an ice chest. They continued their digging through the afternoon. They did find charred wood, indicating where pottery was fired or food was cooked. They also uncovered a shell mound where oyster shells were obviously thrown away after meals. Mac had found a large shell that Will said had been used as a hammer. It had been a productive day.

"People will ask us what we found today," Mags said to Will.

"Well, the important question isn't 'what did you find'? The question to ask is 'what did you learn'?"

"Ah, good differentiation. OK, Dr. Marks, what have we learned?"

"Well, Mrs. Mason," Will said with a grin, "We are learning more about how the Calusa lived thirty-five hundred years ago, what they ate, and where they lived."

"Indeed, sir. If ever I am on 'Who Wants to Be a Millionaire', I hope they ask a question about what Calusa ate for supper!" Will gave a polite chuckle, but it was clear that he did not find the comment all that funny.

At 4:00 PM, Mac said, "I think Mags and I will be going. I need to go to the administration office and print some items that have been sent to me, and set up some files on this investigation."

Kate came over, "Thanks for the help today. We couldn't have done as much without you two. Mac, we'll miss you. Come down and check in with us when you can. We promise we won't put you to work."

Mac and Mags got into their golf cart and began their trip back to *The Mistress.*

As Mac and Mags were riding back to the dock, Mac suggested, "Mags, why don't we eat at the Inn tonight. If you are as tired as I am, you probably don't feel like cooking. I know I don't."

"That's a good idea. We'll both need showers. You smell a little ripe right now, and I'm sure I do too."

Mac and Mags walked the dock towards *The Mistress* just as Mac's phone rang.

He looked at the screen and said to Mags, "It's Adam."

"Hello, Son," said Mac. "I didn't expect to hear from you until Monday."

"I didn't expect Barnes to get back to me so soon. He talked to the Director and I've been relieved of my duties as Section Head so that I can put full time into the case that you've uncovered. We have human trafficking at the top of our list of concerns. If that is what this turns out to be, the Director wants us to give full cooperation. By the way, did you know that the Assistant Director knows you? He was at the conference where you spoke on human trafficking in Miami a couple of years ago. He was very impressed with you. He had no idea that I was your son. He is okay with our working together professionally, even though we are, you know, sort of kin!"

"Great! Is your boss Pete Barnes?"

"Yeah, Dad. He reports straight to the Director."

"I remember him also. We went to lunch together. He's a good man."

"Yes, he is. Now when would you like to meet and where?"

"I think Joseffa would be a good place to meet. Mags is continuing on the dig, although I won't be able to. Too much going on! I wonder, Son, if you can you drive to Fort Myers? If so, I will pick you up there. We three---you, me, and Travis--along with Sheriff Walton, will be the nucleus of the task force, but I would expect others to join as we define our needs. I'll arrange with Bob or Pat for a conference room in the auditorium. We can center the investigation there for the next week at least."

"That sounds fine. When will you pick me up?" Adam asked.

"How about around 10:00 AM Monday at the Fort Myers Marina? Jim Travis will meet us there also. You can stay on *The Mistress,* if that's okay with you. I'll arrange for a condo for Jim. The sheriff will probably choose to stay at home."

"Sounds good to me. See you Monday, Dad."

Mac called down to Mags, "Hon, I need to make a couple of phone calls and then I'll be down."

"OK, Hon. I'll be out of the head in a few minutes," Mags said, using her nautical jargon.

Mac quickly called Jim Travis and filled him in on the arrangement to meet at the Fort Myers Marina. It would be a two and a half hour drive for Travis. Mac then called Sheriff Walton.

"Bud, this is Mac Mason. I've arranged for FBI support for our investigation. Can you come to the first task force meeting Monday?"

"OK, Mac. That'll work. I can be there. Where and when?"

"Do you need a place to stay since the meetings will be on Joseffa?"

"Mac, I'd prefer to stay at home. My wife, Peg, is expecting, and I'd like to be at home in the evening. I'll tell you what, I'll bring my boat over to the island instead of you picking me up. When should I be there?"

"Bud, I have to pick up Jim Travis and my son in Fort Myers Monday morning. Why don't you just plan on being on Joseffa Tuesday morning at 8:00 AM?"

"That's fine with me. See you then."

Mac disconnected from the call and went down the ladder to the main salon where Mags was sitting, styling her wig. She had on a pale blue sundress with white open-toed sandals.

"You look lovely, Mrs. Mason."

"Why thank you, sir. However, you do not!"

"Give me a few minutes and I'll make myself presentable," Mac smiled.

Mac stripped and went into the master bedroom bath. He quickly showered, brushed his teeth, and combed his hair. He chose a pale blue polo shirt and a pair of khaki Dockers. As he sat, putting on brown socks and loafers, he thought "This investigation will be quite a challenge. But, if the result is what I hope it will be, it will be well worth it."

Mac went into the salon and took Mags' arm. "Are you ready, my lady?"

"Ready and starving to death," Mags replied.

The couple headed for their golf cart and the Inn.

35

ARRIVING AT THE INN, MAC approached the welcome desk.

"Good evening, Peter. I didn't call for a reservation. Can we get into the casual side?"

"Yes, Mr. Mason. In fact, Mr. And Mrs. Gardner are in there now."

Just as Peter was leading Mac and Mags to a table, Susan Gardner jumped up and rushed to them. "Mac and Mags, would you join us? We are just getting ready to order."

"That would be wonderful," Mags replied.

Bob stood as Mac and Mags approached the table. He held Mags' chair as she sat. Mac held Susan's chair for her.

On the table in front of Bob, was a very tall glass of dark liquid. "Is that your drink of choice?" asked Mac.

"It's the elixir of life, Mac. My caffeine-free Diet Dr. Pepper! They see me come in the door and it arrives at the table before I do."

Elyse arrived at the table carrying her order pad and menus. "Good evening, Mr. and Mrs. Gardner and Mr. and Mrs. Mason. What can I get you to drink?" she asked, looking at the Masons.

"I think I'll just have water," said Mags.

"Make it sweet iced tea for me," added Mac. Looking at Bob he asked, "What looks good tonight?"

"Well, the rib eye is great, and we have lobster tails," Bob offered.

"I don't need to ask what you're having, Mags," Mac stated.

"Ah, husband, you know me well. I'll have the lobster, of course."

"And Elyse, I'd like the rib eye," stated Mac.

"How would you like it, Mr. Mason?"

"Rare, just make sure it isn't still mooing."

Mac and Mags turned their attention back to Bob and Susan. "It's been quite an exciting week."

Bob responded, "Yes, Pat has been keeping me abreast of what's been happening."

"There's probably a lot you don't know. I'll fill you in quickly and then I have a couple of requests for you."

Mac quickly brought the Gardners up to date on the latest non-confidential information and then turned to Bob and asked, "Could you make a condo available for Jim Travis? He's the head of the Major Crimes Division of the Miami Police Department. I'd also like to reserve the small conference room in the auditorium for next week, if possible. Plus, since I'll be busy with the investigation, can you provide a golf cart for Mags to get to and from the dig?"

Bob smiled, "You don't ask for much, do you?"

"I'd only ask a good friend, Bob."

"Sure, Mac, we can arrange that. I'll let Pat know."

"Also," Mac added, "Is there internet access in the conference room?"

"We just added wireless internet last month. I'll provide you with a secure password for access. Let me give it to you now."

As Bob was writing on the back of one of his business cards, Elyse arrived with the dinners. Susan had also chosen the lobster and Bob had picked the rib eye.

"Great minds agree," Bob offered.

The two couples shared what was going on in their lives. Bob and Susan announced that their son, Donald, was due to become a father and would be visiting Joseffa over the Christmas holidays. Mags shared about her upcoming trip to MD Anderson for radiation treatments after the first of the year. Mac told Bob and Susan of his chance meeting with Eve and the fact that she was dating Pat.

"He seems quite smitten, if that is still an 'in word' today," Susan said.

"Yes, he came into my office and asked for the name of a good jeweler," Bob smiled.

"What?" Mac almost yelled, causing the people at the next table to look over.

Mags put her hand over on Mac's arm and said, "Relax, Hon, she's a grown woman."

Mac sputtered, "I know. I know, but....." He fell silent. His little girl? Married?

The two couples finished their meals. Mags asked, "Will we see you at the beach front worship service tomorrow?"

"We'll probably be there. We weren't last week since we were off-island."

As Elyse brought Mac the check, Bob said, "Elyse, let me have that one." He signed his name and the couples rose and left the Inn.

Outside, Mags said, "Thanks for the wonderful dinner, but most of all, thanks for the wonderful friendship."

"Ditto," said Mac, as the couples parted.

Mac and Mags walked to their golf cart. "I wish we had walked here," Mags said, "it's so beautiful tonight."

"We can take a walk when we get back to the dock, if you'd like."

"Let's do. I'd like to walk the Promenade to the north end of the island."

Mac and Mags rode back to the dock, parked their golf cart and walked the short distance behind the Administration Building to the Promenade and turned to the left.

"Mags, you know I love to show off the island." He made as if he were tipping his hat and added, "Madam, may I give you a guided tour?"

Mags rolled her eyes. "This," Mac began "is the older part of the island, as far as modern history goes. These cottages are among the oldest on the island. The middle cottage on the northern point is where Bob Gardner stayed when he made his decision to buy Joseffa in 1976. The island was a jungle and all the cottages were in a poor state of repair. He brought Joseffa back!"

"Excellent tour, sir. Seriously, I can't believe what Bob has gotten done here. He is a man of vision; that's for sure!"

Mac added, "Susan helped make it happen. He'd be lost without her."

"Well Mac, as they say, 'Behind every man is a....'"

"Oh, so true, Mags, oh, so true!"

Upon reaching the northern most point of the island, the couple turned and began their walk back. Mac was holding Mags hand tightly. "I don't know what I'd do without you, Mags." He didn't see as a tear rolled down Mags' cheek.

36

MAC ROSE EARLY ON SUNDAY morning. He took eggs and grated cheese from the 'fridge. He set up the griddle and began to fry a pound of bacon. "We can freeze what we don't eat and use it for bacon, lettuce and tomato sandwiches," Mac thought. He broke four eggs into a bowl, added a little milk and a large handful of grated cheese and prepared to scramble them for breakfast. He then took out two pieces of toast and put them into the toaster.

Just as he was taking the crisp bacon off the griddle, Mags came into the galley. "Making breakfast, again? Joseffa Island is a good influence on you."

"Just taking care of my love," Mac smiled.

"And your stomach!"

The couple sat down at the table in the salon and quietly ate. Afterwards, Mac looked at his watch and said, "Well, we need to dress for the worship service."

"I saw how people dressed last week. I think I will just wear capris and a sleeveless tee." Mag went to their stateroom and selected light green capris and a white tee. Again, she chose her white, open-toed sandals.

Mac wore khaki shorts and a yellow polo shirt. He also chose to wear sandals.

After dressing, the couple walked down the dock towards their golf cart. Mags stopped halfway down and looked into the water. "Look at those huge fish, Mac."

"Those are mullet. To continue your guided tour, madam: An early owner of Joseffa had a rancho here where he caught mullet, salted them, and shipped them to Cuba. It was quite a business for a number of years."

The couple moved on to their golf cart and headed to the windward side of the island. There were even more people gathered for worship than there had been the previous Sunday. Christmas hymns, photocopied on white paper, were handed out and the gathered congregation sang several before a man stood and announced, "Do we have any joys or concerns to share this morning?"

Bettina McCauley stood and announced, "I think we should pray for our safety. Since two people were murdered on our island, I'm not sure we are safe. And I've heard rumors of people being taken from their beds and sold into slavery in some third-world country."

The leader of the service responded, "Ms. McCauley, I think we are all safe here. From what I hear, those bodies were buried eight years ago and I've heard no evidence of kidnapping citizens."

Mac leaned over to Mags and whispered in her ear, "Well, so much for keeping anything confidential here. I wonder how that word got out."

Mags whispered back, "It's kind of like a small town. There are no secrets at all."

Bettina looked at Mac and said, "Mr. Mason knows what is going on. What can you tell us, Mr. Mason?"

Mac said simply, "I'm not at liberty to give you any information you haven't already heard. I must caution everyone not to spread rumors. I'm sure Bob Gardner or Pat Jefferson will update residents and members if there is any new information that impacts the island."

Bettina sat down with an audible "Humph!"

After a number of joys were shared and Bettina read off a list of people to pray for, most unknown to the residents, a prayer was said by the leader and then he offered a short homily on the parable of the Good Samaritan. The closing hymn, 'Hark, the Herald Angels Sing' was sung. Mac leaned over to Mags. "I love the Christmas hymns, but it is hard to believe that today is December 8."

Upon completion of the hymn, the service was concluded with a brief benediction.

Mac and Mags drove the golf cart back to *The Mistress* and spent their afternoon reading and napping. It was a good day to relax. They spent the evening watching a movie on a DVD that they had brought with them and went to bed early.

The following morning, Mags got up, dressed, kissed Mac goodbye and took the golf cart down to Will and Kate's condo where she had been invited for breakfast. Mac had prepared a lunch for her to take to the dig since he would be away on *The Mistress*.

After Mags left, Mac made a large thermos of coffee that he carried to the flying bridge of *The Mistress*. The Harbor Master came from his office, which overlooked the dock, and offered to help Mac cast off. With all lines free, Mac eased *The Mistress* away from the island. Using his onboard navigation system, he set his course for the Fort Myers Marina and filled his coffee mug. As he passed out of the No Wake Zone, he eased his craft to a cruising speed of twenty knots. Shortly after 10:00 AM, Mac radioed the Fort Myers Marina and asked permission to pick up two passengers. Permission was granted and Mac navigated to the long dock. From a distance, he saw Adam waiting, a large bag in hand. Next to him stood Jim Travis, also with luggage. Mac pulled up, slowed to an idle, and eased against the dock. He went to the main deck just as Adam handed his bag onboard and stepped quickly on deck. Jim followed.

"Hey, Dad, you made good time."

"It's a short trip over here, Son. Thanks for driving down." Looking at Jim, Mac said, "Welcome aboard *The Mistress*."

"First time I have seen your toy. Fantastic!"

"Thanks." To both men, Mac said, "We should be on Joseffa in time for lunch. We can debrief then and have our first official meeting tomorrow morning when Sheriff Walton arrives."

Mac navigated out of the Fort Myers harbor and set the GPS system for Joseffa. He pushed the throttle forward and set *The Mistress'* speed at twenty knots.

Mac chose to navigate from the lower cabin instead of the flying bridge so that the three men could talk. "Have you ever been to Joseffa, Jim?" Mac asked. "No, in fact I had never heard about it until you and Mags bought your membership there."

"It's quite an island with a fantastic history. Maybe after lunch we can stop by the museum and you can see what I mean. Adam, you've seen the museum, haven't you?

"No, Dad, I haven't. The only time I was on Joseffa was for that party that Bob Gardner gave you and Mags on your tenth anniversary. The museum had closed for the day."

"It'll be a treat for you also. Son, since you know your way around down below, why don't you fix us something to drink?"

"Beer, soda, or water, Jim?"

"I will take anything that is diet," Jim responded.

"Same for me, Son."

"Dad?" Adam said with some urgency.

"Yes?" Mac responded.

"Do you think you could call me Adam while we're working together? I'm uncomfortable with 'Son'. I feel like maybe I should be taking out the trash or cleaning my room."

Mac, laughing, said, "Yes, Agent Mason."

"I wouldn't go that far, Dad...errrr...I mean Mr. Mason."

Joseffa Island came into sight. Mac eased into the berth that he had left just a few hours earlier.

After tying up and getting Adam's luggage into the guest stateroom, Mac said, "Jim, let's get you settled and then have lunch."

They walked towards the Administration Building.

Bob rushed out to greet them. Mac was surprised to see Mags with him. She was obviously upset. Mac rushed to her: "Hon, are you all right? What's wrong?"

"They told me not to call you. They didn't want you to be upset."

"What happened? What's going on?"

Mac hugged Mags tightly as Bob spoke. "Mac, there has been an incident."

Mac's nerves froze.

"While you were gone, someone—we have no idea who it was—put a bullet into the boat docked where you usually have *The Mistress*. I think it was intended for you."

"Why do you think that?"

"We got a call at the office and a voice said, "Tell Mason that the next one will be for him.""

"Have you called the sheriff," Adam asked.

"Yes, he's on his way."

Mac looked at Adam and Jim. "The word spread quickly about my suspecting human trafficking, or maybe the murderer of the Morrison brothers has decided to stop my investigation. It could be either."

Adam spoke up. "How does anyone know about the possibility that this is tied to human trafficking?"

"Adam, I don't know. Maybe someone heard me talking about it to Bob or overheard my phone conversations with you two, as well as Sheriff Walton. Or, there is another possibility. I took all the files sent to me by Dr. Garcia and my other correspondence and reports to the Administration Building computer to print them out. That could have been hacked. I'm sure the internet system here is not 'hacker proof'. If someone knows of my suspicions, they'll know I have called in a task force. Let's be careful to keep everything we find as confidential as possible."

Jim added, "Mac, I'm concerned about your and Mags' safety. Do we need to get extra security for you two?"

Mac thought for a moment. "Whoever fired those shots is on the island or has access to Joseffa. We'll talk to Sheriff Walton and see if he can provide security for Mags. I can take care of myself."

Adam did not hesitate using his familiarity with Mac. "Dad, I worry about you, too. Believe me; I am not leaving your side until we get to the bottom of this."

Mac, Adam, and Jim entered the Administration Building and retrieved the keys to Jim's condo, as well as a golf cart for him to use. Pat came from his back office and placed a key in Mac's hand. "Here's a key for the small conference room you want to use. The lock was changed and this is the only key to the room. We've put in a white board, an easel with a flip chart, legal pads, pencils and dry erase markers."

"Thanks, Pat, I think you have thought of everything we'll need."

The three men left the Administration Building and drove two golf carts to the White Sands Condo on the Promenade. Jim carried his suitcase, placed it on the bed in the back bedroom and then said, "Let's go check out the conference room we'll be using."

Mac shook his head negatively and said, "No, I want to check on Mags first. She seemed pretty upset. I'd like to keep her with us until we arrange security for her."

"Good idea!" both Jim and Adam agreed.

They headed back to Administration where Mac had asked Mags to wait.

Mac found Mags sitting in Pat's office. With a worried look on her face, she asked, "Are you okay, Mac?"

Giving Mags a hug, Mac replied, "I'm fine. I want you to stay with us until we can arrange for security for you. I'm going to see if the sheriff can do that."

"Is that necessary?" Mags asked. "Is that really necessary?"

"Absolutely!" Mac answered, leaving room for no debate.

"Let's go down to the boat where the shots were fired. I wondered why our normal berthing space wasn't available when we came back from Fort Myers."

The four walked from the Administration Building, down the long dock to the boat in what had been *The Mistress'* space. Two island employees were standing on the dock next to the boat. The three approached the two young men who immediately blocked the entrance to the deck of the Bayliner that looked similar to Mac and Mags' boat. Mac stepped forward, "I'm Mac Mason." He flashed his identification. "This is FBI Special Agent Adam Mason and Detective Jim Travis. We need to check this boat out."

One of the young men said with an authoritative air, "One minute." He spoke into a two way radio, listened for a minute and said, "Sorry Mr. Mason. I had to check with Mr. Jefferson before I allowed anyone onto the boat. You can go onboard now."

Adam nodded and the four stepped onto the main deck. As they looked around, they immediately noticed a side window shattered. Entering the cabin, Jim handed the others protective gloves which they put on with a snap of the wrist band.

"I doubt anyone was aboard, but we do want to protect from contamination in case anyone did come aboard," Jim declared.

The three men began looking at the shattered window and allowed their eyes to follow what was probably the trajectory of the bullet. On the wall opposite the window, there were several holes. "I think we might have evidence here," Adam noted. Mac took a small pocket knife from his pocket and carefully cut around one of the holes. "Yep, we have bullets."

Jim took a plastic zip lock bag from his pocket and with his gloved hand, Mac dropped the bullet into the bag.

"You really come prepared. Gloves and evidence bags!" Adam said obviously impressed.

"Old habits die hard, Adam."

Mac checked the other two holes and found two more slugs that he also dug out and dropped into the bag.

About that time, a voice sounded from the dock. "Mac, are you down there? Bud Walton here."

"Sheriff, come on down." The two island workers stepped aside allowing Bud to step onto the deck and down the ladder to the salon.

"We've found slugs in this wall. Do you think Raul might get something from them?" Mac asked.

"Good work. I'll get them to him as soon as I get back to the mainland."

Mac looked around the cabin and said, "I don't think the shooter was trying to hit me. I think this was just a warning. But, I'm glad *The Mistress* wasn't in this berth. I hope the owner of this boat has insurance."

Sheriff Walton and the others walked back to the main deck. Two deputies stood next to the young island employees. "My men and I will start questioning anyone on the dock or in the boats tied up here. I'm surprised the Harbor Master didn't see anything."

One of the young men spoke up. "The Harbor Master went up to the boutique next to the administrative office to get a soda. This happened while he was gone. He did say he saw someone he didn't recognize leaving the dock when he came out, but didn't suspect anything at that time. He didn't even hear the shots."

The other young man spoke up. "You know Josh and his hearing. If he doesn't have those hearing aids turned up, he is almost deaf."

"Yeah," the other young man replied, shaking his head.

"Bud, let me know if you or your deputies find out anything useful. It's late and I think we'll call it a day. Will we still see you tomorrow?" Mac inquired.

"I'll be here bright and early."

"Oh, one more thing, Bud, I'm a little concerned about my wife's safety. Can you provide her with security until we get this worked out?"

"Mac, I can provide someone for a day or so, but I'm so short-staffed, I can't promise anything beyond that."

"I understand, Bud. If you can cover tomorrow and maybe Wednesday, I'll make arrangements for after that."

"I'll bring two men with me tomorrow," the sheriff said as he turned to go.

Mac looked at Mags. "Do you think we can provide these two men with dinner tonight?" Mac said, motioning to Adam and Jim. "I'll help you. Just say 'no" if you need to. This stress cannot be good for your..."

"Why don't you grill and I'll take care of side dishes and a salad," Mags said, not letting Mac complete his sentence.

The four walked down a perpendicular dock and to *The Mistress*.

When on board, Mac said, "I could use a beer. How about you guys?"

Both nodded their heads and said almost in unison, "Oh, yes!"

37

On Tuesday morning, Mac, as usual, woke up early, long before Adam or Mags. He showered, dressed, and went to the galley. He prepared a strong cup of coffee and added his usual three spoons of sweetener, one spoon of sugar and a small amount of milk. Sitting on the sofa, he began looking through his cell phone contact list.

He made his selection, Phil Phillips detective agency. He pressed the icon on the phone and placed his call.

A young, female voice answered. "Phillips' Investigative Services, how may I direct your call?"

"Phil Phillips, please. Mac Mason calling."

A somewhat gruff, but friendly, voice came on the line. "Mac, you old son-of-a-gun! I haven't heard from you in years. How's retirement?"

"Busier than I ever thought it would be, Phil. How are you?"

"The same here, a little of this and a little of that."

"Phil, I need your services. Can you provide me with two of your people for security?"

"That can be arranged. You don't need bodyguards, do you?"

"Not me, Phil. I want them for Mags."

"Mags? You bet I can do that. Is this anything you can share with me?"

"Not now. I'd only need them during the day. We're on Joseffa Island. I can arrange transportation for them from the Bokeelia

Marina on Pine Island. They can catch the Joseffa Island Shuttle at 8:00 AM and return to the mainland on the 5:00 PM shuttle each day."

"When do you want them and for how long?"

Mac thought a moment. "Let see, how about Thursday morning and until further notice? Just bill me for their time and expenses."

"Can you tell me what they should be looking out for?"

"Just keep her safe. This is a personal safety detail. She will probably be working at an archaeological dig Thursday through Saturday, and after that I don't know."

"They'll be there Thursday, Mac. Give Mags my best."

Mac disconnected from the call just as Adam came from the guest stateroom.

"Starting early, aren't you, Dad?"

"I just arranged for security for Mags. I'll feel much better knowing professionals are looking out for her."

At that moment, Mags came from the master stateroom already dressed in jeans and a tee shirt. "Did I hear you say security for me, Mac?"

"Yes, and I want no arguments from you, Darling."

"Yes, Dear, you're right," Mags said with a smile. "Always right."

"Wow, how did that feel coming out of your mouth?" Mac said, quoting a line from one of his favorite movies, *The Blind Side*.

"You two sound like Kelly and me!" Adam said with a grin.

"Are you going to the dig this morning, Mags?"

"Yes, I thought I would. I feel like we've let Will and Kate down."

"Let's have some breakfast and you can head that way after Sheriff Walton's deputies get here. I want them with you at all times."

"Yes, Dear," she said, perhaps with a touch of impatience.

Mags took the bacon from the freezer, warmed it and prepared eggs and toast.

The three ate and went to the upper deck just as Jim Travis walked toward them on the dock. Behind him were Bud Walton followed by two uniformed deputies.

"Did you get a golf cart key from Pat?" Mac asked Mags.

"Yep, got it right here. I'm off," she said as she introduced herself to the two men who would be her shadows for the day.

Mac turned to Adam, Jim, and Sheriff Walton and said, "Let's head to the conference room in the auditorium." He, Jim, and Adam picked up bags that contained their laptop computers and assorted files and walked toward the auditorium where Mac unlocked the door to what would become their command post.

As soon as they sat down, Pat knocked on the door. The four men exchanged glances. "Be careful," Jim said, as Mac got up to go to the door.

"Who is there?" he called out.

"Pat Jefferson. I am alone."

Mac opened the door just a crack and then seeing that Pat was indeed by himself, opened it widely.

"Come in," Mac said. "As you can see I made an A in Paranoia 101!"

Pat came into the room. "I just wanted to make sure you had everything you need. If you'd like, I've got someone bringing in a pitcher of water, ice, and glasses for you."

"That would be great, Pat. Thanks. Oh, another question for you. What are your thoughts about who might have fired those shots in the boat yesterday?" Mac asked.

"I've been thinking about that. It either has to be someone working, living or visiting on the island. Or, someone could have come on the island using one of the many private docks. There's no way we can monitor all of those."

"OK, I have another question. How secure is your computer system in the administrative offices?"

Pat thought a moment. "I'd like to say very secure but that probably isn't true. I'm arranging for our system support person to add to our security, but he hasn't come to do that yet. Is there a problem?"

Mac replied, "I don't know. I printed documents there two nights ago and we're trying to figure out how confidential information became public knowledge."

"Mac, you know this island. If anyone overhears anything, it spreads like a wild fire. Someone could have overheard you, Bob, or me when we were talking."

"Well, Bettina seemed to have gotten something from someone and I'm very curious."

"Would you like to talk to Bettina? I can arrange for her to come here."

"That is probably a good idea. Would you ask her to come see us?"

"Oh, she'll love that," Pat laughed.

"She might, but when we get through with her, she won't!"

Pat left and soon after, a young man knocked on the door. "May I come in?" a familiar voice asked.

"My turn," the sheriff said. He went to the door. "Who is it?"

"Uh, Peter from over at the Inn."

Mac nodded an okay.

Walton unlocked the door and opened it slowly.

Mac looked up. "Peter? They have you doing more than greeting people at the Inn."

"Yes, Mr. Mason, we work more than one job on Joseffa. I deliver catered meals to all the cottages during the day and work the welcome desk at the Inn in the evenings."

"Thanks, Peter, for the water and ice."

"Just call the Inn if you need refills, or if there is anything else I can do." Peter closed the door as he left. The sheriff turned the lock.

Mac settled back in his chair. I think the first thing we need to do is decide who will be the spokesperson for our task force. Any ideas?"

Adam spoke up. "When I spoke to Pete Barnes, the Assistant Director, he said he was very comfortable with Mr. Mason heading the task force as long as I kept him abreast of our findings. The Director wants frequent updates from Pete. I think they recognize that this is not 'business as usual' for any of us."

Mac looked at his son and said, "OK, Adam, I understand your not wanting me to call you 'son' in a professional setting, but I can't handle 'Mr. Mason'. Can we agree that you call me Mac here? When you say, Mr. Mason, I look around to see if your grandfather is here."

Adam smiled, "Yes, Mac."

"I'm not asking for a leadership role, but since I am really not directly linked with any law enforcement agency, maybe that will solve problems that might arise over which agency is in charge. Do you agree?"

All three men nodded their agreement.

"OK, I think the first item of business is to review the jurisdictions represented here and why each is involved."

Mac continued, "First, Sheriff Walton has two killings that have taken place in Lee County. He also has direct contact with Dr. Raul Garcia, the County Medical Examiner. On top of that, there is the shooting that took place in an attempt to intimidate me. Since it happened on Joseffa, that also falls within Bud's jurisdiction. Can anyone add anything to that?"

No one spoke, but gave acknowledgment that the sheriff's involvement was justified.

"Next, I'll cover Adam's involvement. As you know, he is Section Chief attached to the FBI in Tampa. Sheriff Walton gave me the authority to invite the FBI to become involved in solving the two murders. I asked for that support for two reasons. First, I wanted the resources that the FBI could provide. Secondly, I've had the gut feeling that the murders might have something to do with human trafficking that has been a major issue for the Miami Police Department since I was on the force. Both the murdered brothers and the suspected killer have had ties to two organizations that are suspected of heading the trafficking threat in Florida."

Mac continued, "Jim Travis is the Head of Major Crimes for the Miami Police Department. He has knowledge of the Miami crime world, as well as resources that no one else may have. The suspected killer - at least the one I am beginning to suspect - did spend time in Jim's jail until released on bond. He skipped and we need Miami PD's help apprehending him."

Mac looked down and frowned, "That brings us to me. Why in the hell am I involved?" He laughed. "It seems I am in the middle of this whole thing. While consulting with the Miami PD, I helped apprehend Jim Barber. I have been taught and have also taught law enforcement agencies how to cooperate together and investigate human trafficking. Then, I was one of the people to find the bodies of the Morrison brothers and then someone shot up a boat thought to be mine. So, here I am, retired, but working harder than I did while on the force."

"Does that about cover the four of us?"

"Good job, Mac," Jim said as all three men nodded in agreement.

Just as Mac was about to move to the next topic, someone tried to open the door without knocking. There was an impatient rapping on the door and a voice called out, "Open up!"

Mac walked to the door, unlocked it, cracked it enough so he could see, and there stood Bettina McCauley. She looked into the room as if searching for any tidbit she could learn and said, "You wanted to see me. Well, hurry up! I have a hair appointment and I don't have all day."

Adam spoke up, "Mac, let me handle this."

"Mrs. McCauley, I'm Special Agent Adam Mason of the FBI. I'm Section Chief headquartered in Tampa. Please sit down."

Bettina sputtered, "What does the FBI want with me?"

"I need to ask you some questions and I advise you to answer them fully and truthfully."

Bettina frowned, but just looked ahead, but not at Adam. "Whacha want?" she asked.

"Mrs. McCauley, I am required to tell you that I am recording your statement. Do you understand this?"

Bettina again sputtered, "Yes, but….."

"Mrs. McCauley, It has reached our attention that you have shared publicly that you heard that human trafficking might be involved in the murders committed on Joseffa."

"Human Trafficking? What is that? I never said anything about human trafficking!"

"I believe your words were 'people kidnapped out of their beds and taken to a third world nation'. That's human trafficking. Where did you hear that?"

"Young man, that is none of your business. I don't divulge who tells me things!"

"Yes, madam, that is my business. Human trafficking is a federal offense. It would be wise for you to tell me where you heard that, or you might not be sleeping in your own bed tonight."

"Are you threatening me, young man?"

"No ma'am, I'm telling you that holding vital information from a federal officer of the law is illegal. I'm promising you that if you do not tell me, charges can and will be brought against you."

"But...but...but, I heard this in confidence."

"Well, I can assure you that you had best break that confidence and now!"

Bettina looked down. Her hands were visibly shaking. "Don't I get a lawyer?" she said quietly.

Then, she continued: "Well, I heard it in the beauty shop here on the island. One of the stylists heard it from someone she met on the mainland. It was some man who she had dated a few times."

"Is that the only place you heard it, Mrs. McCauley?"

Stuttering, Bettina said, "Yes, sir. That's where I heard it."

"What is the stylist's name?"

"Do I have to tell you that?"

"Yes, I'm afraid you do."

"Her name is Cathy Holmes. That's Cathy with a 'c'."

Adam looked around the table and asked, "Do you gentlemen have any further questions for Mrs. McCauley?"

Everyone shook their heads indicating no.

"One last thing Mrs. McCauley. You will not and cannot discuss any of this conversation with anyone. If you do, I will have to put you in custody until our investigation is complete and you would not be held in the comfort of Joseffa Island. Do you understand that?"

Bettina nodded her head indicating yes. "No, Mrs. McCauley, you must give me a verbal answer. A shake of your head will not do."

Bettina said in a very quiet voice, "I understand."

"You may go, Mrs. McCauley. Thank you."

Bettina stood, held the back of her chair for support and looking years older, walked slowly to the door, opened it and left.

Everyone applauded and Mac said, "Wow, Adam, you're tough. But, you got what we needed to know. I expect Bettina headed straight for the nearest bathroom. I was afraid she might have soiled herself before she could get to a toilet."

Mac looked at the group and said, "I think we need to talk to Pat Jefferson before we move to the next topic."

Mac picked up his phone, called Pat, and asked him to come to the conference room.

In a few short minutes, Pat knocked on the door. Mac answered.

Pat was smiling. "Boy, you guys must have put the fear of God into Bettina McCauley. She came to my office, and I swear her pants looked, shall we say, 'damp'. She told me she was going to her daughter's on the mainland and might not be back anytime soon. Is it okay for her to leave?"

Mac replied, "I think it would be okay as long as we know how to reach her if she is needed again."

"I have her daughter's address and phone number, as well as her contact information up north where she and her husband have another home."

Mac responded, "Good, now do you have a hair stylist by the name of Cathy Holmes?"

"Yes, we do. Do you need to see her?"

"Yes," Mac answered, "Can you ask her to come here?"

"I'll go get her. I saw her in the beauty shop earlier, so I know she is on the island."

Pat left the room and the four men stood, stretched and each poured a glass of water.

38

WITHIN A FEW MINUTES, THERE was a gentle knock on the door. Mac stood, opened the door and admitted a very scared looking young woman. She was blonde with hair past her shoulders. She was wearing blue slacks and a navy blue smock over a white blouse.

"I'm Cathy Holmes. Did you want to see me?"

This time Adam spoke up. "Yes, is it Miss or Mrs. Holmes?"

"It's Miss, but you can call me Cathy. Most folks do."

"Thank you, Cathy. I'm Special Agent Adam Mason with the FBI. These gentlemen are Sheriff Bud Walton, Detective Captain Jim Travis of the Miami Police Department and Mac Mason. I need to tell you that this is a formal investigation and I will be recording your interview. Do you understand and agree to that?"

"Yes, sir, but I don't know what you could want with me."

"Miss Holmes, errr Cathy, do you know a Mrs. Bettina McCauley."

"Yes, she is a customer of mine. She had an appointment scheduled for today but she didn't show. Is she okay?"

"Yes, Cathy, she's fine. Do you remember sharing some information with her about a friend of yours who is dating a man who spoke to her about something we call human trafficking?"

"Oh, no, Mrs. McCauley told you that?"

"She had no choice, Cathy. The information is important in an ongoing federal investigation. I'd advise you to be completely honest with us, as well."

"I don't want to get my friend in trouble."

"If she hasn't done anything illegal, she will be fine. What is her name?"

"Her name is Rachel Adams. She works at a small boutique in St. Pete. We went to high school together a few years ago."

"What's the name of the boutique?"

"Wallace's; its name is Wallace Boutique. It's on Pine Street."

"Do you know the name of the man she has dated who talked to her about people being taken into or out of the country illegally? That is human trafficking."

"I only know his first name is Bill. She talks about Bill this and Bill that."

"Is there any other information you have heard from your friend that might be on this subject or any other that might be questionable?"

"No, sir!"

"OK, thank you, Cathy and I need to caution you not to discuss anything we have said here with anyone. Do you understand?"

"Yes, sir! Is my job okay here? I don't want to lose it."

"We'll tell Mr. Jefferson how well you cooperated and how appreciative we are."

"Oh, thank you so much."

Cathy stood and left, much less impacted by the interview than Bettina McCauley had been.

Mac stood and said, "How about some lunch? We've had a full morning."

When Cathy Holmes got back to the beauty shop, one of her co-workers handed her an envelope. "That Mrs. McCollie or McCauley or McSomething came by here. She was in a hurry, but said she wanted to leave you a tip even though she didn't get to her appointment."

"Thanks." Cathy stepped to the counter at her chair in the shop. She gripped the envelope in both hands. No one seemed to notice the unease with which she looked at her name scrolled across the cover. The others resumed the general hum and chatter that filled the days at the shop. Cathy touched the shelf on which she had a photograph of her poodle, Gracie. She shifted a peppermint from one side of the shelf to the other. Then, she nervously fingered a copy of the island shuttle schedule.

"I'm stalling," Cathy said to herself. "I am scared to open this envelope." She turned to see if anyone was watching. No one was paying her any attention. Gingerly, she tapped the envelope so the contents fell to one side, and then she carefully tore off the end. She peeked inside. There was a twenty dollar bill. And then she noticed a small slip of paper.

She pulled out the note and read to herself: "They made me do it. I do not want to go to jail. If they make you talk, tell the truth. I did."

Cathy thought back over her interview in the conference room. "I told the truth," she said, surprised when others looked up, because she had said that out loud.

The four men entered the Inn and were led to the casual dining room by a young woman Mac knew as Jessica. Upon reaching the table Jessica had selected, Mac heard his name called out. He looked and there at a corner table sat Will, Kate and Mags. At a table nearby, two uniformed deputies sat silently studying a menu.

"Hi, Mags, we're just taking a short lunch break. Have you ordered yet?"

Jessica looked at the group and asked, "May I put two tables together for you?"

"That would be great," responded Mac.

About that time, Bob Gardner came into the dining room and waved. "Why don't you make that for eight, Jessica" Bob suggested.

As soon as the orders were placed, Mags said, "Well, I have never had a security detail before! You won't believe what happened a while ago. I wanted to go to the ladies room—let me rephrase that: I *needed* to go to the ladies room. As I walked up to the door, one of the men said, 'You can't go in there alone.' So, I said, 'It's either that or, if you'll pardon my French, I'll go right here!'"

The group leaned forward, listening intently.

"He said, 'Ma'am, we have to check out that room before you go in. Lo and behold, he pushed the door open and went right into the ladies room. He kept hollering out, 'Cleaning crew! Cleaning crew!' I suppose he did that so any women in there could get presentable. Evidently, there was no one in there, because he came back out and said I could go in. But I want you to know he stood outside the stall the whole time I was there."

Will tried to hide a giggle, but it didn't work.

Kate tapped him on the arm. "Will, do you have any idea how embarrassing that would be for a lady?"

Mac turned to Bob. "Well, fellow, don't you think it is time that the island got into the twenty-first century. Unisex toilets! That's the answer!"

"It's not funny, Mr. Mason", Kate said, with just a touch of ice in her voice.

Mags tried to defuse the emerging tension. "Well, enough of that! Does anybody know how the Duke game came out last night? They played UConn, if I remember correctly."

Jim whipped out his cell phone and punched in some numbers. "Why won't my WiFi connection work here? I was going to check on the score."

Bob replied, "Sorry. Only in certain places on the island."

Jessica walked over and began delivering drinks and sandwiches. The conversation did a world tour: floods in Europe, new premier in Somalia, Atlantic Coast Conference basketball, upcoming football bowl games, new tax proposal before the State Legislature, the recent national elections, the declining value of the Euro, and reports on children and grandchildren. No one mentioned security personnel or ladies restrooms.

"How about a break before we go back to the dig?" Will proposed. "Maybe we can meet there is a couple of hours."

"OK by me," Mags said. "I'm sure my two guards will allow me that!"

The two deputies got up to follow as Mags walked toward *The Mistress*. They nodded at Sheriff Walton with a discrete "thumbs up" sign.

"No rest for the weary," Mac lamented. "We best get back to the conference room."

Jim, Mac, and Adam stepped into the conference room. They looked carefully around the room, making certain that things were as they had left them. "It's an old trick," Jim said, "but I still use it. I put a small thread across my materials. I can tell if anyone has tampered with my things just by looking to see if the thread has been disturbed."

"And your report is…?"

"Mr. Mason of the Tampa variety," Jim teased, "in answer to your question, let me report that all is well."

"All is well, except where is Bud?"

"He was following us, I thought. Maybe he has gone to check with his men about their security detail work with Mags."

"Dad, uh, Mac, do you want me to check on him?"

"Oh, he's a big boy. He'll be along. Maybe he had to call back to his office."

They waited another ten minutes.

"Let me try to call him." Mac touched the call button and listened as the phone's persistent ring went unanswered.

Another ten minutes went by. "Now, Mac, I am getting a bit worried, Maybe we ought to take Adam up on his offer to go check on things."

"Where would he check?"

"I'll start at *The Mistress* and then see if anybody at the Inn has seen him."

"OK, Son—uh, Adam, maybe you better go looking. We'll stay here and will call you if he shows up here."

Adam stepped out the door. Jim locked it back.

"While we are waiting," Mac began, "let's make a list of everything we know up to now. We can check it out with Adam and Bud when they get here. Can you make a recording as we go along?"

"Yeah, I can do that." Jim flipped the switch on his recorder.

Mac began, "Well, for starters, we've got two dead bodies discovered in an archaeological test pit here on Joseffa Island. Forensic tests show one was shot in the head and the other was shot in the chest."

"One is named William Morrison and the other is Daniel Morrison. Brothers. This was based on the DNA taken from the marrow of the bones."

"Also there is the medallion that you contacted me about. It was found in the grave, uh, the pit."

"And we know of a Jim Barber who has a tattoo that matches the design of the medallion, plus Barber's fingerprint was found on the medallion. Had I told you that?"

"Interesting. Interesting. Jim Barber was also apprehended for certain crimes in Miami. He was charged, but was able to get bond and skipped."

"Shots were fired into a boat thought to be mine and a warning phone call was made to the Joseffa offices threatening me."

"The slugs taken from the wall of the boat were sent to Dr. Raul Garcia, the Medical Examiner in Fort Myers, for analysis."

"Word has gotten out that we suspect that the murders might be connected to concerns about human trafficking. Bettina McCauley spread that rumor based on something she heard from her hair stylist, Cathy Holmes."

"Cathy Holmes has identified the person who she heard the rumors from, a Rachel Adams. Rachel is dating a man named Bill who divulged to her his knowledge of human trafficking."

"Rachel works at a boutique kind of place, a dress shop, I think, in St. Petersburg and has yet to be interviewed."

Mac thought whether he had covered all known information and concluded that it was all he knew. "That pretty much sums it up. Jim, do you have anything else to add?"

Jim responded, "No, Mac, I think that pretty much says all we have. I have bulleted this and will print it out for each of you."

"Good, Jim, Thanks."

At that time, Mac's phone began playing "The Fifth Symphony" by Beethoven. He looked at the caller ID and saw the name of Dr. Garcia.

Mac held up one finger, saying, "I'd better take this. It's Raul Garcia." He put his phone on speaker.

"Hello, Raul."

"Mac, I have news for you. The slugs you sent me have been analyzed and they do not come from the same gun used in the two murders."

"OK, Raul. Thanks."

Mac disconnected from the call, looked at Jim and said, "Jim, would you add that to our analysis of information gained up until now?"

"Already have it, Mac," Jim responded.

At that moment, there was a rap at the door. Mac eased over and asked, "Yes? Who is it?"

"Sheriff Walton, Mac."

Mac unlocked the door and opened it enough to see a uniformed Bud. Then, he opened the door and Bud stepped into the room.

"Where's Adam?" There was some concern in Mac's question.

"I thought he would be here. I don't know about Adam. Is he missing?"

"Well, he went looking for you because we thought you were missing!"

For a moment, Bud looked puzzled. Then he gave a quick smile. "Just because I know where I am does not mean that you know where I am! Sorry about the delay. I think it was important."

"Did you discover something?" Jim asked.

Before Bud could answer, Mac spurted out "Hold it! This is Adam!" He reached for his cell phone.

Mac answered hurriedly, "Yes, Adam. Are you all right?"

Jim and Bud motioned for Mac to put the phone on speaker.

Adam's voice was clear and calm. "Code two four."

Mac replied, "Code four two."

"Code one two."

"Code two one."

"Code nine four."

"Code nine five! Code nine five!" Mac put the phone back on top of the table.

"What in the world was that about?"

Mac grinned, looking relieved for the first time in a while. "When Adam was growing up, he wanted to play, what else, 'cops and robbers.' I played with him and we developed this imaginary code. 'Two four' means 'I am okay.' When I reversed the numbers and said 'four two,' that meant that I received and understood his message."

"And the next number—what was it, one three?"

"Oh, not 'one three'! That one means 'I have to stop and go to the bathroom.' He used 'one two.' That is code for 'I did not find anything.' He meant he had not found you, Bud."

"And 'two one' mean you understood."

"I think Adam must still be a boy at heart!" Bud said.

Jim looked bemused. "And the final code? I don't remember the numbers—nine four?"

Mac beamed. "I'm proud of me for remembering all these boyhood codes! 'Nine four was Adam's way of saying 'I'm on my way home.' I did not say 'four nine.' That would have meant, 'OK, I understand.' Instead, I said "nine five." By adding one to 'nine four,' my message was 'Run, don't walk, run until you get here!'"

"Amazing, and only half as confusing as hieroglyphics in an ancient cave." Sheriff Walton just shook his head. "How do you remember all that?"

The bang on the door indicated that Adam had returned. He came in, a bit of out of breath. He spotted Bud Walton: "Sheriff! There you are!"

"And there you are, Adam!"

Adam quickly explained his futile search for Bud, and the others turned to Bud to explain where he had been.

"Just before we got back to the Administration Building, I spotted something out of the corner of my eye. There was a man at the side of the building, working with some kind of electronic device. I remembered our concern about a wiretap or electronic eavesdropping, so I decided to watch him for a while. I did not want to call out to you to let you know what I was doing because he would have heard me. And I certainly did not want to answer my phone, in case he was listening in on our calls."

"Makes sense."

"I kept my eye on him for a good twenty minutes. He was using earphones to listen to something or to test some equipment. I couldn't tell. I was probably thirty feet from him. I did not want him to see me."

"What do you think he was doing?" Adam asked. "Is he still there?"

The sheriff touched his holster. "No. He is not."

"You shot him?"

"No," Bud chuckled. "As I was watching him, Pat Jefferson came up and spoke to him. It turns out that he is the technician that Pat had working to make sure protective firewalls and safeguards were installed to protect the island's internet. He wasn't trying to monitor us. He was assuring we were protected."

"And you are sure you can trust this guy?" Adam wondered out loud.

Mac said, "Code three eight."

Adam answered, "Eight three."

Jim threw his hands up as if to say "I don't get it."

Mac gave a broad smile. "That is more or less Mason code for 'Dumb question.' Of course, I trust Pat Jefferson to have checked him out completely."

The quartet reviewed the afternoon's work and went in a variety of directions, each one holding a cell phone to his ear.

39

On Wednesday morning, Mac and Adam awoke early and prepared a bowl of cereal and fresh fruit. The previous afternoon, the decision had been made that Mac, Adam, and Jim would take *The Mistress* to St. Petersburg and meet with Rachel Adams. Adam, sharing his FBI affiliation, had called John Thompson, the police chief of St. Pete, and apprised him of their possible desire to locate "Bill," Rachel's boyfriend. If Adam, Mac, and Jim located Bill and found it necessary to apprehend him, the chief promised full cooperation, including the use of the St. Petersburg SWAT team.

Mags had prepared for her day on the dig and just as Mac was ready to send her off, a female voice sounded from the dock. "Mr. Mason, may we come aboard?" Mac went to the main deck and saw two individuals standing there, a young woman and a large, beefy man.

"Yes, come aboard," Mac called out.

The woman was first to board. When Mac saw her, it was like looking at Mags, only thirty years younger. She was tall, maybe five foot eight, slender with hair the same color as Mags'. The man was huge, approximately six feet, seven inches tall and easily over three hundred pounds. He looked as if he did not have an ounce of fat on him, with arms as large as Mac's thighs. The woman approached Mac first and introduced herself.

"I'm Brenda Vinson from Phillips' detective agency and this is Brad Williamson." Mac shook Brenda's small hand and then reached for the hand of Brad.

As Mac reached to shake hands with Williamson, he found his hand enclosed in a grip that had Mac trying hard not to wince. "Mr. Mason, just call me 'Moose,'" the large man said, with a wide smile on his face. Both Moose and Brenda showed Mac identification.

Mac tried discretely to rub his aching hand on the leg of his Dockers. "It's good to meet you, too. My wife, Mrs. Mason, is below. I'll get her," Mac said, as he called below.

Just at that moment, Mags came up the stairs.

"Mags, this is Ms. Vinson and Mr. Williamson. They will be spending the next few days with you."

Ms. Vinson said, "Mrs. Mason, please call me Brenda."

Brad quickly added, "and call me Moose. Only my mother still calls me Brad."

Mags smiled, immediately liking the two. "Call me Mags, please."

Adam stepped onto the deck and, after introductions, said, "It looks like quite a day for all of us!"

Mags turned to Mac. "I guess we'll get down to the dig. I've packed a bag for several nights in case you don't get back tonight. I'm sure I can stay in Will and Kate's extra bedroom. You guys be careful," she said as she kissed Mac. With a slight, uncertain hesitation, he finally turned and walked toward the dock.

The three began the short stroll along the dock to Mags' waiting golf cart. Moose carried Mags' bag as if it weighed nothing.

As they moved toward the dig site, they greeted Jim Travis coming towards them, dressed, as Mac and Adam were, in slacks and polo shirts. Mags smiled: "I can't guess where you're going, Jim!"

When Jim reached *The Mistress*, he called to Mac, "Am I late?"

"No, Jim, you're right on time. We'll shove off as soon as we get these lines untied."

Adam released the stern and bow lines. Mac turned the key and started both of the powerful 330 horsepower engines and eased *The*

Mistress away from her berth and slowly moved away from the dock. Mac entered the data into the GPS system. The trip to St. Petersburg began.

Even cruising at twenty knots, *The Mistress* didn't reach St. Pete until shortly before noon.

Mac, explaining, not apologizing, said, "We could have driven this trip, but by the time we docked in Fort Myers, had one of your cars delivered by the valet, and driven to St. Petersburg, it would have taken almost as long. Besides, this gives the two of you an opportunity to enjoy *The Mistress* and gives us more comfort and the opportunity to talk."

After Mac radioed for permission to dock at the Mariner's Cove Marina, he eased *The Mistress* into the assigned berthing space.

Meeting an employee of the marina, Mac arranged for payment for the berth and left instructions for the diesel fuel tanks to be topped off. "While you are at it, would you top off our water tanks and purge the brown water?"

The dock worker replied, "Yes, sir. How long will you be?"

Mac responded, "We are not sure at this time. We may stay overnight. It just depends on how long it takes for our business to be concluded. I'll let you know. Has there been anyone asking for Agent Mason here?"

"I believe that might be the man standing next to the office up there," the employee pointed.

Adam looked and said, "Yes, that's Jeff Rose, one of my people. He will be with us for as long as we need him."

Jeff led Adam, Mac, and Jim to a black SUV and asked about the address of Wallace Boutique. Mac responded, "201 Pine Street." Jeff keyed the location into the GPS.

The group drove in silence until Adam said, "I think only two of us should go into Wallace's, and I think that we should see the manager first before approaching Rachel."

Jim spoke up. "I agree. Why don't you and Mac go in while we wait outside?" Jeff turned onto Pine Street and pulled into a parking space a half block from Wallace's. All four exited the SUV. While Jeff and Jim looked into the windows of shops along the way, Mac and Adam entered the small dress shop.

"Is your manager in?" Adam asked an older lady who had inquired, "May I help you, gentlemen?"

Adam asked again if the manager was available.

The older lady responded, "I'm Mrs. Mabel Wallace. I'm the owner."

Adam introduced himself and took out his FBI identification. Mac also produced identification. Adam asked if Rachel Adams was available.

Mrs. Wallace looked carefully at Adam's and Mac's identification.

"Yes, she is helping a customer in the rear of the store."

"We would like to speak to her somewhere private if possible," Adam stated.

"You can use my office. Is Rachel in some kind of trouble?"

"We just have some routine questions for her, ma'am."

Mrs. Wallace walked back to where Rachel was helping the customer, motioned to Adam and Mac and pointed toward a door at the back of the shop. Rachel frowned and walked towards the two waiting men. Mrs. Wallace continued with the customer.

The office was small with only a desk and two chairs in the room. As they entered, Adam said, "Rachel Adams?"

"Yes," Rachel responded.

"I'm Special Agent Adam Mason and this is Mac Mason. We will be asking you a few questions. I must advise you that I'll be recording this interview." Adam pulled a small recorder from his pocket.

Rachel slumped into one of the chairs.

"I have no idea what this is about, but I have nothing to hide. Certainly I'll answer your questions, but you can understand that this does make me more than a little nervous."

"It is imperative that you provide us with honest answers to all of our questions. This is a federal investigation and we believe you have information that is important."

"I do? Me? What's going on? Do I need a lawyer?"

"Only if you think you have a reason for one. If you are just honest with us, I see no need for a lawyer," Adam advised.

"OK, what do you need to know?"

"First, do you know a man by the name of Bill?"

"I date a man named Bill. Has he done something wrong?"

Adam looked at the obviously nervous young woman and said, "Bill might be a man we are looking for."

"Ohhhh, I can't imagine Bill doing anything wrong."

"Perhaps he hasn't done anything, but we have reason to believe that he has information that we need in our investigation. What is Bill's last name?"

"Barber," Rachel replied.

Adam looked at Mac as they thought, "He didn't even change his last name."

Mac reached into a file that he brought with him, withdrew a photo and held it up to Rachel. "Do you recognize this man?"

With a look of astonishment, Rachel said, "Yes, that's Bill except he has a mustache and beard."

Adam looked at Rachel and said, "Our conversation must be absolutely confidential, not shared with anyone, not even your boyfriend. Do you understand and agree to that? Divulging anything we might share today would be a violation of an ongoing investigation. Do you understand that charges of being an accessory could be brought against you if you divulge any of this to anyone, including Mr. Barber?" Adam repeated.

"Yes, I understand and agree," Rachel said nervously. "You sure I don't need a lawyer? This sounds serious."

"Whether or not you call a lawyer is up to you. If at any point you want to stop our conversation, just say so. Here is why we are checking in with you; we have received evidence that Bill Barber talked to you about 'human trafficking'."

"Human trafficking. I didn't know what that meant when Bill used the term and I still don't know. Bill only said something about bringing people in need of work into the country and that the police sometimes thought that was a crime. He laughed about it. Can you explain more about that to me?"

Adam looked at Mac, "Mr. Mason, can you explain the definition of human trafficking to Ms. Adams?"

"Let me give you the text book answer, Ms. Adams," Mac said as he organized his thoughts.

"Many people are brought into this country or taken out of this country illegally and find themselves trapped in lives they had not expected. Usually, they are tricked into leaving their home country or they are taken by force or threat. They are often beaten, starved, and forced to work as prostitutes, or to take grueling jobs as migrant, domestic, restaurant, or factory workers with little or no pay. All law enforcement in the United States is working hard to stop human trafficking—not only because of the personal and psychological toll it takes on society and the victims, but also because it facilitates the illegal movement of immigrants across borders and provides a ready source of income for organized crime groups and even terrorists."

Adam added, "We have reason to believe that because of Mr. Barber's comments to you, he might know something about this kind of federal crime."

"I had no idea, Agent Mason. I still can't believe that Bill could be involved in something as hideous as that," Rachel said, defending Barber. "Do you think…surely not!"

"When did you meet Bill Barber?" Mac asked.

"Let me think. I would say it was sometime in the early or middle part of November. I've only gone out with him a few times."

Both Mac and Adam realized that the timing of Barber's arrival in St. Petersburg coincided with when Barber had jumped bail.

"Do you know where he lives?"

Rachel quickly responded, "No, I don't. He's always picked me up here after work, or met me somewhere. I know that he said he had a small apartment in the area, but I have never been there."

Adam asked, "Do you have a phone number for him, or are you planning on meeting him anytime soon?"

"I don't have a phone number for him. I thought it strange that Bill didn't give me one. But, I do have a date with him this evening."

"What time, Ms. Adams?"

"Six o'clock. He's coming by when my shift is over."

"OK, here is what I need you to do. We will be here. When he comes in, I want you to act as natural, as possible. We will handle the rest. Can you do that?"

Rachel looked down at her feet, thought and then said, "Yes, I can. But why?"

"At this point, Ms. Adams, you simply have to trust us. We are trying to get information and Mr. Barber may have some knowledge we need. Go about your business here. If you see Mr. Mason or me, do not acknowledge either of us."

Rachel replied, "Yes, sir! But, you know, this is scary! I've never been involved in anything like this."

"You'll be fine," Mac offered as reassurance.

Mac and Adam turned and left the small office. They met Mrs. Wallace, and Adam simply said, "We will be here in your shop for the rest of the afternoon. We'll try to look inconspicuous and simply be shopping for gifts for our wives. I am a federal agent and we might be making an arrest here this evening. You are in no trouble and neither is Ms. Adams, if you just do what we ask."

Mrs. Wallace nodded her agreement; concerned both about these mysterious visitors and about the impact these events might have on her business. "If you say so," she said.

Mac and Adam left the shop and walked across the street and into a small alley where Jim and Jeff met them.

"We have the information we need. Barber didn't even change his last name. He should come to the shop around 6:00 PM," Adam told Jeff and Jim. "I need to call John Thompson, the police chief here in St. Pete, and advise him. I'd like him to provide a couple of his men to be on hand before six."

Adam took out his cell phone and contacted Chief Thompson and brought him up to speed. Within a few minutes, two men in plain clothes parked their non-descript car and looked up and down the block.

"They couldn't be more obvious, could they?" Jim said to Mac.

Adam walked over to the two men. There was some very quiet conversation and the two men walked to the end of the block and turned left.

"I've asked the two detectives that Chief Thompson sent over to cover the back door of Wallace's. At about 5:30, Mac and I will go into the store. I want Jim and Jeff to position themselves here until you see Barber enter the shop and then move to block any escape attempt through the front door. Please do not fire your weapons, unless it is absolutely necessary!"

"The wait shouldn't be too long," Mac thought. "We are definitely making progress."

40

Six o'clock was approaching. Mac and Adam were inside Wallace Boutique looking at dresses as if looking for the right sizes. Since it was a few minutes before closing, there were no other customers in the shop. Rachel Adams had disappeared into the office in the rear of the store, as had Mrs. Wallace.

A few minutes before six, the front door opened causing a small bell to ring. Mac and Adam positioned themselves behind a large display case of ladies dress shoes in the center of the shop. Jim Barber entered.

Adam circled around one side of the store and Mac circled the other side as they came up behind Barber. Adam stepped out. "Jim Barber, place your hands behind your neck and do not move."

Barber looked round and made a dash toward the rear of the shop. Mac was right there. He grabbed Barber, whose right hand swung. Mac ducked, landed a hard left to Barber's midsection and then a right cross to his chin. Barber collapsed on the floor. Adam rushed up placing handcuffs on Barber securing his arms behind him and began to frisk him. Inside Barber's short jacket, Adam found a Glock in a shoulder holster. "Jim Barber, you are under arrest!"

Looking at his father, Adam said, "Good job for an old man!"

Mac just smiled.

Mac went to the front door of the boutique and motioned Jeff and Jim to enter. With Barber being held by Jim, Jeff, and Adam,

Mac went to the back door of the shop and motioned for the two detectives there to enter.

Mac looked at the two detectives and said, "Can you escort our guest here to your headquarters?"

Barber seethed with anger, "What are you arresting me for? I haven't done anything!"

Adam spoke up, "Let's start with carrying a concealed weapon, unless you can show me a carry permit. We'll add resisting arrest, a Florida charge of skipping bail, a possible charge of murder, attempted murder, and a federal charge of human trafficking. I think that should keep you in custody for a while."

Barber looked down at his feet and said, "I ain't telling you nothing!"

Adam looked at the two detectives and said, "Book him and make sure you 'Mirandize' him."

As the two St. Petersburg detectives wrestled a resisting Barber out the front door of Wallace, Mac could not help but hear one of the detectives saying, "You have the right to remain silent..." The voice faded away as the detectives placed Barber into a sedan parked down the block.

"What do you want to do now?" Adam asked Mac as Jim and Jeff looked on.

"I'd like to call Mags and tell her we won't be back tonight and then I'd like to go to the St. Petersburg Police Department and begin questioning Barber."

"Jeff, I'd like you to stay with us until we can arrange for a car to use," Adam stated.

Jeff answered, "I'll call the office and have your car brought to the police department. When you leave, I can arrange to have it picked up at the marina."

Adam looked at Mac and Jim. "I wish I had room to put you up at my condo, but it only has one bedroom. It's temporary until Kelly sells the Biloxi house and moves here."

"That's okay, Adam. Jim and I can stay on *The Mistress*. But, I'm not sure we'll get much sleep tonight. I think we'll be spending most of it with our friend, Jim Barber."

"I will definitely be with you for the questioning," Adam stated.

Mac looked toward the back of the shop. "Let me go tell Mrs. Wallace that she can close up the store and I guess I need to let Ms. Adams know that she doesn't have a date tonight!"

"You know guys, we missed lunch entirely." Jim offered. "Can we get some dinner before we go to our sleepover with Barber?"

"Sounds like a plan. There's an okay place to eat near police headquarters," Adam suggested.

After dinner, Jeff drove Mac, Jim, and Adam to the St. Petersburg Police Headquarters on First Avenue North. An agent was waiting outside the door; she handed a set of car keys to Jeff and left in another black SUV.

"Here are the keys to your wheels, Adam," Jeff said handing the keys to yet another black SUV to Adam.

The four men walked into the large, imposing building, introduced themselves to a sergeant on duty at the front desk, and walked in the direction he pointed.

On the way down the hallway, a hefty and very impressive man with prematurely gray hair joined them. He was dressed in a dark blue uniform. There were three stars on each shoulder. "I'm Chief Thompson," the man said, holding his hand out in greeting. Adam quickly introduced Mac, Jim, and Jeff to the chief.

"We have your customer locked up in solitary right now. He hasn't said a word since he was booked. I'll take you there."

The group walked the length of the hallway and entered an elevator. The chief pushed a button labeled "B". "We keep people we don't want to have access to the general population down here," Thompson shared.

The chief signaled an officer behind an enclosed room. Mac heard a click and a door swung open. The group walked through.

In a cell on the right, Mac and the others saw Jim Barber, sitting with his head in his hands.

"We have an interview room across the hall from his cell. There's an adjoining viewing room with a one way mirror so that witnesses can watch the interrogation. The interview room is also equipped with video and a sound recording system. These devices can be operated from the viewing room if you want to."

"Thank you, Chief. Do you want to stay with us?" Adam asked.

"No, I have a meeting with the Mayor, so I need to get to that. I'll check in with you later. If you need anything, just ask the officer you saw as you came in here."

Chief Thompson left in the direction of the locked door and the elevator.

"How do we want to handle this?" Mac asked.

Adam responded, "Good cop, bad cop? I don't really like that cliché, but sometimes it works! Maybe we could start with both of us questioning him. You can represent Lee County and the murders and I'll represent federal concerns and the FBI. Does that sound okay?"

"Yes," replied Mac, "and I'm certain you want the role of 'bad cop!'"

"You know it, Dad!" Adam said, laughing.

Barber was led by a uniformed officer to the interview room, shackled in handcuffs connected by a chain to ankle cuffs.

Mac looked at the officer and said, "Can you take those cuffs off? He'll be a good boy, won't you Jim?"

Adam looked at Mac and simply said, "Humph!"

The officer removed the cuffs and said, "I'll be right outside if you need me."

Mac looked over at a long mirror on one side of the room knowing that Jim and Jeff were recording the interview and watching.

Mac sat down in the chair facing Barber. Adam stood behind Mac looking with pure hatred at Barber, playing the role of 'bad cop' perfectly.

"Mr. Barber, I'm MacKenzie Mason, special consultant to the Lee County Sheriff's Office."

"I know who you are. You grabbed me in Miami even though I didn't do nothing!"

"If you were so innocent, why did you skip out on your bail bond?"

"I was innocent, but no one was going to believe me."

"Skipping bail is only one reason we apprehended you today."

Adam broke into the conversation, "Mason, you're going too slow." He looked at Barber and said, "Why did you kill those two men on Joseffa Island?"

"What two men? I ain't never been on no island."

Mac intervened. "Jim, we know you worked on Joseffa Island for two years. We've also found evidence that implicates you in the murders of William and Daniel Morrison. We have ballistics evidence. We have fingerprint evidence, as well as pretty strong circumstantial evidence against you. We also have a witness that can tie you to some questionable conduct in the area of human trafficking."

Jim and Jeff watched Mac as he made the statements to Barber. Jeff looked at Jim. "That last statement was pretty flimsy. I'm not sure that will hold up." Jim responded, "Mac's just softening Barber up. If he thinks we have something, he's more than likely to divulge more."

Mac continued questioning Barber, but didn't seem to be making any headway. The accused just sat and looked at the floor. Mac offered, "Do you want something to drink or eat?", again playing the good cop.

"I want a smoke," Barber almost shouted.

"Sorry, can't help you there. Besides, it's bad for your health."

"You're bad for my health!" Barber did shout this time.

The interrogation went on for an hour, then two hours. Mac repeated the charges over and over again. Barber denied, showing stronger and stronger anger with each question Mac asked.

Finally Adam intervened. Mac stood up, stretched and left the room. Jim came in and stood behind Adam who had taken the chair vacated by Mac.

"OK, enough of coddling this guy," Adam said to Jim.

"Barber, we have more than enough evidence to convict you on the murder charges. We have your fingerprints on the medallion we found next to the bodies. I am sure that we will tie the slugs from the killings to the Glock we took from you today. Do you really think any jury in this state will fail to convict you? You are looking at a date with a needle unless you want the chair. In Florida, that is your choice. And, if you're lucky enough to beat the death penalty, you'll be put in the general population of the prison. Human traffickers are not so popular there. Of course, you're still pretty enough that you might get a boyfriend to protect you."

Fear seemed apparent in Barber's eyes for the first time.

I didn't murder those two SOB's. It was self-defense. They came to Joseffa to kill me. I just defended myself."

Mac and Jeff looked on through the one-way mirror. "Well, we got him on that one."

Adam continued. "Why would the Morrison brothers want you dead?"

Barber thought for a minute. "Can't we make a deal here? If I tell you everything, can we make a deal?"

Adam softened. "Barber, it all depends on what you tell us and what the Florida prosecutor says. I can make sure the prosecutor knows you cooperated. He might be willing to take the death penalty off the table, and he might be able to guarantee you a cell away from the general population."

Jim and Adam left the interrogation room and joined Mac and Jeff in the viewing room.

"I think we should give him a day to ponder his next step," Mac said, looking at the other three.

"I think we all agree with that. We could come back Friday morning and see where he stands," Adam allowed.

The decision was made that Adam would stay at his condo in Tampa and Mac and Jim would spend the night on *The Mistress*. Jeff returned home agreeing to meet the others at police headquarters early Friday morning.

41

On Friday morning, after reviewing how they wanted to approach Barber, Mac, Adam, and Jim arrived at police headquarters, finding Jeff already there.

Adam and Mac joined a waiting and nervous Barber in the interrogation room.

Before any questions could be asked, Barber spoke up.

"What about...if I can tell you about...whacha call it? Human trafficking and the death of the Morrison brothers? Can I get a deal?"

Again, that is up to the DA in Florida, but also the Federal Prosecutor. But again, depending on what you tell us, we can tell them that you cooperated. That's the best we can do."

Sweating now, Barber said, "OK, here's the whole story."

Barber hesitated before beginning his narrative. "I need some kind of agreement that the Federal Prosecutor and the State will guarantee me no needle or chair, and that I won't be put in the general population of any prison, if I'm found guilty."

Adam looked at Jim, called the guard outside the door and asked him to stay in the room until they returned.

Adam went to the viewing room, took out his cell phone and called Pete Barnes, the Assistant Director and his immediate superior.

"Pete, this is Adam. We've got Jim Barber in custody and he's ready to talk. We are sure he has information on human trafficking, as well as confessing to killing the Morrison brothers. He's asking for a deal."

"Well, Adam, the State Prosecutor in Florida will have to be contacted regarding the killings since that is in their jurisdiction. What is he asking for that we can provide?"

"He wants a guarantee of no death penalty and no integration into the general population of any prison."

"Let me get back to you. I have a contact on speed dial who can make those guarantees. Do you really think Barber's testimony will be helpful?"

"Yes, sir, I do, but I can also promise him leniency only if his statement proves true, and aids in our further investigation."

"Adam, I was going to suggest that. Give me ten minutes and I'll get back to you."

Adam turned to Jim. "Your turn, Jim. See what you can do about the murder charges."

Jim turned away from the others and selected a name from his contact list and placed his call. He spoke on the phone for a few minutes and said, "Thanks," and hung up.

"It looks like the state can assure Barber our cooperation in meeting his requests, as long as he gives us helpful information. I hate doing this, but if we can break a major crime organization with Barber's help, it will be worth it. He may never see the light of day again, anyway."

Adam's phone rang. Pete Barnes name displayed on the screen. He answered.

"What do you have for me, boss?" Adam asked.

"If Barber can give us reliable information concerning human trafficking, we can give him a guarantee that we'll share his testimony with the prosecutors and suggest some leniency, but I repeat, only if his information aids in our apprehending those who are guilty, and he is willing to testify."

Mac and Adam returned to the interrogation room, relieving the officer who had been standing watch over Barber.

Mac spoke, "OK, Mr. Barber. We have a guarantee that your testimony will be taken into account when sentencing is pronounced. Are you ready to tell us your story now, and are you willing to testify in court later?"

"Yes, I'd suggest you sit down. This will take a while."

"Jim, we are going to record this, as well as video tape it. We have advised you of this. I will offer an opening statement and then you can begin."

Taking a deep breath, Barber said, "OK."

Adam began, "It is Friday, 5:00 PM, December 14, 2012. Mac Mason, special consultant to the Lee County Sheriff's Office and Special Agent Adam Mason are speaking with Jim Barber. He has been promised that special treatment will be provided to him if his testimony proves true and helpful in the investigation before us, and he must be willing to testify in court, if needed. Mr. Barber has declined the presence of an attorney."

Adam looked at Barber and said, "The floor is yours."

Barber took a deep breath. "It all started in 2004. I was the second in command to Triple J, working out of Miami."

"Triple J? Then you are part of his organization. We had him on our watch list for years," Mac commented.

"No, I am not involved with him any longer and haven't been since 2004."

In the viewing room, Jeff looked at Jim Travis. "Triple J? Who is that?"

Jim responded. "Triple J is the street name for Jackson J. Jackson. His parents must have had a weird sense of humor. When he was born, he was named Jackson Jackson Jackson. He preferred being called Triple J."

Back in the interrogation room, Adam asked, "Why did you part company with Triple J?"

As you guys in Miami probably knew, there was bad blood between Triple J's organization and Big Mama's."

"By Big Mama, you mean Marjorie Malone?"

"Yes, Big Mama Malone. She had all but wiped out Triple J's organization. Triple J left the country. The last I heard he was somewhere in the Caribbean living off what he had stashed there."

"Now, sir, can you give testimony that Triple J's organization was involved with transporting human beings into this country and out of this country. In other words, can you give testimony about the Triple J organization being involved in human trafficking?"

"Yes, I can. I know everything there is to know about Triple J's involvement."

"What about Marjorie Malone's organization? What can you share about that?"

"I know for a fact that Big Mama was up to her size thirty neck in what you call 'human trafficking'. That's what brought about the turf war between Triple J and Big Mama."

"OK, continue," Adam said.

"I took it on the lam too. I had heard of this private island off the southwest coast and went there looking for a job. I figured nobody would ever look for me on a private island off the coast. I got a job there as a grounds keeper under the name, John Thomas. I knew I wasn't safe from Big Mama since our last score had cost her in excess of seven hundred grand. Triple J had taken most of that money with him, but I had managed a good nest egg for myself. I knew Big Mama would want it back, plus she felt she had unfinished business with me."

"So you got the job on Joseffa Island back in 2004?" Mac asked.

"Yes, and everything went alright until some friends of mine contacted me and said they thought Big Mama had found me. I started making plans to leave the island when the Morrison brothers showed up one night. I had been warned that they were close. I was supposed to sneak off the island and make contact with my friends who had a fishing boat I could swim to."

Before I could pack to leave, the Morrisons found me. I heard them coming in spite of a storm that had settled on the island. I took them out before they could get me. As I told you, it was self-defense."

"What happened next?" Adam asked.

"I wrapped one body at a time into rugs that had been taken up from the floor of my apartment. I loaded the bodies in a trailer connected to a grounds keeper golf cart and carried them to the south end of the island. It was three in the morning. I buried them there. That was where I must have lost my necklace. I found their rubber raft hidden in some mangroves near where I buried them and I paddled it out to my friend's fishing boat. I dumped their pieces, as well as what I took from their pockets in a hundred feet of water."

"Where did you go from there?" Adam asked.

"I had a pretty healthy amount of cash so I just travelled, always looking over my shoulder for Big Mama's men. I eventually made my way back to Miami. That's where I made my mistake. I got involved with a gang, did some drugs, sold some drugs and got picked up by Travis and Mason here," Barber said pointing at Mac. "A lawyer I knew got me out on bail and I skipped. I headed for St. Pete and that's where you found me."

"What about your shooting up that Bayliner last week, thinking it was my boat?" Mac asked.

"Whoa, what shooting? What Bayliner? I've been straight with you. I didn't shoot up no Bayliner. I ain't been back on Joseffa since 2004!"

Mac looked at Adam. They were both thinking the same thing. Then, who was out to get Mac? Who had made the threatening call to the administration office phone?

Barber had finished. He had nothing more to say.

Adam asked Barber one more question. "Now, you understand that you will be called as a witness when and if Jack Jackson or Marjorie Malone is brought to trial?"

"Yes, I understand." Barber moaned. "Now can I have something to eat and use the head? It's been a long day!"

Adam advised Barber that everything he had said would be transcribed for his signature. "Is what you have said your full and complete testimony concerning your knowledge of human trafficking and your confession to killing the Morrisons?"

"I told you it was self-defense."

"Barber, that will be up to a judge and jury to decide, but we'll provide both the federal and state prosecutors with your full statement."

Adam and Mac joined Jim and Jeff in the viewing room. "You guys get it all?"

"Yes, but it looks like we aren't at the bottom of this, yet," Jim said.

"No, and we still don't know who has threatened Dad," Adam said forgetting his professionalism and putting his arm around Mac's shoulder.

42

MAC TURNED TO ADAM, JIM and Jeff and said, "We can go grab some lunch and by then Barber's testimony will be transcribed. We can get it signed and then head back to Joseffa."

Mac pulled out his cell phone. "Oh, no, I turned my phone off while we were talking to Barber and I have six messages."

Mac turned his phone on and keyed in the codes to listen to his voice mail. The first message said simply, "Call immediately!" It was from Brenda Vinson, one of Mags' security team. Before responding, Mac listened to the second message, "Please call!" It was also from Brenda. Mac didn't listen to the remaining messages. He quickly pressed the necessary buttons to return a call to Brenda.

"Vinson here," a voice answered.

"Ms. Vinson, Mac Mason here. You called?"

"Mac, Maggie is missing!"

Mac went numb. "Missing? How can that be? How can she be missing?"

"It's a long story. We have our people, as well as Sheriff Walton, looking. Please get back here as fast as you can. We'll explain when we see you."

Mac disconnected and turned to Adam and Jim. "We have to get to *The Mistress* and back to Joseffa as fast as we can. Mags is missing."

Adam turned to Jeff and quickly said, "Jeff, can you handle getting Barber's signed testimony? When you have our copy in your hands, call me."

"Yes, sir," Jeff replied.

As Mac, Jim, and Adam ran down the hallway toward the elevator and the entrance to the Police Department Headquarters, Chief Thompson intercepted them. "Whoa, men, what's the hurry? What's wrong?"

"No time to talk now, Chief. My wife's been taken or something. She's missing," Mac shouted. "We've got to get back to Joseffa."

"You came by boat, didn't you tell me? It'll take you three hours to get there. Let me help."

Mac stopped, looked at the chief, and said, "How?"

"We have a helicopter available. I can call it. It will land on the roof of this building. You'll be on Joseffa in a half hour."

"God bless you, Chief." He turned to Adam and Jim, "Do you think you can get *The Mistress* back to the island?"

"Sure we can," Adam said. "I piloted half the trip here. I might be a little rusty docking her, but we can do it."

"If anything has happened to Mags, I don't know what I'll do," Mac said holding back a tear of worry that threatened to roll down his cheek. Adam placed his hand on Mac's shoulder, gave it a squeeze and said, "It'll be okay, Dad," not really knowing whether it would or not.

Following Chief Thompson, Mac took the elevator to the top floor and followed up the steps to the roof.

Adam and Jim left the building and drove to the marina. Within thirty minutes, they were navigating towards Joseffa Island.

The chief had been correct. Within half an hour of lift off, the helicopter was hovering and then settling on the emergency landing area across from the Joseffa Fire Department building. Parked in a golf cart were Bob Gardner and Pat Jefferson.

As Mac alighted from the copter, Pat spoke first, "Mac, Ms. Vinson and Mr. Williamson are in my office. They will fill you in."

Bob added, "And, friend, I hope you know we're sorry. We'll do whatever it takes!"

Two men drove slowly along the two lane highway on the mainland when the ring of a cell phone startled them. The larger of the two men answered.

"Yes?"

A hoarse voice thick with the effects of too many cigarettes spoke, "Did you do it?"

"Yes, mission complete."

"Were there any problems?" the voice said, coughing.

"No, it went just as you planned it."

"Good, maybe this will keep Mason off our backs."

"I still think you should have let me handle it the way I wanted."

"Are you telling me I was wrong?" an angry voice almost shouted.

"No, Mama, Never!"

"Good, get back here then."

"Yes, ma'am," the larger man said rolling his eyes at the younger man.

Upon reaching the Administration Building, Mac slammed through the front door, past the cluster of desks and back to Pat's office.

Brenda was on the phone and Moose was standing next to her.

Mac listened as he heard Brenda's side of the conversation. "Yes, sir, we've sent one team out to search the island. They found nothing. They've left for the mainland to join our other team. But, there are so many places they could have taken her, Fort Myers, Pine Island, Sarasota, or even as far as Tampa or St. Pete. And..." she hesitated, "there is a lot of water around here where..." She stopped without completing her sentence.

Brenda listened and then said, "Yes, Mr. Phillips, Mr. Mason is here now. We'll fill him in. Yes, sir, I'll tell him. Good bye."

Brenda turned to Mac. "I know you want to know how something like this could happen. Let me fill you in."

In anger, Mac almost shouted, "YES, please do!"

Brenda began. "This morning we arrived at Bokeelia to catch the early shuttle as we were directed to do. The worker at the marina told us that the shuttle had mechanical problems and would be late. About thirty minutes later, the shuttle arrived. We went straight to the dig site where we talked with Dr. Marks and his wife. They wondered why we were there. They said that two security people had shown up at the site, had explained that you had been in an accident and that your wife needed to go with them to St. Pete and to the hospital where you were. Mrs. Mason was in a state of panic. She left with them around 8:30. We did not get to the site until around 9:00. We immediately called Mr. Phillips at our office and Sheriff Walton. Our teams, as well as the Sheriff's deputies, are looking everywhere. There's been no sign of Maggie."

Mac cooled down and took on his professional persona. "It's not your fault, but we have to find her."

Pat had been listening at the door. "There's more, Mac. The mechanical issues with our shuttle were not accidental. When our people began to check, we found fuel lines damaged. They were not broken. They had been cut. This was no accident. It was well planned. By the time we discovered the problem and could send a second shuttle to Pine Island, thirty minutes had passed."

Adam looked at Mac. "Who could have done this?"

"Well, we know it wasn't Jim Barber. My money is on Marjorie Malone. She has learned we have Barber. She knows about our investigative efforts. And, now she has Mags." Mac had been calm, but was beginning to lose it again.

Bob put his arm around Mac's shoulder and said, "Mac, we've got to think this through and find Mags. That's most important right now."

"Yes Bob," Mac said, "this is a time that Mags needs us."

Mags pulled the blindfold down from her eyes and squinted from the bright sunlight. She then rubbed her bruised wrists where the restraints had dug into her skin. She looked around. "Where am I?" she asked out loud. She was on a sandy lane with only a marsh on one side and canal on the other. The murky water was cluttered with tall weeds and debris. Across the thirty-foot canal, giant lily pads dotted the view. Stacked up behind some of the plants were discarded cups and thrown-away cans. "Not exactly a Chamber of Commerce view," she thought.

"I sure hope there are no gators around here," she said to herself. "No, I know there are gators out there. I just hope they don't know I'm here!" She stood still for a moment and wondered, "Which way now?" In the far distance, she saw a semi passing. "The main road must be that way" she again said out loud. She began to walk. Reaching the main road, she turned right towards a sign that read, "Welcome to Matlacha."

"Oh, no, this is too ironic. I'm kidnapped and dumped off near the town where Mac was born. This is just too much." Although no one could hear her, she still spoke aloud.

Mags walked into the first store that she came to. "I need to call the Sheriff's Office," she said to a person at the counter.

"Are you alright? What's happened? Can I help?" an older man asked.

"I'm okay. I just need to reach Sheriff Walton."

The older gentleman placed the call and handed the phone to Mags.

"Sheriff's Department," a female voice answered.

"This is Margaret Mason. I was kidnapped and I need Sheriff Walton."

"Yes, ma'am. Half our department is out looking for you. Are you okay?"

Mags replied, "Yes, I'm okay." She turned to the older gentleman and asked, "Where am I?"

"You're at Ike's Emporium in Matlacha."

Mags repeated the location to the deputy on the phone.

"I'll radio the sheriff right now. Stay where you are and someone will pick you up in a few minutes."

Mags hung up. The older man offered Mags a soda, which she gladly accepted. He pulled out a chair and suggested she sit down. "Looks like you've had quite a day, young lady," he said. As she sat, sipping her Diet Cola, she looked down. She hadn't noticed it before, but a piece of paper was pinned to her shirt.

Mac felt helpless. Phil Phillips and Sheriff Walton's people were searching everywhere for Mags. He wanted to help, but thought that he would wait for Adam and Jim's return. That would be at least two more hours. In frustration, he decided to drive down to the dig site and update Will and Kate.

As Mac approached the dig site, he saw that there were still people digging, screening, and bagging found archaic material. Kate was the first to see Mac approaching.

"Mac, you're back! Have you heard anything about Mags?" Kate asked as Will joined her.

"Not yet and I'm really worried. This was a planned kidnapping. I've never wanted Mags involved with my work, but it seems she is this time. I just have to have faith in Phil Phillips, his people, and Sheriff Walton."

"Phil Phillips? Who is he?" Will asked.

"Phil is a private investigator; he owns the detective agency that supplied Moose and Brenda. We go back ten years or more. When I was on the Miami Police Department I recommended his people when a citizen might want to supplement our efforts. He has always worked well with me. I trust him. This isn't his fault. I should not have left Mags. I'll never forgive myself if..."

"Mac, is there anything we can do, anything at all?"

"Just keep praying that she is okay and that we find her. Won't you be gone? Isn't the dig ending today?"

"We'll be sticking around through next Wednesday to close down the dig, catalogue some of the finds, and get everything ready for our return to Cedar Key," Will explained.

"Well, I probably need to get back to the Administration Building. Moose and Brenda are monitoring all the search activity. I just wanted to update you guys and ask you something else."

"What's that, Mac?

"You saw the two men that came for Mags. Right?"

"Yes, we saw them," Kate responded.

"Do you think you'd recognize them again? Do you think you could describe them?

Will looked at Kate. "I think I would know them anywhere. What about you Kate?" Will asked.

"Yes, I think I'd know them if I saw them again."

"Good, we may need you to look at some pictures and see if you can pick them out. I'm willing to bet that they are in one of our mug books. And if that doesn't work, we can bring in a facial composite artist who can create a likeness of the men."

"We'd be glad to do that and if it can't be done by Wednesday, we'll stay as long as you need us."

Mac expressed his appreciation and went to his golf cart for his return to the Administration Building. Just as he was turning his golf cart around, Beethoven's "Fifth Symphony" sounded on his phone. His screen displayed "Bud Walton."

"Bud, Mac here," Mac said in a rush.

"Mac, we have her. She's fine. We're bringing her back to Joseffa and should be there within the hour."

Mac sat silently for a moment before saying, "Thank God."

He continued to sit quietly for a moment, with his head bowed, praying a prayer of thanks. Will and Kate had rushed over to his golf cart. Mac filled them in and said, "I'm going to the dock. I've got to see that she is safe and unharmed." He headed to the dock area.

43

MAC SAT ON THE DOCK, watching the horizon for incoming boats. Within fifteen minutes, he saw a boat approaching. As it got closer, he could see a name emblazoned on the side, "Lee County Sheriff." Mac stood in excited expectation. Sure enough, on the back deck, sitting on a bench seat, was Mags. Mac excitedly waved and smiled as Mags returned his wave.

The sheriff's twenty foot vessel settled into a berth near where Mac stood. After the craft was tied up to the dock, Sheriff Walton took Mags' arm and helped her to the dock. Mags ran into Mac's waiting arms.

"I was so worried, Mags. Are you okay?" Mac asked, with tears in his eyes.

"Yes, Hon, I'm fine. Except for having my hands bound with those plastic locking fasteners," she said as she rubbed her bruised and chafed wrists, "and being blindfolded, I wasn't touched."

"Are you tired? Do you need to rest? Do you need to see a doctor? Can you tell me the whole story?" Mac spewed out the questions with machine gun rapidity.

"Whoa, Mac! Let me catch my breath. Yes, I am tired. No, I don't think I could rest. No, I don't think a doc is necessary. Yes, I can tell you as much as I know."

"Mags, why don't we go relax at the Inn, get a bite to eat and wait for Jim and Adam to get here. Then, we can go over what happened."

"That works for me!"

Mac turned to Sheriff Walton and said, "Moose and Brenda are in the Administration Building. Would you go and bring them up to speed, and we'll come join you as soon as Jim and Adam get here. They should be here within the hour."

Bud Walton nodded his understanding and walked up the dock towards Administration.

Mac put his arm around Mags' waist and they walked the short distance to their golf cart and they drove to the Inn.

Elyse met Mac and Mags at the door of the Joseffa Inn. "Mrs. Mason, I heard what happened. Are you alright?"

"I'm fine, Elyse, just a little hungry."

Elyse smiled and said, "We can sure take care of that!"

Mac and Mags were shown to a table and given menus and Elyse said, "Mr. Gardner was in earlier and said that whatever you wanted was on the house, so eat hearty."

Mac and Mags both looked at their menus. They both chose grouper sandwiches, curly fries, and diet sodas.

Mac spoke first. "Mags, I was so worried. I've been told how this happened, but I'm anxious to hear what happened after you were taken from the island."

"Well, do you still want to wait for Adam and Jim? By the way, where are they?"

"As you know, we were in St. Pete when I got the call about your being taken. Chief Thompson, of the St. Petersburg Police Department, offered his helicopter to get me back here fast. Adam and Jim are coming on *The Mistress.*"

Elyse returned carrying a tray weighted down with their order.

Mac and Mags both dug in. "Mmmm, this is good," Mags said as she took her first bite of the fried grouper sandwich. "It's been a long time since breakfast."

"For me, too," Mac agreed.

Just as Mac and Mags were finishing their meal, an excited Adam and Jim rushed in. Adam threw his arms around Mags saying, "Thank goodness you are alright. Dad was worried sick. We all were!"

Mac spoke up. "We've finished here. Why don't we go to the conference room and let Mags fill us in on all that's happened. Can you guys hold off on lunch?"

"Not a problem. Let's go over where the sheriff is."

Calling Elyse and trying to pay for the meal, Mac was rebuffed. "No way, Mr. Mason. Mr. Gardner made that crystal clear."

Mac put a $10 bill in Elyse's hand. She tried to refuse, but Mac said, "Bob might tell you what to do about our check, but he can't tell me what to do about showing you our appreciation. Thank you!"

The four walked out of the Inn, and getting in Mac's golf cart, made their way to the Auditorium and to the conference room.

Mac unlocked the conference room door and pulled out his cell phone and called Sheriff Walton. "Bud, we're in the conference room. Can you come on over now? And bring Moose and Brenda with you!"

In just a few minutes, there was a knock on the door. Mac asked, "Who is it?" and hearing Bud reply, "Sheriff Walton, Moose, and Brenda," Mac opened the door.

The group sat around the conference room table and Mac said, "I think the place to start is with Mags telling us what she remembers about the abduction."

Mags began. "First, I had no idea that it was an abduction or kidnapping, or whatever you want to call it. The two men looked like security. I was so worried about Mac that I just did as they asked. I went with them. My suspicions were somewhat aroused when they didn't walk towards the main dock, but instead led me to a dock on the east side of the island. I asked why and they just told me, having not been to Joseffa before, they didn't know where to dock and chose one of the private docks on the east side. That made sense to me," Mags paused.

"As soon as they got me aboard the boat and we had gotten some distance from the island, the smaller of the two men grabbed me, bound my hands and blindfolded me. That's when I knew they had lied to me."

"I don't know how long we were in the boat. I tried to count seconds. You know? 'one Mississippi, two Mississippi'. I'd estimate that we were on the water about forty-five minutes. When we docked, the men led me to a car and pushed me into the back seat. We drove about an hour and then they pulled to a stop. I was conscious of a number of turns and then felt we had left the paved road. When they stopped, I was near panic. I had no idea what they were going to do to me. One of the men pulled me out of the car, cut my wrists free and said, 'Don't touch the blindfold for five minutes, or you will wish you hadn't.' At some point, one of them had pinned something to my shirt. Then one of the men said, 'This is just a sample of what could happen to you. We can get to you anytime we want. Remember that!' I waited and listened as the car pulled away. I did wait the five minutes and removed my blindfold. I found myself on a narrow, sandy road and had no idea where I was. I walked to the main road and saw that I was on the outskirts of Matlacha. I stopped in a place called Ike's Emporium and called the sheriff's office. Bud," she smiled, "picked me up in less than a half hour. He took me to his boat and brought me here. That's all I remember."

"What did they pin to your shirt?" Adam asked.

"In the excitement of being free, I forgot all about that. Here it is," she said, handing the note to Mac.

Mac took a pair of rubber gloves and opened the note. He read it aloud, noting that the note had been typed. "This is only a warning. We can get to you anytime. Tell your husband to stop what he is doing, or he will lose you permanently." Mac muttered, "No signature."

"Who do you think did this?" Sheriff Walton asked.

"I don't think it was done by anyone associated with Jim Barber, but we can't be sure. From our interrogation of him, I think he has taken himself out of circulation for some time. My suspicions are that it's that other crime outfit we suspect are messed up in this human trafficking scheme."

"Who?" asked Jim Travis. "Big Mama?"

"That would be my guess," said Mac.

"Big Mama," Sheriff Walton asked. "Who is she?"

"Jim, why don't you tell us all about Big Mama," Mac suggested.

Jim began. "Big Mama is the name used to refer to Marjorie Malone. In Miami, she is well-known. No one knows what she looks like except those closest to her. But, from what we have heard through informers is that no one in her organization would dare call her 'Big Mama'. All her people are scared to death of her. We hear that she is well over three hundred pounds and stays out of public view. She leaves all her dirty work to two lieutenants who lead her organization. We've had her people on our watch list for a long time. We want her for human trafficking, but haven't gained sufficient evidence to find and arrest her yet. But, with Jim Barber's testimony, we might be able to do that now. We just might."

"Thanks, Jim. And maybe I should say 'thanks' to the *other* Jim, too!"

I know Mags is tired and we've all had a long, stressful day. I'd advise that we stop here and meet again tomorrow afternoon around two." Mac suggested.

At that moment, there was a knock on the door. "Who is it?" Mac asked.

"Bob Gardner and Pat Jefferson," Bob's voice answered.

Mac opened the door, admitting the two.

"We just wanted to see if you needed anything and to make sure Mags is okay," Bob said.

Mac answered, "We are just about to break this up for today. Mags is okay, but I do have a request. Could you arrange lodging for Mr. Williamson and Ms. Vinson for the night? We're going to meet again here tomorrow at two."

Pat responded, getting a nod from Bob, "We can arrange that."

Bob and Pat left after telling Moose and Brenda to stop by Administration to pick up keys to the two adjoining duplexes they would occupy.

Mac looked at Jim and asked, "Do we still have a facial composition artist at the Miami Police Department?"

Jim answered, "Yes, she is new and a great asset to us. She can either do free hand sketches or use the facial recognition software. She is a master at either."

"Could she be here tomorrow afternoon? I know it will be Sunday, but I'd like to get Will, Kate, and Mags with her as soon as possible."

"I'll call her right now. Her name is Chantal Smithson. If anyone can get us composites, she can."

"Call me and let me know," Mac asked. He then added, "Unless anyone else has anything, I suggest we adjourn until two tomorrow."

Everyone agreed. Mac, Mags, and Adam headed back to *The Mistress*. Bud walked with them to the dock and to his waiting boat. Moose and Brenda walked toward the Administration Building while Jim walked toward his condo.

Adam said goodnight as soon as he boarded *The Mistress*. Mac and Mags both showered and were soon in bed and asleep.

44

MAC AWOKE FIRST, AS USUAL. He went to the galley and put a pod of Columbian Dark Roast coffee in the Keurig. He was just adding his sweetener, sugar, and milk to the cup when Mags came from the master stateroom.

"Good morning, Darling. Did you sleep well?"

"Like the dead," Mags answered. Mac grimaced at the use of the term, dead.

"How are you feeling?"

"OK, my wrists were hurting but I put some ointment on them and they feel better this morning."

"Are you up to church today?" Mac asked.

"Yes, today, more than many days. I have so much to be thankful for."

"We both have a lot to be thankful for. Why don't you just relax on deck and I'll fix you a nice breakfast."

Mags smiled and gave Mac a kiss. "You're my hero!"

After having a very well prepared breakfast of sausage and French toast, Mac and Mags took turns in the master bath and bedroom, preparing for the island's beach-front worship service. They walked to their golf cart and drove to the east side of the island. Mags pointed to a dock as they passed. "That's where the men docked their boat that took me from the island," she stated. "That was less than twenty-four hours ago, but seems like a week."

As their golf cart approached the crowd gathered for worship, Mac and Mags were surprised to see Will and Kate as well as Adam, Jim, Moose, and Brenda. Hugs and handshakes were shared among the eight, as well as with many island residents.

Before the service began, Mac turned to Mags and said, "That Moose is one huge guy."

Mags responded, "Yes, I learned more of his story when talking with him the other day. It seems he attended Grambling University, was a first round draft pick of the Atlanta Falcons, and was an All-Pro Tackle for them before blowing out his knee in his sixth year. He always had an interest in law enforcement and security and took the job with Phil Phillips. He's quite a guy and quite a Christian working with Campus Crusade and speaking all over the country."

"That is quite a resume, Mags," Mac said, just as the leader of the service announced the time for Joys and Concerns.

Someone that Mac and Mags didn't even know gave thanks for Mags' safe return to the island.

Someone else spoke up and asked, "Where is Bettina McCauley?" No one seemed to know until one person spoke up and said, "I saw her and her shih tzu, Puffball, boarding the shuttle a few days ago. Maybe she's going up north." Mac and Adam just smiled.

The opening hymn was an old African-American song, short but beautiful, "Thank You, Lord." After the closing words, Mac leaned over to Mags and said, "Amen."

At the conclusion of the service, a dozen residents came up to give Mags a hug and share their happiness that she was back among them and unharmed.

Mac and Mags joined the others who would meet with Sheriff Walton at two o'clock and went to the Inn for brunch. Bob, Susan, and Pat were already there. Bob quickly arranged for a large table to be set and the group enjoyed a great Sunday morning repast.

As two o'clock approached, Mac and Mags returned to *The Mistress* to gather some files that Mac had taken to the boat with him the previous evening. Together, they walked the short distance to the Auditorium and the conference room.

Upon arriving at the room, Mac noted that Sheriff Walton was already waiting. Adam and Jim arrived followed closely by Moose and Brenda. The group took seats around the table.

Mac spoke first, "Did you reach Chantal Smithson last evening, Jim?"

"Yes, I did. She will be here around three-thirty. I told her to just catch the three o'clock shuttle from Bokeelia. I cleared that with Pat Jefferson."

"Good. Would you go and check with Pat as to whether we can use the other conference room across the hall and then call Will and Kate and ask them to be here at three?"

"I'm on it," Jim responded.

"OK," Mac said, as he turned to the rest of the group. "We have several issues to discuss this afternoon. I think the first is to find Triple J. Jim Barber said that he thought Jackson had fled to the Caribbean. That jibes with information that Jim Travis shared with me when we discussed Triple J in St. Pete. Is that right, Jim?"

"Yes, Mac, that's right. When he fled the country, we didn't have enough evidence of serious crimes to extradite him. We did learn that the last anyone knew, he was in Aruba. It's a part of the Kingdom of the Netherlands. We do have an extradition treaty with them."

"Adam, how do we go about finding Triple J and getting him back here? Barber has agreed to appear in court as a witness against him."

Adam thought. "The first thing we have to do is get the extradition orders drawn up and a warrant for his arrest. Then, we have to find him. The KPA will cooperate with us in finding and apprehending Triple J, or Jack Jackson."

Sheriff Walton scratched his head. "The KPA, what is that?

Adam smiled, "Saying 'KPA' is easier than saying the Korps Politie Aruba, which is the police force of Aruba." Adam continued, "I have a suggestion. With my boss, Pete Barnes' approval, I could send Jeff Rose and another of my agents to Aruba to represent the United States in the search and recovery effort."

Mac responded, "That will take care of that issue. How long do you think it will take to put that into motion?"

"If I call this afternoon, I think we can have the legalities taken care of by tomorrow morning. Jeff could be in the air by tomorrow afternoon. Is that fast enough?"

"Perfect. Now on to our next topic. Big Mama Malone."

Sheriff Walton asked, "Now, this person's name is Marjorie Malone. Right? Why Big Mama?"

Jim was the first to answer. "From what we understand, Malone is huge. She is never seen except by her top lieutenants. She supposedly tops three hundred pounds, maybe three hundred fifty. Rival gangs refer to her as Big Mama, although none in her organization would ever address her that way and live."

Mac spoke up. "I think finding Malone will require that we go back to St. Petersburg and talk to Jim Barber again. Chief Thompson e-mailed me and told me they were keeping him in solitary and away from others for his own protection. He has an officer stationed outside his cell at all times."

Mac looked troubled, "I don't want to leave Mags alone again."

Brenda spoke up. "Mac, Moose and I will not leave the island or Mags' side again. I can promise you that."

Sheriff Walton added, "I can also place a couple of deputies on the island, if that would help."

Smiling at Mags, Mac said, "That would make me feel much better." He then added, "Adam, let's you and I leave at daybreak tomorrow. We can talk to Barber and be back before dark tomorrow evening."

Adam thought for a moment. "Mac, I think I have a better idea. Let me call Chief Thompson and see if he could send his helicopter for us. That would save us hours. Whacha think?"

"Great idea, Adam. Would you make that call? Tell him we'll be ready to leave at 6:30. That would get us to the police headquarters by 7:00. We could probably be back here by noon."

"Making the call now, Dad." Adam said smiling.

Mac took the leadership role again and said, "Now, if we find Malone is in Miami, which I expect, we'll need to move our operation there. Sheriff Walton, I don't think we need for you to accompany us. Malone is not wanted in your jurisdiction, but we will keep you informed."

Sheriff Walton responded, "Not a problem, Mac. Just let me know if there is anything I can do."

Adam looked at Moose and Brenda. "Brenda, can you and Moose go with us? I'd like to have you there to keep an eye on Mags' security."

"You've got us as long as you need us. And, Mac?"

"Yes?"

"We would be doing this even if you hadn't hired Phillips detective agency. It's payback time for us."

Moose added, "And, we've kinda become attached to Mags." If Moose's dark complexion had not hidden it, they would have been able to see him blushing.

Adam returned from his phone call and reported. "The St. Petersburg Police helicopter will be here at 6:30 in the morning."

There was a knock on the door. It was Will and Kate, accompanied by a young woman whom they introduced as Chantal Smithson. They all stood and introduced themselves.

Smithson, with Mags, Will, and Kate in tow, was shown to the conference room across the hall.

Sheriff Walton asked, "Anything else you need from me today, Mac?"

"No, Bud, but I can't thank you enough for all you've done to help us. We'll be in touch."

Walton said his goodbyes to everyone and left.

Mac, Adam, Moose, and Brenda huddled around the table and began to plan on the future steps to be taken, assuming a trip to Miami.

◈ ◈ ◈

Chantal Smithson removed a computer from a bag she had hung over her shoulder. She also removed a small projector and connected it to the computer, pointing it to an area of the white wall to her right. She set the computer up at one end of a table and asked Mags, Kate, and Will to sit where they had a good view of a projected image on the wall to her right. She then gave them instructions.

"It's important that you each agree on the images I ask you to decide between. When you have all three agreed, we'll move to another image. Is that understood?"

Mags, Will, and Kate all nodded their heads in agreement.

"We'll start with the first man. How should we identify him?"

"Mags answered, "One man was larger and appeared to be the leader."

"OK, we have a large man and a small man. Right?"

"Yes, that would be correct," Mags affirmed.

"OK, first, how would you describe the shape of the head of the larger man? Which of these images," she asked pointing at the wall, "would be the closer?" Will indicated one image. Kate said, "I think just a little thinner, higher cheek bones."

Mags agreed. Will studied the image and said, "Yes, that's better."

Smithson continued showing images of hair styles, eye shape, lips, nose, ears, and complexion. The three witnesses looked, debated, and finally agreed on their choices. The larger man's image was complete.

Will exclaimed, "That's amazing. That is exactly as I remember him."

Mags and Kate agreed. "That's him!"

Smithson saved the first finished image and the process was repeated as the three made choices of features of the second, smaller man.

Upon completion of the image of the second man, Will, Kate, and Mags all agreed that both were excellent composites.

Smithson spoke. "Our next step is to share these with Special Agent Mason and the others, and then I'll run the images through our facial recognition software. If these men have been booked and photographed in the past, we ought to be able to get a hit."

The four crossed the hall and knocked on the door where Mac, Adam, and Jim were still working.

Adam, Mac, and Mags walked the short distance to the dock and on to *The Mistress*. They had no more than boarded the boat when they heard a voice call out, "Ahoy, Mate!"

Mac went to the upper deck and saw Will and Kate there.

"Welcome, strangers. It's been forever since I've seen you," Mac laughed.

"We wanted to come over and ask if you think you needed us any longer. If not, we thought we'd load up all our equipment and our specimens and get back to Cedar Key," Will said.

By this time, Adam and Mags had joined the others on the deck.

"Have a seat. Adam, why don't you get some drinks for all of us?"

"What will you all have?" Adam asked.

The men agreed on beers. The women agreed on a glass of Merlot. Adam said, "Be right back!"

Mac spoke up. "Guys, I am so sorry that I was of so little help to you on the dig. I hope you'll invite us again and we'll do our best not to get involved in murders and abductions."

"It's okay, Mac," Kate stated. "After all, you still don't know the difference between a scallop and an oyster shell."

"But, I like to eat them both. That should count for something."

"What do you think we learned from the dig, Will?" Mags asked.

"Well, we've confirmed that the Calusa inhabited Joseffa thirty to thirty-five hundred years ago. They were probably seasonal in their habitation, though. We also know more about what they ate and that they were quite adept at making tools from the resources available to them. This dig, and the one in April, has certainly added to our knowledge base. Now, we face months of examining and cataloguing the items we're taking back to our labs. The work has just begun."

The five visited for another hour until Will and Kate excused themselves.

"It was great finally meeting you, Adam," Will said. Everyone hugged and promised to get together again soon.

Soon after Will and Kate left, Mags, Mac, and Adam went below deck and prepared for bed. Mags looked thoughtful which Mac picked up on. "You're thinking of something, Mags. What is it?"

"You know that older gentleman at Ike's Emporium? I'd like to do something for him. He was so nice and helpful. Maybe I could call Sheriff Walton and ask him to pick up a gift certificate and a nice card of thanks."

"I'll get him on the phone and ask him if he'd do that. I'll send Bud a check for fifty dollars. Is that enough?"

"That would be great, Mac," Mags said placing a kiss on Mac's cheek.

Mac waggled his eyebrows again and said, "Ready for bed, Wife?"

"I know what you want, Old Man."

45

PRIOR TO SIX THE FOLLOWING morning, Mags gave Mac and Adam a ride to the helicopter landing pad. Moose and Brenda, accompanied by Jim Travis, followed closely behind.

"They didn't need to get up so early and follow us here," Mags commented.

"Oh, yes they did! Mags, please don't go anywhere without them. I've asked them to stay on *The Mistress* near you. Jim will probably be there, too."

"Yes, sir." Mags agreed, snapping a quick salute to her husband.

Within five minutes, the helicopter landed and Adam and Mac climbed aboard. They waved as the group below disappeared from view.

❖ ❖ ❖

Thirty minutes later, the helicopter landed on the pad atop the St. Petersburg police headquarters. Chief Thompson was waiting.

The Chief shared, "Barber has hired a lawyer, but he still stands by the statement he signed. He feels confident that a jury will either acquit him or find him guilty of a crime lesser than first degree murder. As to the human trafficking charge, he says that he has been out of that for over eight years and he will testify against both his past boss, Jack Jackson, and also provide testimony on Marjorie Malone."

"Good," replied Mac. "We do have some questions for him today."

Mac and Adam were led to an interview room where Barber and another man waited. Barber was dressed in the standard issue orange jump suit. His lawyer was in a rumpled seersucker suit.

Mac and Adam introduced themselves to Jim Barber's lawyer. "I'm Patrick Gonzalez," the attorney said.

"Mr. Barber, may I record our interview with you today?" Adam asked.

Barber looked at his lawyer who nodded "yes."

Adam began, "Mr. Barber, in our conversation three days ago, you agreed that you'd help us in the apprehension of Marjorie Malone. Is that true?"

"Yes, I did agree to that in exchange for some guarantees."

"Those agreements are still in place," Adam responded. "We really have just one question for you."

"OK?"

"Do you know from where Marjorie Malone is now operating and how to find her?"

Barber looked at his lawyer and leaned over, whispering something. The lawyer covered his mouth as he spoke to his client, and then Barber said, "I think I can help you, although my information is a little old."

"What do you know?" Mac asked.

"The last I heard was that Big Mama is still operating in the Miami area. I don't know where her headquarters are, but I might know someone who does know."

"Who is this person?" Adam looked intently at Barber, waiting for this answer.

"His name is Billy Hastings. His brother was killed by Big Mama's boys. He doesn't have the manpower, or the brains, to take Mama down. I think he might be able to help you if he thinks you can do it."

"OK, how do we find this Hastings?" Mac asked.

Barber reached for the lawyer's legal pad and his pen. He wrote something.

Adam asked, "Is this the address where Hastings lives?"

"I think so but I can't be sure. I talked to him about two weeks ago. However, I stayed in close touch with him while I was on Joseffa. In fact, he was the one that told me that Malone's men had found me, and with his friends, got me to the mainland on their fishing boat. "

"Any other questions, Mr. Mason?" Adam asked as he looked at Mac.

"No, I think that will do it."

Mac and Adam left the interview room and met Chief Thompson again.

"We might have what we need. Thank you so much for picking us up on Joseffa. If I can ever do anything for you, call me." Adam handed Chief Thompson a business card, and he and Mac made their way back to the roof and the waiting helicopter.

When belted in and with earphone on, Mac asks Adam, "Where is this Hastings located?"

"He's in Miami."

"OK, we leave for Miami tomorrow. OK?"

"Yes, I'll need to arrange lodging for Moose and Brenda. I assume Jim will stay at home, and we'll go on *The Mistress* and stay on her?"

"That sounds like a good plan to me, Son."

The helicopter landed on Joseffa thirty minutes later. Mac and Adam began their walk north to the dock and *The Mistress*.

◈ ◈ ◈

Mac and Adam reached *The Mistress* shortly after noon. When they got to the dock area, they saw one sheriff's uniformed deputy standing near the entrance. Another was standing in the vicinity of *The Mistress*. Mac and Adam, not knowing the deputies, both showed their identification. Sitting on deck were Moose and Jim.

"Greetings," called out Jim. "How did it go?"

"It went well. We leave for Miami early tomorrow morning," Mac replied. "Where's Mags?"

"She's down below with Brenda. I think they are watching some cooking show. That was too much for us," Jim replied. Moose just grunted. "We've been arguing up here as to who is the better team this year, the Falcons or the Dolphins."

"When you get to college basketball, let me know. I can tell you who the best Atlantic Coast Conference team is," Mac smiled.

Now interested, Moose looked up. "And, who's that?"

Mac pretended a look of shock and turned to Jim. "You've been with this man for all this time and you haven't shared the truth with him?" Mac turned to Moose, "The Blue Devils, of course."

"Oh, no, we may have issues. I've always been a Tar Heel fan," Moose said with a smile.

Mac just looked at Moose sadly, shook his head, and then turned his thoughts back to the trip to Miami.

He looked at Adam, Jim, and Moose. "I hope we don't need it, but how are we fixed for firepower?"

Moose patted the holstered pistol on his hip. He added, "Brenda is armed too."

Jim indicated a shoulder holster under his light jacket.

Adam said, "I have my 9 mm service pistol down below."

"I also have a 9 mm below and a .357 magnum. How about ammo?" Mac asked.

"We've come with plenty," stated Moose.

Jim said, "A full magazine and two extras."

"I've got several boxes of 9 mm below. We probably won't need it, but I'm still thinking about that note left with Mags. I don't think we've seen the last of whoever took her."

"We'll be ready," Moose, Adam, and Jim all agreed.

Changing the subject, Mac said, "Why don't we grill up some steaks tonight and then get to bed early? It will be a long day tomorrow."

"Sounds good," Moose said, rubbing his belly.

Mags and Brenda came topside, while Mac went below to pull six one-inch thick rib eyes out of the 'fridge. "I'm glad Mags took these out of the freezer last night," Mac thought to himself.

Brenda raised her hand. "I make a killer salad and can sure bake a potato."

Moose gave her a skeptical look. "Cut it out, Big Guy. I CAN cook!" Brenda chided.

"Uh huh," was the only response from Moose.

A person, looking at the six, would see only a group of friends enjoying an evening on a great boat. They'd never suspect that this was the eve of an exciting and somewhat terrifying day.

46

MORNING CAME EARLY AS USUAL for Mac. Around six, he found the Harbor Master and asked that *The Mistress* be topped off with fuel and potable water, apologizing for not remembering it the day before. Adam came on deck with two cups of steaming coffee.

"Mom up yet?" Adam asked.

"Not yet. I think I'll go down and whip up some baggie omelets and fry another pound of bacon," Mac said. "I wonder if Jim, Brenda, and Moose will want breakfast. I'll make enough for everyone. Will a cheese omelet work for you?"

"Yes," Adam replied, "with double cheese."

"You are my son," Mac beamed.

Just as Mac was turning to go below, he saw Jim, Moose, and Brenda coming down the dock. "Good. They're here. We'll leave as soon as we eat."

Mac went below and put two large pots of water on to boil. He then took a pound of bacon out of the 'fridge and placed the bacon strips on the griddle. Within thirty minutes, he had a platter piled high with bacon and cheese omelets ready to take topside. Jim, Moose, and Brenda had come below and prepared coffee for themselves and a cup for Mags who had dressed and joined the group on the upper deck.

"Great breakfast," Brenda said as the others agreed. "I need to find a man who knows his way around the kitchen."

Mags beamed, "Breakfast and grilling are just two of Mac's talents." She smiled and winked at Mac.

"Let me get those dishes," Moose offered.

"Wow, such domestic men," Mags said. "I'll help you." Brenda went below with Moose and Mags.

The Harbor Master had topped off the fuel and water tanks on *The Mistress* while the group had been eating.

"Let's get started. Adam, would you free the forward and aft lines?" Mac asked.

"Got 'em, Captain," replied Adam.

Mac eased *The Mistress* away from the dock, set the onboard GPS and pointed the boat toward Miami.

Mac piloted the boat from the upper flying bridge, joined there by Adam and Jim. Mags, Brenda, and Moose settled in chairs on the lower deck.

❖ ❖ ❖

The azure water seemed calm. A slight breeze matched the wind flowing from the boat's "full speed ahead" mode. The morning sun sent a friendly light across the bow. As they pulled deeper into the Gulf, Mac waved at passing vessels. All in all, it was a pleasant, winter cruise. Only the roar of the powerful engines intruded on what, to all appearances, was a routine outing.

An hour into the cruise, Jim tapped Mac on the shoulder. "This doesn't look right. What do you think? Look to aft on the starboard side. There's a runabout gaining on us quickly, two men in it. It's coming straight for us."

"Tell Mags to get below and tell the others to be ready in case this is more than just a careless boater," Mac directed.

As the other boat drew nearer, Mac saw it was about thirty feet in length with the trademark logo, "Outlaw," emblazoned on the side. "That model can reach speeds in excess of fifty miles an hour. If they are after us, we can't outrun them."

As the approaching boat got within one hundred yards, Moose, looking through binoculars, shouted up from below. "They have guns."

Mac began a crisscross pattern as the armed five drew their weapons. As the runabout closed distance, one of the men from the approaching boat began to fire a semi-automatic rifle.

Shots hit the side of *The Mistress*, and Mac heard a window below deck explode. "Check on Mags," Mac shouted.

"I've got it," Brenda responded.

Jim, Moose, and Adam from behind cover began to return fire. "It's five against two. Just keep low," Moose yelled.

Mac kept zigzagging *The Mistress*, trying to keep their boat away from the approaching shooters.

Mac kept his head low. He was a prime target on the upper flying bridge. Adam and Jim had gone to the lower deck. Bullets ricocheted off the area near Mac, shattering glass.

Moose, Jim, and Adam emptied their clips at the approaching "Outlaw." Brenda was firing through the blown out window below, keeping Mags flat on the floor of the salon. After the barrage of return fire, one of the attacking men grabbed his chest and fell from the boat. The runabout did a quick circle, coming back to the man in the water. The pilot of the runabout, looked down at his fallen comrade, turned the boat and opened the throttle. In a few moments, the powerful craft was almost out of sight.

Mac pulled back on the throttle of *The Mistress*, idling her. He ran down to the lower deck. "Everyone okay?"

Several voices shouted "Yes."

Mac hurried below. "Everyone okay down here?"

"We're okay," Brenda said, as Mac took Mags into his arms.

"I'm okay, Mac. I wish you had given me a pistol. I could have used it."

"Next time, Hon, but let's hope there's not a next time."

Mac and Mags took the stairs to the main deck.

"Dad, let's see about that man we hit."

Mac, from the lower bridge, pushed the throttle forward and circled where a body floated nearby.

Adam and Moose took a grappling hook and pulled the body near the aft of *The Mistress*. They lifted the man onboard. His body fell into a lifeless heap. For some time, no one made a sound.

Adam spoke first. "Folks can say what they want to about death, but to me it is never pretty. Why would I be feeling sorry for a man who just tried to kill me?"

Jim touched Adam on the arm. "I suppose it is a good thing that we never get used to it."

Moose gently turned the body so they could see his face. "I just have to do this," he said, as he leaned over and carefully pulled the man's eyelids closed.

Mac began, "I always wonder who will mourn a death." He paused, "That's for later. We still have work to do. For starters, it's too bad we don't know who this is, or who the other man is."

Mags eased toward the body and said, "I know who he is. That's the younger of the two men who kidnapped me."

Mac looked closely at the body. "That composite Chantal did was accurate. It looked exactly like this guy."

Adam looked away from the gruesome scene. "I guess I need to be in my professional mode, so let me ask, Is there any serious damage to *The Mistress*? We still have a ways to go."

Mac walked from bow to stern, leaning over frequently to look at the side of the boat. "Some minor damage, but nothing that will reduce her sea worthiness. We need to call the Coast Guard and report this."

Adam pulled out his cell phone and keyed '911.' A voice answered, "911, where is your emergency?" Adam explained, asked Mac for the coordinates of their location and passed that on to the operator. He told what had happened.

In a short time, a Coast Guard cutter pulled alongside. A young lieutenant came aboard. Adam took out his credentials and introduced the others. The officer took notes and ordered two of his men to offload the body to the cutter.

"We will need to find out everything we can about the dead man. Where will he be taken? "Jim asked.

"We'll take him to the morgue. You'll need to follow us to Miami to give a full report."

Jim showed his Miami PD badge. "We were headed to Miami anyway. We'll follow you."

"Detective Travis, do you have any damage to your boat?" the young officer asked.

"The boat belongs to Mr. Mason, but, no, there's no damage that will hinder our following you."

One of the Coast Guard crew stayed on *The Mistress*. The cutter pulled away and Mac eased the throttle of *The Mistress* forward and fell in behind.

An hour later, the cutter pulled into a small area where other vessels were tied up. A sign on the side of one building read "U. S. Coast Guard." Mac docked *The Mistress* where a coastguardsman on the dock indicated.

"This was not how I planned on arriving in Miami," Mac said, with only a slightest trace of a grin.

47

As the group began to climb out of *The Mistress*, an officer approached. On his lapel, he had the insignia of a commander. Adam stepped forward.

Adam held out his hand, "I'm Special Agent Mason of the FBI. These people with me are special consultant McKenzie Mason, Detective Captain Travis of the Miami PD, Brad Williamson and Brenda Vinson, security specialists, and Maggie Mason, Mac's wife"

The Commander looked the group over and said, "I'm Commander Wilson, Commanding Officer of the Coast Guard unit assigned to Miami. I believe I have met Special Agent Mason before, and I've heard of Mac Mason by reputation. I hear that you really ran into some trouble out there," the Commander said pointing to the open Gulf.

Mac spoke up. "Commander, I'm the head of a task force assigned to investigate murders that took place on Joseffa Island, as well as looking into suspected human trafficking. It's beginning to look as if the murder and the human trafficking are tied to one another. We believe the attack on my boat was perpetrated by an outfit that is suspected in the trafficking of humans. Bad stuff. We were on our way to Miami to find and interview a person of interest."

"Human trafficking is probably a number one priority for the Coast Guard right now. Is there anything I can do to help?"

"Yes, Commander. We can give you a description of the runabout that attacked us, and a possible composite picture of the man who piloted the boat. The body on the cutter is the other man who attacked us. Can you put your patrols on the lookout for that runabout? Detective Travis can give you the description."

"Yes, Mr. Mason. I'll put out a bulletin to all our patrols immediately."

Mac asked, "How long until we can leave and dock at the Miami Marina?"

"Let me get your statements. As soon as that is done, you'll be free to leave."

Another Coast Guard officer came aboard *The Mistress* and a complete report of the attack was taken.

The interviewing officer stated, "I think I have all the information I need. We'll forward the body of the dead man to the morgue where the Medical Examiner will autopsy the body, and try to identify him."

"Good, can you contact me if the M.E. makes an identification?"

"We can do that!"

Adam gave the officer the business card that contained his cell phone number.

Adam untied the lines securing *The Mistress* to the Coast Guard dock and Mac piloted the boat toward the Miami Marina.

As the craft moved toward the Miami Marina, Mags and Brenda taped plastic over the windows blown out by the runabout attack. Although no one mentioned it, the uneasy feeling gave way to nervous pacing; someone may be lurking, ready to spring another bullet-ridden surprise.

Mac radioed ahead to the Miami Marina, asking permission to dock there. As he approached the marina, a dock worker indicated a berth for *The Mistress*. Mac edged closer and completed the mooring.

Mac, back in full business mode, said, "Our first item of business is to set up a command post. We can do that at the Miami PD, can't we, Jim?"

"Yes, I'll call ahead and get us an assigned task force room," Jim offered.

"Good. And transportation?"

"I'll have my assigned SUV brought here immediately. I'll also arrange for a car for Moose and Brenda and one for you, Adam, and Mags." Jim continued, "I've arranged accommodations for Moose and Brenda at a hotel immediately across from Miami P.D."

Mac smiled and said, "I knew I had recommended a good man to replace me. Let's get to police headquarters and get organized. I want Mags with us, unless it gets dangerous, and then I want Moose and Brenda with her at all times."

Within a half hour, three SUVs pulled up at the marina. Moose and Brenda got into one. Jim climbed in another. Mac, Adam, and Mags went to the third. Mac got into the driver's seat saying, "I know my way around Miami. I'll drive."

Mags, laughing, said, "Don't you always?"

The three vehicles made their way through the heavy Miami traffic and entered the parking garage of the Miami Police Department.

Upon entering the building, the group was met by a tall, slender man in full uniform.

"Chief Talbot," Jim stated, shaking the man's extended hand. "You remember Mac Mason." He went on to introduce the others.

The chief nodded a greeting. "We have your task force room set up for you. Just keep me informed of your progress. I'm ready to assist you in any way."

"Thank you, Chief," Jim replied. "We may need to call on you."

Mac and his team were led to the task force team room by Chief Talbot. Everyone set up a laptop and found a chair at the table.

"Our first job, as I see it, is to find Billy Hastings. He's our connecting link to Malone. Barber gave us a phone number and where Hastings might possibly live. How should we proceed?" Mac asked.

"I think we try to get a fix on the cell phone. That can be done here, can't it, Jim?"

"Yes, we have the technology to do that. But, I need to find out if a court order is necessary. If we have probable cause to find this person, one is not necessary in Florida," Jim replied.

"I think we have probable cause, don't you?" Adam asked.

"Yes, I do. I'll go to the department that can do that for us and see what I can come up with. Mac, can you give me the number?"

Mac reached in his pocket, pulled out the piece of paper given to him by Barber, copied the phone number onto a note pad and gave the sheet to Jim. Info in hand, Jim left the room.

"Let's assume we find a location for Hastings. Do we need backup to apprehend him?" Mac looked at Adam as he asked the question.

"I don't think so, Mac. With the five of us, we should be able to handle it."

"I want Mags to stay here. She should be safe. I'll alert officers here to keep an eye on her," Mac said.

Mags wasn't happy with the plan to leave her behind, but thought, "They don't need to be worrying about me while they are out there. It probably is better I stay behind."

Jim returned to the room. "We are in luck. They pinged the cell phone and it is stationary. It's at a location on First Avenue. That's under ten minutes from here even with traffic."

"Let saddle up," said Mac. "We should take two vehicles in case we do find him and want to bring him back here." He added, "Moose. Brenda. You are not law enforcement officers. You don't have to go with us unless you want to."

"Are you kidding?" they both replied, pointedly.

Moose threw his hands over his head. "I won't arrest anybody. I'll just hold 'em until you get there!"

Mac smiled at the teasing and pointed his finger as if aiming a pistol. "Sounds like a plan!"

The five went to the parking garage and settled into two of the SUVs. Jim had been right. In less than ten minutes, the team had departed their vehicles a block from the address given to them.

It was decided that only two, Adam and Jim, would approach the house. Mac would stay on the street out front. Moose and Brenda would cover the back.

Adam knocked on the door.

"Who's there?" a voice called out.

"Friends of Jim Barber," Adam answered.

There was the sound of heavy footsteps and something being knocked to the floor.

"He's running," shouted Jim.

A moment later, a voice called out. "We got him!" Moose came around the house pushing an unwilling person with his arm twisted behind his back.

Mac approached. "Are you Billy Hastings?"

The man said angrily, "Who wants to know?"

IDs were shown to Hastings before Mac said, "We just want to talk to you, but we need to take you downtown."

Mac and Adam placed Hastings into the back seat of their SUV. Adam slid into the backseat beside him. Jim drove back to police headquarters.

After bringing Hastings into the team room, Adam offered the tense man a chair at the head of the table.

"What do you want from me?" Hastings asked.

"Jim Barber really did send us. I understand you have a pretty big grudge against Marjorie Malone," Mac stated.

"Big Mama? You bet I do! She's responsible for the death of my brother. I'd like to get at her, but her security is too tight. I don't have the manpower. Nothing I can do."

"We want her. If we can apprehend her, we have a case that will stick. Human trafficking is a federal offense and we have a witness who will testify against her."

Hastings thought a minute. "Count me in. You'll have two witnesses if you can get her. Are any charges being brought against me?"

"We don't want you. Once we have Malone in custody, you will be free to leave." Jim offered.

"OK. Big Mama lives outside the city on a bit of coastline south of here. Her place is like a fortress. It's really a compound surrounded by eight foot walls. She has men patrolling the perimeter twenty-four seven."

"What's the address?" Jim asked.

"10128 Beach Road," Hastings answered. "I've driven by dozens of times just wishing I could get in."

"We'll get in!" Mac said emphatically.

"OK, Hastings. We appreciate your help, but we will have to keep you here in protective custody until we apprehend Malone. No charges, just protective custody." Jim advised.

"OK by me. If you get Big Mama it will be a small price to pay. They will feed me, won't they?"

"We'll see that they order out for you. You can have whatever you want," Jim said, smiling.

◇ ◇ ◇

Mags waited patiently at police headquarters for the group's return. The female officer who had been left outside the task force room door checked frequently on Mags' wellbeing. After two visits, Mags invited the young woman to come and sit with her.

"I know that your husband was once the head of the Major Crimes Division here. I also know he retired. I've seen him back here a few times with Detective Travis. Can you tell me what he does now, if it isn't confidential?" the woman asked.

"No, it's not confidential. He consults with the Miami police and a number of other law enforcement agencies across the country."

"Flunked retirement, did he? And, do you work outside the home?"

"Why, yes, I still do a little modeling and also have a cosmetic company that I own and manage," Mags answered.

The woman looked at Mags and then said, "I know you! You're Maggie Miller! I've seen you on TV and all over magazine covers."

"You're very observant. I haven't been on many covers lately, but there are still some ads running for my products. In fact, there will be a whole new series of ads starting in mid-January for my newest product."

"I use some of your line now. What's coming out next?"

"It's a new perfume called Mmmm. If it is well-received, there will be other items with the same fragrance coming out later, things like body oils, shampoos, body wash and the like."

"I hate to ask you this, but would you give me your autograph? I'd say it was for my daughter, but I don't have a daughter." Laughing, she said, "It's just for me."

"I'd be glad to," Mags said, asking for the woman's first name.

Late in the afternoon, Mac, Adam, Jim, Moose, and Brenda returned to the task force room.

"Let's just meet for a few minutes." Mac suggested.

After all five were seated around the small table, Mac asked, "Jim, what do you think we should do next?"

"I would think we'd want to take a look at Big Mama's compound, perhaps get some satellite images of it so we could learn the layout."

Adam spoke up. "I can order those images. I can call Pete Barnes and put that in motion now."

"Sounds good, Adam," Mac responded.

Adam got up from the table and walked to the end of the room with phone in hand.

"When do you think we could schedule the 'hit' on the compound?" Mac asked Jim.

"I'd say that it will take us most of tomorrow to get everything in place, study the satellite images, and prepare the assault team. I doubt Malone is going to open the gates and invite us in," Jim responded.

At that moment, Adam returned. "Barnes is onboard. We're getting more than just images. The images will be heat-sensitive. We'll be able to determine how many people are in the compound."

Mac thought for a moment. "OK. Let's tentatively plan the action for sunset tomorrow evening."

Brenda took out her cell phone and keyed in some information. "Sunset tomorrow night will be 5:37 PM."

"Let's set this for 6:00 PM sharp then," Mac responded.

Jim spoke up. "We'll most likely need explosives to open the gate and quite a significant force to guarantee success. We want to avoid casualties and take as many of Malone's people alive as possible. There may be children there. We really won't know much until we get the surveillance information, both visual and via satellite. Moose and Brenda, this is more in your line of work. Why don't you do a drive by this evening at around six? Find out what you can see from the street and surrounding area."

"Not a problem, Jim. Moose and I do that type of recon frequently. When we dress down, we'll look just like a couple of tourists out for a stroll. There is one thing I don't understand though."

"What is that?" Mac asked.

"If it was this easy to find Big Mama, why hasn't she been arrested before?"

"Brenda, we just haven't had any real evidence against her. We've known about her for some time and we've had our suspicions, but her organization is run so tightly that it took Barber and Hastings to give us the information we needed."

There was a knock on the team room door. It was Chief Talbot.

"I've got some news for you. We have positive identification on the man killed while attacking Mr. Mason's boat. And, we have gotten hits on the facial recognition composites Officer Smithson completed."

Mac spoke up, "Who are they?"

"They are brothers, Paul and Win Baxton. Win is the one who was killed. In addition, they have been suspected to be part of Marjorie Malone's organization."

"The web tightens," Mac offered.

Jim spoke up, "Chief, we've gained the information that we think we need to apprehend Malone. If all our indicators prove out tonight and tomorrow morning, we'd like to hit her compound at 6:00 tomorrow evening. Could we count on your SWAT team to assist?"

"Definitely, Jim. I'll have Lieutenant Starling, the SWAT team leader, come by to coordinate with you as soon as you want."

"How about 10:00 tomorrow morning? By then, we should have our satellite images and a report from Moose and Brenda," Jim responded.

"He'll be here," the Chief assured.

Mac looked at Jim. "Again, I'm impressed. As much as I hated leaving Miami PD, I couldn't have left Major Crimes in better hands."

Mac then looked at the group. "What do you say, we call it a night? Sorry that you have to work, Moose and Brenda."

"Hey, this is when it starts getting fun," Moose said, as he gave a fist punch to Brenda.

They scattered for whatever rest they could get.

Adam went to the guest stateroom early, telling Mac and Mags that he was exhausted, wanted to read for a while and get a good night's sleep.

Mac and Mags turned on the flat screen TV in the salon and settled on the sofa. Mac had the remote, as usual. He chose a show entitled, "Searching for Sasquatch."

"Mac, why in the world do you watch that show? They never find any firm evidence of a Sasquatch. And, why are all the so-called photos and videos so poor that you can't really see anything? Then you watch those shows about UFOs. But, again, they never discover anything conclusive. Let's just say that Sasquatch wouldn't hold up in court!"

"Mags, if you asked me if I thought Yetis were really roaming the forests across the U. S., I'd have to say, 'I don't know!' If you asked me if UFOs exist, I'd have to say 'Yes.' After all, UFO means unidentified flying objects. There are definitely objects flying that aren't identified. If the objects, sometimes appearing as flying saucers, are real, are they alien? Are they a new craft being developed by our country or another country? Or, as some far out researchers think, are they our descendants who have perfected time travel and are just coming back to see how we are doing? In answer to all these theories, I'd have to say, 'I don't know.'"

"You are really into this stuff, aren't you? You even record all those old 1950's sci-fi movies."

"Mags, I guess it is just the boy in me coming out," Mac laughed. "I'll believe in a Sasquatch when one runs across the road in front of our car. I'll believe in flying saucers when one lands in our backyard. It's just fun to speculate."

"Well, Mac, I've had enough speculation for tonight. I'm going to bed."

"I'm ready too. Let's go!"

The couple settled into their king sized bed. The soft rocking of the boat soon put them both fast asleep.

48

MAC AND MAGS AWOKE LATER than usual. Neither had slept well. Both admitted that they just had too much on their minds. Adam joined them in the galley as Mac and Mags, together, prepared breakfast.

Mac's cell phone played its usual "Fifth Symphony" by Beethoven.

"Mason here," Mac answered.

"Brenda Vinson here, Mac. Just wanted to make sure you guys are up before we come over."

"Hi, Brenda, have you and Moose had breakfast?"

"Yes, we just finished eating. Jim joined us for breakfast here at the hotel."

Mac thought for a moment. "We are just now eating, but you three come on whenever you want. We're here."

Mac, Mags, and Adam ate, cleaned the galley and went up to the main deck. Fifteen minutes later Moose, Brenda, and Jim approached *The Mistress.*

The six settled into padded benches and deck chairs before Mac, looking at Brenda and Moose, asked, "What did you guys find out last night?"

Brenda began. "What Hastings told us was pretty accurate. There is a front gate that faces west, and it appears that anyone entering must either enter a security code or call in via a speaker and ask for entrance. No one came into or left the compound while we were there.

There was a person in a small building, monitoring the entrance. We couldn't tell if he was armed, but I'm sure he was. As Hasting said, the walls are eight feet tall. There is no razor wire on top. I guess that would raise too many questions from neighbors or those passing the house. We did see a man inside the wall circle from the north and another from the south. They stopped to talk to the man at the gate, and then turned and circled back. If they were armed, they had their weapons concealed. I would guess side arms, no heavy weapons. We assume that there is a man patrolling, not only the north and south walls, but probably the east wall, as well. Looking through the gate, we could only see the main house. There did appear to be a garage building with six doors on the north side of the house. It was very close to the north wall. That might be an entry point. The guard has to walk around the garage and can't walk along the wall there. We couldn't stop and look more carefully. We didn't want to raise suspicion. The house is about a hundred yards beyond the gate. The house is huge. That's about all we can report. We didn't see anyone other than the three men we assume to be guards."

Moose took out a sheet of paper. "Last night, after returning to the hotel, we drew a layout of how we perceived the compound. We can compare that with the satellite images when we get them."

"Good report," said Mac. "We'll share that with Lieutenant Starling at our 10:00 meeting. We haven't heard from Pete Barnes about the satellite surveillance images yet. I hope soon."

"Do you think we can get into the compound without jeopardizing our people?" Mac addressed the question to Moose.

"It won't be easy. The north wall behind the garage would probably allow one team to enter, but beyond that we'll definitely meet resistance. Starling can probably advise us best. That's his job."

The group broke up into separate conversations. Mac and Mags conversed with Brenda, while Adam spoke with Moose.

Moose was showing Adam a copy of the drawing he and Brenda had made of the compound. With pencil in hand, Adam was marking different areas on the drawing.

Adam's phone rang.

"Mason here," Adam answered. "Yes, Pete. OK, I'll watch for it to arrive. Thank you, sir."

Adam turned to the group. Barnes has the satellite images and is e-mailing them to my laptop now. We don't have a printer on board *The Mistress*. The marina has a small business office for the use of guests here. We'll need to go there to print them."

Mac responded, "Why don't you and I go there? Moose, you, Brenda, and Jim stay with Mags in case Lieutenant Starling gets here early."

Leaving Mags, Moose, Brenda, and Jim on the main deck of *The Mistress*, Mac and Adam headed for the main offices of the marina.

Adam quickly logged onto the business office internet, retrieved the images, and printed them, making ten copies. Mac reached over and tapped the icon "Erase File." "Old habits die hard." Then the two men walked back the short distance to *The Mistress*.

A few minutes before ten o'clock, a tall man approached *The Mistress*. He was tanned and wore faded jeans and a tee shirt that clung to his muscular body. As he came near, he called out, "Detective Travis, are you aboard?"

Jim looked up and responded, "We're here, Lieutenant Starling. Welcome aboard."

Jim made introductions and the group went below and gathered in the salon. Mags disappeared into the master bedroom.

Jim led the discussion. "Moose and Brenda did a surveillance of the compound last evening and brought back information that might be helpful. They also drew us what they could see from their brief scan from the street. Brenda, why don't you tell the lieutenant what you saw?"

Starling interrupted, "Jim, why don't all of you just call me Karl."

Brenda again gave a full account of the surveillance she and Moose had done the previous night.

"Good info, ma'am," Karl said, as he looked over the drawing of the compound.

"We've also received heat sensitive, satellite images of the compound, thanks to the FBI. We have those printed here," Jim said as he handed out copies to each person.

Starling looked at the color copies. "I rarely get intel this complete. This is good work. I do have one question though."

"Yes?" Jim responded.

"Is this an announced apprehension or will we be in assault mode?"

Adam answered, "We have all the necessary warrants to make this an assault. We have sufficient evidence that a felon is residing on the property. We will give anyone we approach the opportunity to surrender, but we have to assume significant armed opposition."

"OK," Karl answered. "Let's look at the images and plan our entry. I see from the images that there were eight persons in the compound last night. We can't be sure of that number today; however. It appears that four persons are stationed around the outside perimeter. Three more were gathered in this room here," Starling says pointing. "There's a lone figure in this large room on the east end of the house."

"Yes," Jim answered. "It is our assumption that person may be Marjorie Malone."

"So we are looking at seven possible combatants, plus Malone. Of course, there could be more if we get there during a changing of the guards. I tend to agree with Brenda's assessment that one point of entry would be the north wall. I think four of my men can scale that wall and take out that guard before he knows what hit him. The rest won't be as easy. I can have two more teams of four men ready to breach the east and south walls. Now, for the hardest part. The main team of eight will have to hit the main gate. We have an armored vehicle designed for just that. It can crash through the gate and, we hope, surprise the guard there. Once that happens, we can expect the three people inside either to come out or to go into protection-mode around Malone. I'd like to suggest that you let us infiltrate the house. My men are trained for this kind of assault. There will be less danger if we do it."

Jim stood up. "OK. Let me make sure I understand." He counted the steps off on his fingers as he reviewed the plan: "Three teams of four men each will breach the east, north, and south walls, neutralizing the guards there. An armored vehicle will crash the front gate and eight of your men will take out the gate guard and enter the house, neutralize Malone's personal guard, and arrest her. What do you want us to do?" Jim asked.

"I know that all of you can take care of yourselves, but I think it best that you let us do our jobs," Starling responded. "Surprise is going to be mandatory and we need to coordinate the breaching of the walls and the crashing of the main gate to the exact second. We have experience and training to do that. OK?"

Jim looked at the others and seeing the nodding of heads, said, "OK, Karl, it's your ball game now."

The afternoon sun sat low in the west. Its rays gave a strange peacefulness to the moment. There was no breeze. The large, palatial estates in the neighborhood seemed remote behind their gated entries. No traffic stirred. The only sound was the quiet hum of a distant lawnmower.

At four o'clock, Starling met with his team, twenty men, dressed all in black, with flak jackets emblazoned across the back with "MIAMI SWAT". They listened intently to the assault plan drawn up by Lieutenant Starling. Every man had his face blackened. Each carried an assault rifle. Three men were designated as team leaders. It would be their jobs to breach the east, north, and south walls with their teams of three. Starling would lead the main force crashing the front gate. Mac, Adam, Jim, Moose, and Brenda were also given flak jackets, although they would remain outside the compound.

Mac typed a quick text to Mags: "Are you okay?"

"Well-guarded!" came the reply.

An area, two blocks from the compound, had been designated the staging area. Surrounding streets were blocked off by Miami PD cruisers. At 5:50, Starling gave the order for his men to take their positions. Each man could communicate through a closed network, an ear piece for listening and a voice-activated microphone for speaking.

"Everyone in place?" Starling's voice came through the ear pieces.

"Team 2 ready," responded one team leader.

"Team 3 ready," responded another.

"Team 4 ready," responded the last.

"Go on my command," broadcast Starling from beside the assault vehicle.

"GO NOW!"

The armored assault vehicle turned from a side street and at a rapid speed turned and crashed through the front gate of the compound. A startled guard in the small shack reached for a phone, but before he could say a word, he was subdued by two of the Team 1 men.

"One down," thought Karl.

Then, one by one, the three team leaders reported. "North wall neutralized."

"East wall neutralized."

"South wall neutralized."

"Four down," thought Karl.

Team 1 with eight heavily armed men, with their weapons raised and ready for immediate firing, converged on the front door of the main house.

Team 2 took position outside the north side of the house. Team 3 took position on the east side, covering rear exits. Team 4 took position on the south side of the house. Malone's house was surrounded.

So far, not a shot had been fired. But, surely those on the inside of the house must have heard the crashing of the front gate.

Starling signaled two of his men to bring a heavy, metal battering ram to the front door. On his command, the ram was driven into the front door. It shattered. Immediately, there was gun fire. One of Malone's men was taken out swiftly. A second fell only seconds later.

"That's six," thought Karl.

Starling with four of his team began up the winding stairway to the second floor.

He called out to a closed door, "Malone! Miami SWAT. Give up, throw out your weapons and no one else has to be hurt!"

One team member raised his boot, kicked in the door and stepped aside. There were no gunshots. The last member of Malone's security had laid his weapon on the floor and was on his knees with his fingers laced behind his neck.

"Don't shoot. I give up!" he shouted.

Behind him, in a huge chair sat a woman, unlike anyone Karl had ever seen. She was massive, only five foot, four inches tall, but easily over three hundred pounds. Her hair had been dyed a flaming red. She wore a muumuu in a clashing red. She said nothing other than, "I want to call my lawyer."

The last man was handcuffed. Malone's wrists had to be secured by plastic fasteners. The handcuffs would not go around her thick wrists.

No one on the assault team had been injured. One of Malone's guards was dead. Another had a shoulder wound, but would live. The remaining had been handcuffed and placed in separate Miami Police Department cruisers. A special vehicle had to be ordered to transport Big Mama. She could not get into the backseat of a squad car.

Karl Starling walked over to where Mac, Adam, Jim, Moose, and Brenda had been watching.

"Mission accomplished. It went like clockwork, just as it is supposed to go. When we searched the house, we found a basement. In one of the rooms, we found six women and two children being held. That should drive more nails into Big Mama's coffin. Of course, she wants a lawyer. She'll get one. But, her six accomplices will be kept separate. I bet we'll get even more from them that will help take Malone down. They just might tell us where the rest of the Malone organization might be. Nothing like a close-up view of prison to help someone start getting friendly!"

Mac spoke up, "Well, we have two others who will give testimony against her. I think she'll be out of circulation for the rest of her life. Now, if they just have a cell big enough for her."

Laughter was restrained, but every face had a huge smile.

Mac looked at the others, "Let's get back to *The Mistress* and Mags. I think steaks are in order for tonight."

Jim spoke up. I know a great place near the marina where I can get fresh lobster. Want to make it surf and turf?"

Moose rubbed his stomach, "Now, you're talkin' man. Now, you're talkin'!"

49

MAC AND ADAM WENT TO pick up Mags from Miami PD. When they entered, with Jim, they passed through an open area before reaching the team room. Everyone stood and applauded. Jim and Mac, knowing most of the detectives gathered, bowed low and smiled.

Mags threw herself into Mac's arms. "Let's go home!" Mac whispered.

Jim picked up his wife, Mary, at their house and then they took Adam, Mac, and Mags back to *The Mistress*.

When they arrived back at the docks, Moose and Brenda were waiting. "We'll spend the night here tonight and head back to Joseffa tomorrow," Mac said.

Adam looking at Moose and Brenda said, "I can sack out on the sofa in the salon, or Moose can have that. Brenda can have the guest state room."

Moose spoke up, "Oh, no, I want to sleep on deck. We may be docked, but I want to smell that sea air. You take the sofa."

Mac said, "I can do better, Moose. We'll go to the nearest inlet, and I'll anchor for the night. It will beat the dock."

"That'll be great!" said Moose.

The seven enjoyed an unbelievable meal of rib eyes and lobster, accompanied by twice baked potatoes and a salad.

Jim and Mary said their goodbyes. Mac moved *The Mistress* to a nearby inlet. All found their bed for the night. Mac gave Moose a self-inflating air mattress, sheets, pillow and a blanket. In the morning, they would head for Joseffa where Moose, Brenda, and Adam could pack their belongings and everyone could head home.

As *The Mistress* completed docking on Joseffa, Mac and Mags saw Bob waving to them. He approached just as the Pine Island shuttle was docking. Stepping off the shuttle was Bettina McCauley, carrying Puffball. She stepped vigorously, as if a woman on a mission.

Mac looked at Bob and said laughing, "Looks like everything is back to normal."

"Unfortunately, yes," Bob said, with a frown.

After saying their goodbyes to Bob, Susan, Pat, Moose, and Brenda, Mac and Mags cast off from Joseffa on their cruise back to Venice.

The last words out of Mags' mouth were, "See you all on the twenty-ninth for the Christmas Bash. Remember, six pm at Chez Mason."

50

Mags and Mac worked all day setting four tables on their lanai, decorating them in red and green. Mags had worked since Christmas Day preparing all her specialties, as well as two twenty pound turkeys. "Dinner fit for royalty!" Mac's compliment was backed up with a hug and a kiss on the cheek.

The guest list included sixteen or maybe eighteen if Moose and Brenda brought dates. Mags had forgotten to ask when she invited them. Also on the list were Bob and Susan Gardner, Will and Kate Marks, Adam and Kelly, Pat Jefferson and Eve, Jim and Mary Travis, Bud Walton and his wife Peg and perhaps one new born infant.

At six o'clock, the first guests began to arrive. Sam, Mac and Mags' feline son, ran for safety behind the sofa. First to arrive were Bud and his wife, Peg. In her arms was a tiny baby. "Surprise!" Bud hooted. "This is Geraldine Walton; we call her Gerry."

"Hey, sweet thing," Mags cooed. "You are going to be the star of the show!"

"You didn't tell us the baby had come."

"Now, Mac, you are not the only one who can keep a secret!"

Bud reached for the baby. "My turn!" he said, as he took the sleeping infant into his arms.

Peg smiled at the father-daughter scene.

There was a knock on the door. Mags answered to find Moose and Brenda. They greeted one another and then Mags whispered to Brenda. "You know, you could have brought a date."

Brenda put her arm through Moose's and said, with a big grin on her face, "I did bring a date." Moose was smiling, too.

Jim and Mary were the next to arrive. Almost immediately, Mary took Mags aside and asked. "You've had quite a December. How are you feeling? Jim tells me you'll be heading back to Houston next month. You must be petrified."

"No, actually I'm doing well, Mary. Of course, I am nervous, but God has been with Mac and me through all of this. I've every faith that God will see me through this part of the journey, no matter where that journey goes." Mary squeezed Mags' hand. "You stay in touch. Promise?"

"Of course. You and Jim are special people in our lives."

More people began to arrive. People began to settle into chairs and on the sofa in the large living room. Some even chose to find places on the floor.

Bob spoke up. "You left Joseffa so quickly that we didn't get to hear the whole story of finding Mags' kidnappers and apprehending the human traffickers. Tell us!"

Mac briefly recounted the event of finding and apprehending Marjorie Malone.

"I've heard that more of her organization has been arrested. Her men that we caught with her couldn't talk fast enough to start placing blame on Big Mama and the Baxton brothers. Of course, Win Baxton was killed, but Paul will probably never see the light of day. He was one of the first to ask for a deal."

Adam spoke up. "Two of my agents went to Aruba and with the help of the Aruba police were able to find and extradite Jack Jackson, you know, Triple J. He'll be standing trial, as well."

Mac continued. "We would have never broken this case without the help of Jim Barber and Billy Hastings. Although every charge against them could not be dropped, I think the judge will go lightly on them."

"So, in one month, we managed to solve two murders and close down two major human trafficking organizations. By the way, we also were able to free six women who were going to be shipped overseas to be future prostitutes and two children that would have been used for God knows what," Mac added.

"Enough of that" Mags says, "Surely we have some other news to share. I'll start. Each of you women has a small gift box at your plate. Some of you have tried my new perfume, Mmmm, but you are getting more. For those of you that haven't tried it, I hope you like it. The bad news is that I have to push my rollout date until late March because of my radiation treatments in Houston, but hopefully the ads will be running and people can preorder before Valentine's Day."

"Well, I have some news," shared Kelly. "We sold the house in Biloxi and Adam was able to find a beautiful home for us in Tampa. We've just come from there, and I love it."

"That is so wonderful," Mags gushed. "What a great Christmas gift!"

"Oh, that's not all the news. Mac, you're going to be a grandfather!"

"A grandfather? I'm not old enough!" Mac said as he rushed to Kelly giving her a hug.

"What about me? Margaret Miller Mason, a grandmother? What will people say? Maybe I'll just have to develop a line of products for seniors. But, I refuse to model Depends." The laughter could be heard a block away.

Eve had remained very quiet since arriving. It bothered Mac, but with all the other guests, he hadn't had the time to give her any attention.

Eve spoke up. I don't know many of you, but this seems to be the night for news. I want to share some good news with you. With a huge smile on her face, she held up her left hand to show a beautiful diamond ring in a gold setting.

Mac looked at Pat and with a smile on his face, shook his fist at him and said, "I just got named 'Granddad,' so don't you dare call me Dad!"

Pat laughed and mouthed the letters: "D...A...D." Mac feigned horror, as he threw his hands up in surrender.

Mac, Mags, Adam, and Kelly rushed to Eve and threw their arms around her. Then, everyone was either hugging Pat or shaking his hand.

Mags asked, "When is the wedding?"

Pat looked at Eve and said, "We haven't set a date yet. We have a few issues to iron out first, but it couldn't be soon enough for me."

The women all gathered around Eve and admired her ring.

"Lovely!"

"Wow! It shines like a lighthouse!"

"Doesn't your finger get tired carrying all that weight?"

"Hold it up again!"

Pat stepped over and embraced Eve. She lightly rubbed his back. "What a night for news!" Mags pointed at the new baby, to the expectant Kelly, and the newly engaged Eve. "What a wonderful night for news!"

As the group began to slip into other conversations, Eve moved closer to Mac. "Can I talk to you in private, Dad?"

Mac led Eve to the master bedroom. "What is it, Eve? I think Mags could give you a better 'birds and bees' talk." When he saw how seriously Eve looked at him, he grasped her hand. "What is it, Honey?"

"Dad, I don't know what to say. I've talked to Pat, and I've even talked to Mom. I've been so unfair to you." Her voice caught. "So much time has passed and you've been so patient. You've shown me over and over how much you love me. Mom even told me that I was not being fair. I really do admire all you've done. I'm so sorry I've been such a..." She paused. "I do love you so much and I want everything to be different now. Will you walk me down the aisle? After all, you are my dad."

With tears in his eyes, Mac said, "You bet I'll walk you down the aisle. Welcome back, daughter!"

From Charles P. Frank

Thanks to all our readers for reading *Digging for Death*, the first of the Mac and Maggie Mason "Digging" series. We hope you have enjoyed reading the book as much as we enjoyed writing it.

Follow the continuing adventures of Mac and Maggie Mason and their friends and family in Book 2 of the series, *Digging Through Time*.

What event could cause the deaths of Mac and Mags? Welcome Moose and Brenda as major characters. What secret has Moose kept from his friends and coworkers? What unexpected skill does Brenda possess that will benefit Mags? What frightening adventures do Mac and Mags experience in New York when Mmmm is rolled out? In what new professional venture will Mac find himself? What will Mags' next trip to MD Anderson in Houston reveal? Will Mac be welcoming a grandson or granddaughter into the Mason clan? What is the major issue delaying the pending marriage of Pat and Eve? And, most importantly, within what mystery or mysteries will Mac and Mags find themselves embroiled?

Find all the answers in *Digging Through Time*. Read more about the three authors who have chosen as their pseudonym, Charles P. Frank. Learn about other books they have written under their given names by visiting their website, **CharlesPFrank.com** or on **Facebook**. The reader may also email the authors at **cpf@CharlesPFrank.com**. We would like to hear from you, our readers.

Made in the USA
San Bernardino, CA
07 June 2014